D0110447

B11/20

YOUNG
DONALD

WEST HARTFORD · PUBLIC LIBRARY · 3958

MICHAEL BENNETT

This is a work of fiction. Names, characters, organizations, places, events, and incidents are either products of the author's imagination or are used fictitiously.

Copyright © 2020 Michael Bennett
All rights reserved.

No part of this book may be reproduced, or stored in a retrieval system, or transmitted in any form or by any means, electronic, mechanical, photocopying, recording, or otherwise, without express written
lisher.

F
BENNETT   s, Inc., Oakland, California
MICHAEL

ISBN: 9781950301133
e-ISBN: 9781950301140

Printed in the United States of America

To my wonderful family and friends who supported me writing this book, despite their occasional fears of unidentified federal troops showing up in camouflage at my door. To the book's original 531 followers on Inkshares who made publication a reality. And to the fabulously talented team at Inkshares (Adam, Sarah, Avalon, Kaitlin, Pam, and Kevin) who brought out the best in me and this story.

Dear Readers,

I'm fifty-five years old, and having worked in law and finance my entire career, I'm not sure I ever expected to have a novel published. I certainly never expected it to happen during a pandemic, or a once-in-a-generation civil rights awakening, or an economic downturn rivaling the Great Depression. And, never in a million years, would I have thought that novel would be a satire inspired by Donald Trump. But here I am—and here we all are.

Donald Trump has been on the periphery of my consciousness for decades, as he has been for most people my age. I think my first memory of him is from my college days in the mid-1980s, when he bought the New Jersey Generals football team. I was in law school in New York City when he made his shameful call to execute Kevin Richardson, Raymond Santana, Antron McCray, Yusef Salaam, and Korey Wise, the so-called Central Park Five. A few years later, I was a young lawyer practicing in Manhattan when his first divorce filled the New York headlines.

After that, I largely lost track of him. I lived and worked in Tokyo and Hong Kong for most of the 1990s, so I missed his next marriage and divorce, as well as many of his bankruptcies. And I was based in Paris in the 2000s, so I didn't notice when he became a reality TV star.

Then came 2016. Like many people, I felt completely overwhelmed watching his march to the White House, but at the same time, I couldn't look away. I became an obsessive follower of all things Trump. My emotions ran a familiar daily course. Confusion and disgust reading his tweets, anger watching Rachel Maddow, and then some relief and laughter watching Trevor Noah.

Up until then, my career had been entirely left-brain. I have always worked in the capital markets and specifically in the quantitative, model-driven field of financial derivatives.

But I realized in watching Donald Trump's rise to power that my left brain alone was not up to the task of analyzing what was happening here in the United States. There's no model for this president.

After awhile, my right brain won out in the struggle to understand the Trump phenomenon, and I decided to try fiction. It was on a United flight from San Francisco to Singapore that I came up with the idea of looking back to Trump's origins in the 1960's. By the time I stumbled bleary-eyed off the plane at Singapore Changi Airport sixteen hours later, I had a crude story outline and a draft of a first chapter.

The axiom that art is the mirror of life is particularly apt in the context of satire. Writing this novel was an iterative process, with each iteration inevitably influenced by what was going on in the country. At first, like many of us, I held out hope that Trump's worst impulses would be held in check by the free press, the courts, and Congress. I hoped that he might just be a crude distraction as president; back then, this story was mainly a comedy. But, as time went on—from "good people on both sides," to family separation at the border, to tear gas in Lafayette Square—it reflected the tragedy of where the nation finds itself.

This is entirely a work of fiction. I didn't research the real Donald Trump, and the characters and events are fully made up by me. There is no New Jersey Military Academy; Teddy Haswell never lived, let alone died; and there was never a pub in lower Manhattan called the Impressionable Dwarf.

While *Young Donald* is a satire, it is also a coming-of-age story. I offer it to you in the hope that we, too, are in our own coming-of-age story as a country, a better self ahead.

— Michael Bennett
   July 2020

This is a work of fiction. The characters and events depicted in the story are a product of the author's imagination. It's not real. It's all made up.

1

Monday, October 7, 1963 (8:02 p.m.)

WHEN DONALD FIRST MET TEDDY HASWELL AS FRESH-
men cadets at the New Jersey Military Academy, he decided
immediately they would be best friends. Teddy was tall,
strong-jawed, and athletic. There were rumors as soon as he
stepped on campus that he would be the starting quarterback
for the football team. It was obvious he would be a popular
boy at the Academy, and Donald believed popular boys made
good best friends.

Technically, at that time, Donald was not in the market
for a best friend, since he already had one. Jerry Stahl, his best
friend since elementary school, was also at the Academy. But
Jerry was shorter than average, pimply, and could barely throw
a spiral. Although Jerry was from a wealthy family (his father
was one of the most successful dentists in central Queens), with
his looks and athletic limitations, he would never be a popular
boy at a military school. Donald determined as soon as he saw
Teddy Haswell that he needed to make a best-friend upgrade.
Jerry was out, and Teddy was in.

The next Sunday, when cadets were allowed to call home, Donald mentioned to his father, a real estate developer in Queens, that Teddy would make a great roommate. He also made sure to point out that Teddy's father was a partner at one of the biggest law firms in Newark. Donald knew to highlight that piece of information, since his father had instructed him, on drop-off day at the Academy, to make friends with boys from successful families. *You can have at least as much fun with rich friends as poor ones*, his father had said.

A week later, after a small donation check had arrived at the Academy, Donald's roommate, Glen Eberhardt (whose father was an electrician), was transferred to another room in the barracks. Teddy took his place in Donald's room.

For the next three years, Donald and Teddy were together almost nonstop. They both played on the Academy's football and baseball teams, went into the city together whenever they got weekend leave, and every summer Teddy spent a few weeks at Donald's family's beach house in Florida. The first time Donald had touched a girl's breast, it was with a blonde Dairy Queen waitress in Boca Raton who had originally shown interest in Teddy. In short, Teddy was exactly the best friend Donald had expected him to become when they had first met freshman year.

Looking down now at Teddy's body sprawled on the granite tiles of Jessup Quadrangle, Donald was sure his best friend was dead. After all, he could see from the light of a nearby lamppost that there was a pool of blood rapidly forming around his head. Teddy was facedown, with his left arm under his body and his right arm splayed out at his side in what looked to Donald like a perfect throwing position, as if, even as he died, Teddy was cocked and ready to launch a touchdown pass.

Donald knew he should be shocked, but more than shock, he felt surprise. The window ledge he was standing on outside Lieutenant Drake's office was at least two feet wide, and Donald was having no trouble keeping his balance. If Teddy couldn't keep his balance on a ledge that wide, he must not have been such a great athlete after all.

Donald looked up from the bloody scene below and peeked through the window from his perch off to the side. Lieutenant Drake, the Academy's mathematics teacher, was sitting at his desk with his back to Donald. The lieutenant's sudden appearance had forced Donald and Teddy to open a window and go out onto the ledge.

Donald and Teddy had snuck into Lieutenant Drake's office to find his grade sheets. Their plan was to change the 67 Donald earned on last week's trigonometry midterm exam to a higher score. Donald's father paid him a hundred dollars for every grade he earned B+ or better. A 67 on the midterm was going to put a B+ for the semester out of reach.

It was faculty poker night in Jessup Cafeteria, and they knew Lieutenant Drake always played in that game. They had assumed his office on the fifth floor of Jessup Hall would be empty and that they would have at least an hour to get in and out before the 9:00 p.m. curfew.

Jessup Hall was the oldest and largest of the four gray stone buildings that surrounded Jessup Quadrangle and formed the center of the Academy's campus. Before it was converted into a school building, Jessup Hall had been a convent. It was built in 1887 by the Catholic Church to be its main convent in New Jersey. On its facade, between the third and fourth floors, were six engraved panels depicting scenes from the Crucifixion. There were three on each side of the building. The architect's original plan had called for fourteen panels, one for each of the stations of the cross, but when construction went over budget, the Church had decided the nuns could make do with just six.

The Academy's library was on the ground floor of Jessup Hall. After class hours, cadets were not allowed anywhere in the building except for the library. Teddy and Donald had gone to the library that evening. They sat down at one of the three long wooden tables in the center of the room and pretended to study for a while. Ten minutes apart, so as not to arouse suspicion, each of the boys—first Teddy and then Donald—had asked the librarian, Mrs. Duncannon, if they could use the bathroom. It was located next to the stairwell, so it was the perfect staging area for their plan.

They met there and then sprinted up the stairs when they were sure no one was looking. If they encountered any faculty in the stairwell, Donald was confident he could talk their way out of trouble. Even if they ran into a teacher who was a real stickler for the rules, with the big game against Westport Country Day coming up on Friday, there was no chance two football players would receive any serious punishment just for being upstairs in Jessup Hall.

The boys reached the fifth floor without being seen, and found Lieutenant Drake's office dark, empty, and unlocked. They closed the door behind them, switched on the lights, and started their search.

Teddy found Lieutenant Drake's black grade book in a desk drawer. He put it on top of the desk and was opening it when they heard footsteps coming toward them down the corridor and the lieutenant's deep and distinctive smoker's cough.

Donald ran back to the door and quietly locked it. Since the boys had found the office unlocked, Donald was hoping Lieutenant Drake might not have his keys with him. By the time Donald turned around, Teddy was already opening the window behind the lieutenant's desk.

Teddy went out onto the ledge first. As Donald reached the window, he heard Lieutenant Drake try the doorknob and then curse loudly when he discovered it was locked. If the lieutenant had his keys with him, it would only be a few more seconds before he would be coming through the door.

Donald quickly went out through the window and onto the ledge. Although the ledge ran the full length of the office, Teddy had not moved down it at all. He was still standing on the spot where he had first come out, leaving Donald without enough space to lean over comfortably and close the window. He could not risk saying something Lieutenant Drake might hear, so instead he tried gesturing for Teddy to move farther down the ledge. But his friend was staring into the office and did not notice Donald waving his hand.

Donald saw the office door start to open and he knew he could not wait any longer. He leaned over to close the window, pushing Teddy slightly with his hip in the process. It was no more than a tiny nudge, Donald thought, and, seeing as Teddy was the Academy's quarterback, with great balance on the football field, it certainly should not have caused him any trouble.

Just as Donald closed the window, he heard a gasp. He turned around, but Teddy was gone. There was a distant thudding sound. He looked down and saw his best friend's lifeless body lying on the hard granite of Jessup Quadrangle, five stories below. He instantly knew Teddy would never be making another game-winning play.

There was nothing Donald could do to help Teddy now, so his focus turned entirely to his own predicament. He could not possibly go back in through the window with Lieutenant Drake sitting there. Even if his father offered to make a large donation to the Academy, it would not be enough to keep him from being expelled.

At the same time, Donald knew he could not stay out on the ledge for too much longer. Soon someone was bound to come through Jessup Quadrangle and see Teddy's body. And when they did, they would surely look up. He would be expelled and, even though Donald was completely innocent, it might look like he had had something to do with Teddy's fall.

Donald moved slightly to one side of the window so Lieutenant Drake wouldn't see him if he happened to turn around. He tried to see what the lieutenant was doing at his desk, hoping to get a clue whether he was planning to stay for long. Just then the office door opened and Stanley Wong entered the room.

Stanley was the only Asian cadet at the Academy. Donald, who was proud of his knack for nicknames, had called him "Fu Manchu" when they had first met freshman year. He also had considered the name "Charlie Chan," but he preferred the way *Fu Manchu* rolled off his tongue. The nickname had stuck, and Stanley became known universally around the school as Fu Manchu. After a while, even some of the teachers had started calling him that.

Stanley sat down across the desk from Lieutenant Drake and started to speak. Donald wondered if Stanley had seen what had happened and was reporting it to the lieutenant. He needed to know what was being said, but while he could make out some sounds, they were unintelligible. As Donald leaned in, trying to hear their conversation, his forehead tapped the window glass. Although Lieutenant Drake did not react, Stanley's eyes shot to the window and locked on Donald.

"Darn it!" Donald whispered to himself. Stanley was Lieutenant Drake's favorite student, and Donald was sure the teacher's pet would rat him out. He stared straight into Stanley's eyes with as tough a look as he could muster, hoping to scare him into staying quiet.

Stanley looked away. Then his eyes began darting around the room as if he were frantically searching for something. Donald wondered if his tough-guy stare had been too effective. He had just wanted to keep Stanley quiet, not cause him to lose his mind.

Stanley stopped scanning the room, rolled his eyes back, and started to convulse in his chair as if he were being electrocuted. It looked to Donald like he was having a seizure. Lieutenant Drake shouted something that Donald could not make out. Then he jumped up from his desk and lifted Stanley to his feet. He draped one of Stanley's arms around his shoulders and staggered to the door like a soldier helping a wounded comrade off the battlefield.

As they were going out into the corridor, Stanley looked back at the window and smiled at Donald. He slightly raised the arm that was slung across the lieutenant's shoulder and for a brief second gave Donald a thumbs-up. Then he seemed to lose all strength again as the lieutenant helped him down the corridor and out of Donald's line of sight.

Donald was shocked. Other than nicknaming him Fu Manchu, Donald had barely had any contact with Stanley Wong during their years together at the Academy. Donald was a jock and Stanley was a brain, and those two groups did not mix much. But Stanley might have just saved him from being expelled.

Donald waited thirty seconds or so before opening the window and going back into the office. He closed the window behind him, ran to the door, and carefully peered down the corridor in both directions. The corridor was empty. Donald guessed Lieutenant Drake was taking Stanley downstairs in the faculty elevator.

Donald wanted to make a run for the stairwell, but he first looked back into the office to see if he had left any evidence behind. On top of Lieutenant Drake's desk, just where Teddy had left it after taking it out of a drawer, was the grade book.

Donald ran back to the desk and opened the grade book. It was a grid-paper notebook, with each page corresponding to a different class. Donald flipped through the pages until he found the one labeled *12th-Grade Trigonometry*. He ran his finger down the column of names to *Donald T.* and then across to his most recent mark, the 67 on the midterm exam.

Frustratingly for Donald, the lieutenant had written everything in his grade book in black pen, so there would be no way to erase that grade. Instead, Donald pulled a black ballpoint from the penholder on the lieutenant's desk and slowly and carefully transformed the offending figure from a 67 to an 87. He considered for a second how easy it would be to change it to an 89, but he decided the risk of detection was not worth the additional two points.

Donald closed the grade book and put it back in the drawer where Teddy had found it. He ran out of Lieutenant Drake's office and hurried down the stairwell to the ground floor. He went through the back door of Jessup Hall to avoid Teddy's body in Jessup Quadrangle.

On his way out, Donald looked up and noticed the engraved stone panel forty feet above his head on Jessup Hall. He could just make out the image from the light of the lampposts on either side of the door. It showed Christ being nailed to the cross. Donald rarely thought about God at all, even during mandatory Sunday services. But, at that moment, staring up at the Crucifixion, he thought that, between two boys on a window ledge, God had made a choice to spare one and sacrifice the other. He wondered what Teddy had done to deserve such a horrible fate.

He turned and ran as fast as he could, feeling like every step was taking him further away from the danger of being caught, expelled, and embarrassed. Donald did not stop running until he was back in his room in the barracks.

2

Wednesday, October 9, 1963 (5:35 p.m.)

THE DEATH OF A CADET WAS A RARE, BUT NOT UNPREC-edented, occurrence at the New Jersey Military Academy. The most common cause of death over the years was car accidents. There had also been a drowning during a canoe trip over summer break several years ago. And once, an overweight cadet with an asthma condition had collapsed and died during a training run. Yet never in the thirty-year history of the school had the Academy's star quarterback been found dead on Jessup Quadrangle.

The Newark police were called in to investigate. Finding no evidence of foul play, they quickly determined Teddy Haswell had committed suicide by jumping from the roof of Jessup Hall. An investigator from the Army Intelligence Service was also sent to campus, since Teddy, like all the cadets, was a member of the army's Junior ROTC. He concurred with the assessment of the Newark police. *Obvious suicide*, he wrote in his report.

As Teddy's roommate, Donald was given a week off from classes to recover from the trauma. The headmaster of the school, Colonel Overstreet, assured Donald that he would receive A grades for all six of his classes that semester. The colonel said it would be unfair to expect him to be able to concentrate on his studies after experiencing such a deep and personal loss. For Donald, that meant he would be making six hundred dollars from his father. It would be his highest paid semester ever.

Since his fake seizure in Lieutenant Drake's office, Stanley Wong had been staying in the Academy's infirmary, under the observation of Dr. Jamison, the school doctor. His absence from the barracks had spawned rumors that Stanley had seen Teddy's bloody body that night in Jessup Quadrangle and suffered a mental breakdown from the shock. Two days later, when Stanley was released from the infirmary, word quickly spread among the cadets that Fu Manchu had not gone insane after all and was now back in the barracks.

Donald heard the news about Stanley on his way to football practice. Coach Mulrooney had given the team Tuesday off in memory of Teddy, but, with only a few days left before the big game against Westport, he had resumed practice so that the team could adjust to Lou Douglas as their new quarterback.

Donald needed to make sure that Stanley said nothing to anyone about what he had seen that night in Lieutenant Drake's office. The day after the incident, he grew so anxious, he began walking to the infirmary to speak to Stanley. Then he stopped. Why would a popular cadet like him need to see Fu Manchu urgently? It would only arouse suspicion. He decided to wait for Stanley to be released.

Once football practice ended, Donald went straight to Stanley's room. The door was open, and he could see Stanley sitting at his desk. Donald walked in, closing the door behind him. Stanley looked up from his calculus textbook.

"Fu Manchu, we need to talk," Donald said.

Donald sat down on the end of one of the two narrow single beds. Each room in the Academy barracks was identical, with two metal frame beds, two metal desks, two metal desk chairs, and two small metal storage lockers, all in the same pale shade of gray.

"Let's talk later, Donald. I need to study now," Stanley said.

"We just need to agree on a few things first," Donald said.

Stanley let out a dramatic sigh. Then he put his pencil down in his book and looked at Donald with a pained expression on his face.

"About what?" Stanley said.

"I need to know what you think happened that night," Donald said, using the tough-guy squint he had copied from James Coburn. He wanted Stanley to know he meant business.

"What night, exactly?" Stanley asked.

"Don't joke around with me, Fu Manchu. You know what night I'm talking about. The night you saw me outside Lieutenant Drake's window."

"I think Teddy killed himself. He jumped off the roof, right?" Stanley said.

"Yeah, but you know . . . What in the world! There's someone else in here!" Donald said.

Donald gestured across the room to a pair of feet in bright white socks sticking out from under the other desk. From the doorway, those feet had been blocked from view by the two beds.

"That's just Dicky," Stanley said. "He likes to study under his desk."

Dicky Daniels, Stanley's skinny red-haired roommate, was famous around the school for two things. He could memorize all the numbers on a whole page of the phonebook in less than five minutes, and he had tried to wear shorts into the shower three years ago on his first day at the Academy. Naturally, the other boys in the shower that day had quickly ripped those shorts off Dicky's very skinny body, and Donald, who was one of those other boys, had nicknamed Dicky "Shower Shorts."

"Scram, Shower Shorts. This conversation doesn't concern you," Donald said in the direction of the feet.

Without saying a word, Dicky crawled out from under his desk and quickly left the room, closing the door behind him. He was holding a thoroughly dog-eared paperback copy of *Crime and Punishment*, which reminded Donald how lucky he was to be guaranteed an A in English class that semester. He had lost his copy of that book, but now he would never need to find it.

Donald had read most of the first chapter already, which was enough for him to know it was just another book about a loser. His father's theory about novels was that people wrote them because they had failed at more useful careers. Naturally, they wrote about other losers like themselves. Donald was convinced his father was right. The only decent novel they had read at the Academy was *The Great Gatsby*. Every other novel they had been assigned in English class had a loser at its center. At least now he would never have to finish *Crime and Punishment*.

"I just want to make sure you know nothing weird happened that night," Donald said.

"Well, Teddy was the most popular kid in this school and he killed himself. That's weird, right?"

"I mean nothing weird involving me," Donald said. "You know, just because I was outside Drake's window and all. Believe me, I had nothing to do with anything."

"It's none of my business," Stanley said.

"That's right. It's none of your business," Donald said. "So, you didn't say anything about that to anybody, right?"

"Like I said, it's none of my business," Stanley said.

Donald could not believe how easy this conversation was going. He had expected he might have to threaten Stanley. His plan had been to stand very close so Stanley could feel how much taller Donald was. Donald's father, who was also tall like him, had taught him that negotiation trick. But intimidation seemed rather pointless now.

"Sounds like we understand each other," Donald said. "We're in full agreement that nothing happened involving me, and there's no need to say anything about me to anybody."

"Like I said before, it's none of my business," Stanley said.

Donald decided three *none of my business*es were plenty to be convinced Stanley was not planning to squeal on him. He got up from the bed to leave.

"I like you," Donald said. "That's why I always tell people that Fu Manchu's a stand-up guy."

3

Thursday, October 10, 1963 (3:48 a.m.)

ROSEMARY DUNCANNON HAD BEEN THE NEW JERSEY Military Academy's head librarian for the past fourteen years. Despite the fact that Rosemary had never married, she had always been known around the school as Mrs. Duncannon. The school's former headmaster had introduced her by that name on her first day of work, and, since she had not bothered to correct him, the title had stuck.

When Rosemary graduated from Montclair State with a degree in library studies, her dream was to work in the library of a major university, like Princeton or Rutgers. But her expectations were tempered after a few years in the workforce. Her first job after graduation was in an elementary school library in a poor section of Newark. Because the postwar baby boom had led to overcrowding at the school, the library had been pushed out of the school building and into an unheated army-surplus Quonset hut on the playground. All winter long she worked

in her coat, hat, and gloves, trying, with little success, to interest students in the library's small collection of very well-used
books.

A friend from Montclair State spotted the Academy's
advertisement for a librarian in the *Newark Evening News* and
sent it to Rosemary. After enduring several winters in that cold
Quonset hut, when Rosemary first saw the Academy's library
in Jessup Hall, she was entranced. The library had been built in
the room that had served as the nuns' chapel during the building's previous life as a convent. There were four stained-glass
windows with scenes depicting the life of Mary Magdalene;
mahogany shelves full of books in good condition; as well as
intricately carved wood molding that ran all along the back
wall, where the chapel's altar used to be. Although it lacked
the large collection of a university library, the Academy looked
like a dream to Rosemary. The very same day the offer letter
from the Academy arrived in her mailbox, Rosemary called and
accepted the job.

Six months later, Rosemary's lover and best friend, Natalie
Coleman, was able to find a job in the Academy's admissions
office. Since then, they had lived together in a small house near
campus. While Rosemary ate like a bird and had been the same
skinny size since high school, Natalie loved lasagna and choc-
olate cake and every year made losing ten or fifteen pounds
her New Year's resolution. Natalie would joke with friends that
they were like the lesbian version of Jack Sprat and his wife.

Over the years, Rosemary occasionally dreamed of working at a bigger library in a more prestigious institution, but
she always decided it would be foolish to risk the comfortable
position she had at the Academy. Having started her career in
a freezing cold Quonset hut, Rosemary was keenly aware there

were worse fates for a librarian than going to work every day at the beautiful library in Jessup Hall.

Rosemary and Natalie enjoyed a quiet life in their house just two blocks from campus. It was a wood-framed Colonial that was by far the smallest house on their street. There were just two bedrooms and a tiny bathroom upstairs, and a living room, powder room, and eat-in kitchen on the ground level.

They bought the house shortly after Natalie had found her job at the Academy. They agreed to split the cost fifty-fifty, and since Natalie was a free spender with not much savings, they needed to find a place cheap enough that Natalie could afford her half of the down payment. They bought the house from an old widower with a cat, and Natalie liked to joke that the man sold the place because his cat needed more space.

Rosemary craved order and structure, and her job at the Academy satisfied her needs in that regard. She worked every day from 1:00 p.m., when she opened the library, until just before 9:00 p.m., when she closed and locked it for the night. During her eight hours in the library, she maintained a very regimented work schedule, with specific times allocated for each major area of her responsibilities. Reshelving, for instance, was always done twice a day for forty-five minutes, once beginning at 4:15 p.m. and then again at 7:15 p.m.

Natalie liked to tease Rosemary that her need for order was abnormal and unhealthy. Rosemary always countered that being well organized was a virtue, but she knew Natalie was not entirely wrong. When she was growing up, Rosemary would watch her mother softly count to twenty every time she washed her hands and lock and unlock the front door exactly five times before she could leave the house, and Rosemary suspected she might have inherited her mother's compulsive gene. In any case, whether her love of order was virtuous or a symptom of an obsessive personality, a well-organized library was the perfect environment for Rosemary to spend her day.

One of Rosemary's duties as librarian was to monitor the cadets' use of Jessup Hall after class hours. To keep track of cadets, Rosemary kept a small notebook at the library's front desk where she recorded each cadet's coming and going. Even if a cadet just asked to use the bathroom, Rosemary would write down in her notebook when the cadet left and when he came back. Given her love of order, Rosemary took great satisfaction in the completeness of her records. Once a notebook was full, she would put it in a cardboard box under her desk.

She estimated there must now be over fifty notebooks in that box. Although she knew it would never happen, she sometimes imagined all those notebooks going on display in the library after she retired. She thought that would be a fitting way to commemorate her many years of diligent service.

Her most recent notebook laid out a timeline of events on the night Teddy Haswell died. Rosemary had read those entries many times over. She simply could not believe a cadet so cheerful and full of life as Teddy would decide to kill himself, and she had a nagging feeling that something in her notebook might provide a clue to what had really happened to him.

According to her notebook, she had last seen Teddy at 7:44 p.m. that night, when he had asked for permission to leave the library and use the bathroom. She did not remember him seeming depressed. Certainly, she had no memory of him looking like a boy who was headed upstairs to jump off the roof.

A few minutes later, at 7:48 p.m., Stanley Wong asked if he could go upstairs to see Lieutenant Drake about his application to MIT. As usual, Stanley had been studying all night in the library. Since the lieutenant had left permission for Stanley earlier in the day, she handed Stanley a green stairwell pass and he left.

Four minutes after that, at 7:52 p.m., Donald had asked to use the bathroom. Teddy had not yet come back, and usually Rosemary would not let cadets she knew were good friends use the bathroom at the same time. She assumed they would be going there to smoke or get into some other kind of trouble.

But Donald was a special case. Rosemary knew if she told him to wait until Teddy got back, Donald would just argue and whine until he got his way. Donald had been that kind of boy from his first days at the Academy, and Rosemary had never liked him. She thought complainers made bad cadets. Besides that, she had always suspected he was responsible for the nickname "Mrs. Dumb Cannon," which she knew the boys used behind her back.

To avoid a prolonged argument, she let Donald go. Two minutes later, at 7:54 p.m., Jerry Stahl left the library. She remembered Jerry saying he needed to get his math textbook from his room and would be right back. Jerry's departure was the last notation in her notebook for October 7.

Shortly after that, Lieutenant Drake came into Jessup Hall and took the faculty elevator upstairs. Rosemary remembered that because she had been surprised to see him. When she had let Stanley go upstairs, she had assumed Lieutenant Drake was waiting for him in his office. She guessed the lieutenant had come in around 8:00 p.m., but she could not be sure, since there were no notations in her notebook about it. The notebook was for cadets only.

Another five or six minutes passed, and Lieutenant Drake reappeared from the faculty elevator supporting a barely conscious-looking Stanley Wong. Rosemary came out of the library to see if she could help the lieutenant with Stanley when suddenly she heard yelling coming from Jessup Quadrangle. Once she learned the yelling was due to the discovery of a dead cadet, she had closed the library early and told the remaining students to go immediately back to the barracks.

It had certainly been an unusual night in Jessup Hall, and she had never had a chance to share what she knew about it with anyone. Both the local police and the army had come to investigate, and she had assumed they would want to interview her. After all, she was the only adult in Jessup Hall at the time other than Lieutenant Drake. If nothing else, her knowledge that Teddy had left the library at exactly 7:44 p.m. should be useful information to them.

But the investigators had never come to speak with her. In fact, she had heard from Florence Kreitzenbach, the headmaster's secretary, that they had barely spent an hour on campus. They went to the spot where Teddy's body had been found, then to the roof of Jessup Hall, and then left. As far as Mrs. Kreitzenbach knew, the investigators had not spoken to anyone at the school other than the headmaster, Colonel Overstreet.

Had Teddy left a suicide note? Had he been acting depressed? Was he having trouble in class or did he just break up with a girlfriend? Had anyone seen him on the roof? Rosemary was not sure if these sorts of questions had even been asked. Although she was just a librarian, she felt sure this was not the proper way to conduct a suicide investigation.

Rosemary also could not stop thinking that the last four cadets to leave the library that night had never returned. She could account for three of them. Stanley had had a seizure, Teddy had died, and Jerry had discovered the body on his way back to the library. *But what about Donald?* she wondered. She was sure he'd never come back to the library, because the next day she had found his copy of *Crime and Punishment* on one of the long library desks. She knew it was his, because he had written his name on the inside cover. Wherever Donald had gone that night, she guessed he had been with Teddy.

So, as far as Rosemary could surmise, a boy who seemed happy and excited about life was with his best friend in a nearly empty school building. That seemed to Rosemary more like a recipe for a tragic accident than a suicide. If it had been an accident, how cruel it would be for Teddy's family to believe he had taken his own life.

Rosemary had gone over her timeline of that night with Natalie, but Natalie had not found it suspicious. Although she agreed Teddy always seemed like one of the happier cadets on campus, she thought a boy could be more depressed than he looked. She also thought there could be hundreds of innocent reasons why Donald had never returned to the library that night. In fact, from what she knew about Donald, Natalie was surprised he had been in the library in the first place.

Despite Natalie's reassurances, Rosemary couldn't get over the suspicion that Teddy's death wasn't a suicide. Thinking so much about that night was making Rosemary an insomniac. She had been tossing and turning in the sheets for hours. All that moving around had made her hungry. She assumed Natalie had fallen asleep by her deep breathing, so Rosemary got up as quietly as she could and tiptoed out of the bedroom.

The wooden staircase creaked loudly with each step as Rosemary went down. When she reached the kitchen, she took a saucepan out of a Formica cabinet and started warming milk to make oatmeal. She had decided it was late enough now that she could go ahead and eat breakfast. Natalie soon appeared in the kitchen doorway as Rosemary was searching in another cabinet for the oatmeal box.

"Sorry, did I wake you up?" Rosemary asked.

"It's okay. What's wrong, Rose? You still thinking about Teddy?" Natalie asked as she sat down at the kitchen table.

Rosemary took the oatmeal box from the cabinet, carried it with her to the table, and sat down next to Natalie. She was not really in the mood to talk, but she knew she could not tell Natalie that without hurting her feelings.

"I just feel like I might know something important," Rosemary said.

"Rose, there was already an investigation. It's over."

"But no one talked to me, and I may have been the last person to see Teddy alive. It doesn't make sense. Don't they want to know how he seemed before he went up to the roof? Isn't that important?" Rosemary said.

"I think you need to let this go," Natalie said, reaching across the small kitchen table to stroke Rosemary's hand. "Maybe Teddy was having problems at home? It's impossible for us to know everything that's going on in these boys' lives."

"I know," Rosemary said.

"And you don't want to be making any accusations about Donald being involved somehow," Natalie said. "You know Colonel Overstreet won't want to upset his father."

4

Thursday, October 10, 1963 (3:02 p.m.)

WHILE STANLEY WONG WAS STAYING IN THE ACADEMY'S infirmary, he had been allowed to place a call to his family in Hong Kong on the infirmary's phone. Dr. Jamison gave him a maximum of five minutes, since New Jersey Bell charged four dollars a minute for calls to Asia.

Dr. Jamison offered to get on the line first and explain his diagnosis to Stanley's family. But since his diagnosis amounted to "unexplained seizure," Stanley did not want to waste any of his five minutes on that. He lied and said his father could not speak English.

It was very late at night in Hong Kong, but his father, Arthur, picked up after only a few rings, just as Stanley knew he would. His father got calls at all hours of the day for his business, so he was never far from the phone when he was home.

Speaking in Cantonese, Stanley explained to his father exactly what had happened in Lieutenant Drake's office. He described how his fellow cadet was stranded out on a window ledge and how he had helped him stay out of trouble by pretending to have a seizure.

His father told him he did exactly the right thing. Stanley had expected that reaction. In his family, informing on a colleague to the authorities was not something that would ever be considered acceptable. In fact, it was something that could get a person killed, seeing as Stanley came from one of the nine most powerful triad families in Hong Kong. His father was the leader, or Dragon Head, of the Ho Fong Triad, a position that had been held previously by Stanley's grandfather and before that, by his great-grandfather.

The Ho Fong Triad had started in the mid-nineteenth century as a secret society in Canton dedicated to resisting the foreign Manchu rulers of the Qing dynasty. To fund its paramilitary activities against the Qing government, the Ho Fong Triad branched out into various lines of business, most of which involved transporting and selling goods along the Chinese coast without paying taxes or customs duties.

When the Chinese Revolution of 1911 ended the Qing dynasty, thereby eliminating the original reason for the Ho Fong Triad's existence, only the business interests remained. By that time, the Ho Fong Triad was already well established as a unique kind of international company active throughout the South China Sea area. It was led at the time of the revolution by Stanley's great-grandfather and included different divisions focused on smuggling silk, lumber, tea, weapons, opium, and people. Then, in the 1920s, when the Nationalist Party, which replaced the Qing dynasty, cracked down on secret societies, Stanley's grandfather emigrated to Hong Kong and established the British-controlled territory as the new center of operations for the Ho Fong Triad.

The British colonial authorities in Hong Kong considered the Ho Fong Triad to be a criminal organization and, in truth, it was involved in many illegal activities, like loan-sharking, extortion, weapons and drug smuggling, and prostitution. It also had significant investments in a range of legitimate businesses, from construction to textiles. As Dragon Head of the triad, Stanley's father ran an enterprise that rivaled any private company in Hong Kong.

Since the first time he had held his newborn son in his arms, Arthur saw Stanley as the key to his dream of extending the Ho Fong Triad's business deeper into the United States. If his son were educated there, at a prestigious American university, and became fluent in American culture, he was convinced the family business on that side of the world would flourish. With Stanley in the United States, the Ho Fong Triad would become a multinational conglomerate.

Arthur's timetable for sending his son to America was accelerated when Stanley was fourteen. That year, the Ho Fong Triad became locked in a bloody dispute with the Shing Yee Triad over control of some warehouses at the Port of Hong Kong. The Shing Yee Triad had a nasty reputation for kidnapping the children of rival triad leaders and cutting off their fingers, their toes, and sometimes even their heads. Arthur decided he could not wait for Stanley to be ready for university to send him abroad. He had to get his only son out of the colony as soon as possible.

Since Stanley grew up speaking English and had always been a top student, his father knew he could succeed at any American boarding school. But he also knew Stanley would need to be strong, physically and mentally, to replace him someday as Dragon Head of the Ho Fong Triad. A military school seemed like the perfect choice. The triad lieutenant he had stationed in New York did some research and discovered the New Jersey Military Academy.

Leaving Hong Kong for the first time, Stanley traveled with his father for two days on Pan Am Clipper jets to Tokyo, Honolulu, San Francisco, and finally New York. They spent another two days staying at the Plaza Hotel and sightseeing around New York before they took a car to the Academy.

During their long travels from Hong Kong to New Jersey, Arthur had given his son a crash course in everything he had previously kept hidden from Stanley about the family business. He described the history and traditions of the Ho Fong Triad, where it fit within the Hong Kong triad hierarchy, and all the varied ways, legal and illegal, that it made its money.

The news that he came from a triad family had not taken Stanley completely by surprise. He had gone to an expensive British-run private school in Hong Kong, where most of his classmates' fathers were bankers, lawyers, accountants, and corporate executives. Stanley had been keenly aware his father was the only one with dragon tattoos down both of his arms.

There had been other hints about the true nature of the family business over the years. Stanley had once found a pool of blood on the back seat of the family car, and he had overheard his father on the phone late one night threatening to chop someone into crab-trap bait over a gambling debt. Half the movies in Hong Kong were about triads, and over time Stanley realized going to the movies often reminded him a lot of home.

Stanley had never had the courage to ask his father about those things, but they had certainly raised his suspicion about what his father did for a living. That his father was a triad leader also explained why he had around fifty heavily tattooed "uncles" who were always dropping by his house at odd hours.

After his long and highly informative journey from Hong Kong, Stanley arrived at the Academy on September 1, 1960. He was the first Asian cadet ever at the school. His father had warned him that this would be difficult, but Stanley did not really understand what his father meant until after he had spent a few days on campus. The other boys generally treated him like a visitor from another planet. They were interested to watch him from a distance, but they did not want to get too close.

On the rare occasions when other cadets did speak to him, they always seemed surprised he could understand them. Even though his English was fluent, and in fact even better than his Cantonese, the other boys looked amazed that English words could come out of a Chinese mouth. So, while the rest of his freshmen class got to know each other and over time develop friendships, Stanley was mainly left on his own.

That kind of isolation was hard enough for Stanley, but on top of that, there was Donald. The first time they met, Donald called him Fu Manchu. The name meant nothing to Stanley at the time, since Fu Manchu movies never played in Hong Kong. It was only later that Stanley learned Fu Manchu was a Chinese supervillain popularized by Hollywood who was always pursuing devious schemes to take over the world. Although he hated that nickname, when Stanley finally saw an image of Fu Manchu in another cadet's comic book, he could not help but laugh. With his long, wispy mustache and Changshan jacket, the character looked more like an old Hong Kong tea seller than an evil genius.

Even after other cadets started calling him Fu Manchu, Stanley assumed it was just a bad joke that would soon get old for them. But it never did get old. After a while, even some of the teachers at the school were calling him Fu Manchu. Almost never hearing his real name made Stanley feel even more alone at the Academy.

Stanley never told his parents he was called Fu Manchu. So his father did not know that the cadet who Stanley had helped on the window ledge was also responsible for his cruel nickname. But Stanley was sure it would not matter in any case to his father. Under the code followed by the Ho Fong Triad, Stanley had done the right thing. He had helped one of his peers stay out of trouble with the authorities.

Stanley was now in Major Burnside's chemistry classroom on the third floor of Jessup Hall. When class ended, the cadets began to file out, but the major shouted his name and waved him over to the lab table at the front of the room.

"Yes, Major," Stanley said.

"How are you feeling, Fu?" Major Burnside asked. "I heard from Lieutenant Drake about the attack you had in his office."

Major Burnside was the only person at the school who had decided to shorten his nickname to just Fu. It was even more jarring to Stanley to hear his racist nickname said so casually.

"I'm okay now, sir," Stanley said.

"What does the doctor think happened to you anyway?" Major Burnside said.

Stanley wished Major Burnside would change the subject, because he hated lying. He had done what was expected of him as a member of the Ho Fong Triad, but that did not make covering up for Donald any easier on his conscience.

"His diagnosis was an unexplained seizure," Stanley said.

"Oh, I see. That sounds kind of mysterious," Major Burnside said. "Have you had unexplained seizures before?"

"No, sir," Stanley said.

"Well, I hope it doesn't come back," Major Burnside said.

"I doubt it will," Stanley said.

"Anyway, I've been meaning to talk to you about your science project," Major Burnside said.

Stanley had assumed that was the reason Major Burnside had asked him to stay. Major Burnside had chosen Stanley to be the Academy's representative in the Morgan Chemical Talent Search, a competition for high school seniors in the New York area. Morgan Chemical, the chemicals-producing arm of the giant J.P. Morgan corporate family (with its famous slogan, "Connecting the World with Plastic"), had sponsored the competition every year since the New York's World Fair in 1939. Chemistry teachers at high schools throughout the region were encouraged to nominate a student to submit a paper based on original research in any area of chemistry. The top prize was a thousand-dollar college scholarship.

Stanley's project was on the dissipation rate from the aerial delivery of chemical defoliants. Major Burnside had suggested the topic. He had worked on chemical warfare programs while he was in the army's Chemical Corps, and believed defoliants would be critical to warfare in the future as more conflicts occurred in the deep jungles of Africa and Southeast Asia. An enemy would not be able to grow food or hide out in the jungle if the army could kill all their crops and strip all the leaves off the trees with chemicals. Major Burnside was also sure that Morgan Chemical, which was a major supplier to the army's chemical warfare program, would appreciate the obvious military applications of Stanley's work.

"We have a little bit of a problem," Major Burnside continued. "Phil Owens has been sniffing around my chemistry lab. He's suspicious about what killed the lawn."

Stanley knew Phil Owens was the Academy's groundskeeper, and that the lawn Major Burnside was referring to was the one just behind Jessup Hall. The experiments Stanley had done for his project involved spraying a form of dichlorine acid from the roof of Jessup Hall to determine the speed at which the acid would break down as it fell to the ground. Not surprisingly, his experiments had laid waste to a large section of the grass.

Major Burnside knew the experiments would damage the lawn, so he told Stanley only to spray acid from the roof after six o'clock, when Phil Owens went off duty. The major had left permission with Mrs. Duncannon for him to go upstairs in Jessup Hall every evening for a week. Stanley would first pick up spraying equipment—bottles of acid and safety gloves and goggles from the third-floor chemistry lab—and then head up to the roof.

It turned out those evenings on the roof were some of the most enjoyable ones Stanley had spent at the Academy. He had carried out the experiments in early September, when the weather was just starting to cool down and usually became a perfect sixty-five or seventy degrees after six o'clock. Stanley had also discovered that the roof of Jessup Hall provided a perfect view of the Newark Airport runways, which were only a few hundred yards from campus. He would often stop working for thirty minutes at a time just to watch the planes land.

"You want me to tell Mr. Owens what I did, sir?" Stanley asked.

"Oh no, absolutely not! Phil would kill me if he knew I agreed to this experiment," Major Burnside said. "Actually, it's just the opposite. I wanted to remind you not to tell anyone about the spraying."

"Sure, no problem," Stanley said.

"You're sure you can keep a secret, Fu?"

"It won't be any problem for me at all, sir."

Stanley thought how shocked Major Burnside would be if he knew the kinds of secrets Stanley was able to keep. He knew his father had once poisoned the Hong Kong chief of police. He knew the best way to smuggle guns into Hong Kong. And he knew Donald had been on the window ledge outside Lieutenant Drake's office the night Teddy died. If he could keep these secrets, he certainly would be able to conceal being responsible for destroying the grass outside Jessup Hall.

"I also wanted to remind you that Morgan Chemical's announcing the winner of the talent search next Thursday," Major Burnside said.

"Oh really," Stanley said, not letting on that, for the last month, he had been counting the days until the announcement.

"I understand they usually name the top ten finalists a few days before the announcement and invite them to the ceremony," Major Burnside said. "So just be ready. You might be going to New York next Thursday."

"You really think I could make the top ten, sir?" Stanley asked.

"Definitely, I think your project could even be the winner," Major Burnside said.

Logically, Stanley knew Major Burnside was not a reliable judge of what kind of project could win the Morgan Chemical Talent Search, seeing as no cadet from the Academy had ever won it before. But still his teacher's words made Stanley happy again for the first time since that night. He really wanted that prize to show the other cadets just how smart he really was.

5

Thursday, October 10, 1963 (3:41 p.m.)

DONALD HAD GROWN VERY BORED NOT GOING TO CLASS. When Colonel Overstreet gave him a week off to mourn his roommate, it had seemed like a great deal. But it turned out that during class hours he was only allowed to go to Jessup Cafeteria for meals or to Jessup Chapel to pray or meet with Chaplain Roberts. The rest of the time, he was expected to be engaged in quiet reflection in his room. Since he had no interest in going to Jessup Chapel, Donald ended up spending all day in his room.

He had smuggled a *Playboy* magazine into the barracks and kept it secretly taped to the bottom of his bed frame. But even that could only entertain him for a minute or two at a time. Since the only other reading material he had was textbooks, quiet reflection had become extremely tedious.

After a day spent mainly lying on his bed, Donald practically ran to football practice at Jessup Field at 3:30 p.m. While he was usually one of the last players to get on the field, this week he was among the first. In recognition of Donald's newly found dedication, Coach Mulrooney asked him to help lead the calisthenics the team did at the start of every practice. Standing in the spot that used to be occupied by Teddy, Donald helped lead the team through their regimen of exercises.

They were finishing their second set of jumping jacks when Colonel Overstreet appeared on the edge of the field, walking quickly toward them. Colonel Overstreet was well over six feet tall with very broad shoulders, but he had a small face and was almost completely bald. Donald always thought he looked like a large man who had borrowed a much smaller man's head.

Coach Mulrooney blew his whistle and the players stood at attention for the school's headmaster. Colonel Overstreet walked straight toward Donald and stopped a few feet from him.

"At ease, cadets," Colonel Overstreet said. "I need Donald to come with me."

That sounded ominous to Donald. His first thought was that Fu Manchu had suckered him and ratted him out. He knew he should have threatened him, but Fu Manchu had been so convincing with his "none of my business" line that Donald had skipped over the horrible things he would do to him if he ever snitched.

Now Donald was walking next to Colonel Overstreet toward Jessup Hall. The shoulder pads under his gray practice uniform felt heavy and itchy, and he started to sweat much more profusely than he had during calisthenics. If Stanley had snitched, Donald was cooked, big-time. He would be expelled and would never be able to get into a decent college. His father would probably sentence him to mixing gravel at one of his construction sites in Queens. His whole life seemed to be coming apart, all because Teddy made a mistake and died. It was so unfair. Why should he have to suffer because of that error?

They walked most of the way in silence. The only sound was the clicking of Donald's football cleats against the concrete walkway, and Donald could feel his heart rate going up with every step.

"Donald, this won't take very long," Colonel Overstreet finally said once they had almost reached Jessup Hall.

"Okay, Colonel," Donald said.

Donald wondered if condemned prisoners were also told "This won't take very long" as they were being marched to the execution chamber. He could not stand the suspense anymore. He had to know if this was his last walk on campus as a cadet.

"Can I ask, Colonel, what this is about?"

"Teddy's parents are here," Colonel Overstreet said. "They want to see you."

Donald exhaled deeply and fought the urge to smile. Stanley had not squealed.

"They have suffered a great loss," Colonel Overstreet continued. "I want to make sure you understand how important it is that you don't upset them."

"I understand, Colonel," Donald said, despite not really understanding.

"Be respectful. Listen to Teddy's parents. That's all you need to do. Do you understand, Donald?"

"Yes, Colonel," Donald said.

"You're a cadet at the second-oldest military academy in New Jersey," Colonel Overstreet said. "As soldiers, when we lose one of our own, we never upset their loved ones. We stay respectfully quiet. You understand, don't you, Donald?"

"Yes, Colonel," Donald said.

Donald was not sure why the colonel felt the need to warn him to stay quiet. It was not like there was a lot he wanted to say about Teddy's death. In fact, even if he had wanted to tell Teddy's parents the truth, he was not sure what the truth was.

That night on the ledge outside Lieutenant Drake's office, Donald assumed Teddy had just lost his balance and fallen. Since then, other cadets kept asking him if he knew his best friend had been depressed. The more Donald was asked that question, the more he wondered if Teddy may really have been depressed despite all of his outward happiness. Donald had begun to think it really might have been a suicide after all. Although it would be strange for Teddy to suddenly decide to kill himself while they were hiding from Lieutenant Drake, it was not impossible. It could have been a suicide of opportunity.

Donald followed the colonel into Jessup Hall. As he went through the front door, he noticed Jerry Stahl walking out of the nearby Jessup Auditorium, and wondered for a second how Jerry would be as a roommate.

Donald had already started considering who would make a good replacement for Teddy. He did not want Teddy's side of the room to stay unoccupied for the rest of the year, because at the Academy there was a stigma attached to living alone. Only cadets with problems, like bed-wetters and nighttime criers, ever got a single room. Living alone would also make him ineligible to win the cleanest room prize at the end of the semester. That prize, which carried with it a weekend leave, only went to roommates. Donald was too competitive to willingly forfeit the chance to win a prize that came with extra privileges.

Jerry certainly paled in comparison to Teddy in every way as roommate material. But Jerry had been his best friend from their first day of kindergarten at Kew Gardens Elementary until the day they both got to the Academy. With their history, Jerry would be easier for him to get used to than any other cadet. Besides that, Donald was already very popular in his own right. He no longer needed the validation of living with a popular boy.

Donald followed Colonel Overstreet into the faculty elevator, and they went up to the fifth floor. It was the first time he had been in the faculty elevator. It was also his first time back in Jessup Hall since that night. As they walked down the corridor, they passed the open door to Lieutenant Drake's office. Donald did not look inside. He had no interest in being reminded of what had happened there.

At the other end of the corridor, they went through the outer room, where Colonel Overstreet's secretary was typing at her desk, and walked into the colonel's large office. The office was on the other side of the building from Lieutenant Drake's. Instead of looking out onto Jessup Quadrangle, the colonel had a view of the green hills that separated the Academy from the runways of Newark Airport.

Teddy's parents were waiting on the sofa inside. They both stood up, and Teddy's mother hurried over to Donald and hugged him so tightly, he could feel her breasts under her sweater. She was crying, and her chest was heaving with each sob. Donald had spent a few days at Teddy's house last Christmas break and had seen how his mother had doted on Teddy, so he had been expecting tears. But this much crying was making him very uncomfortable.

Teddy's father came over next and shook Donald's hand. It was a firm handshake, but not as firm as his own father's, Donald thought. His father had a grip like an industrial clamp.

"Oh my, the sight of you in that football uniform reminds me so much of Teddy," Mrs. Haswell said as tears ran down her cheeks.

"It's okay, Marjorie," Mr. Haswell said, gently stroking his wife's shoulder.

Donald realized he had not been back in the headmaster's office since his first year, when he had gotten in trouble for starting a rumor that the school's English teacher, Major Clark, was a Soviet spy. It turned out Colonel Overstreet took suggestions of Communist infiltration at the Academy very seriously, and he had threatened to expel Donald if he ever said something like that again.

When his father had heard about it, he did Colonel Overstreet one better. Not only would he pull Donald out of school, but he would put him in the army for real if he heard his son had been sent again to the headmaster's office. After that, Donald had been very careful to avoid that fate. Although he had collected more than his fair share of demerits over the years, he had skillfully managed to keep the trouble he got into at a level below the headmaster's radar.

Donald did not want to make eye contact with Teddy's parents. Instead, he scanned the colonel's desk for his famous golden Buddha statue. The rumor at the Academy was that Colonel Overstreet had single-handedly killed ten North Korean soldiers at a temple and then taken a golden Buddha from the altar as a souvenir of the battle. Donald was surprised Koreans had enough gold to make decorations out of it. He always thought gold was reserved only for rich people. The statue, which Donald spotted next to the phone, was smaller than he remembered from when he had seen it as a freshman.

"Why don't we all sit down?" Colonel Overstreet said.

"Actually, Colonel, if you don't mind, we'd like to speak to Donald alone for a minute," Mr. Haswell said. "We just have a few questions, and we think Donald may be more comfortable if it's just us."

Colonel Overstreet stopped halfway to his desk chair and turned around. Donald hoped the colonel would object, since

Donald had absolutely no desire to be alone with Teddy's parents. It would be uncomfortable enough just dealing with a crying mother, without having to answer any questions. *Please, Colonel, say you need to stay.*

"All right," the colonel said. "I have some things to do downstairs. But I'll need to get Donald back to practice soon. We have the big game tomorrow, as you know."

"This won't take long," Mr. Haswell said.

Colonel Overstreet left the room, shutting the door loudly behind him. Donald felt his heart pounding under his football pads. He had not prepared anything to say to Teddy's parents.

"Let's sit down on the couch," Mrs. Haswell said.

Teddy's parents went back to the sofa and sat down at the two ends, leaving the middle for Donald. Although it was a three-seater sofa, Donald, in his full football uniform, felt jammed in between them.

"We know how close you and Teddy were, Donald," Mr. Haswell said. "How are you doing?"

"Okay, I guess," Donald said. "I mean, it's really hard, because I miss Teddy, but I'm okay."

"Teddy was always such a happy boy. We just don't understand this," Mrs. Haswell said, tears still freely flowing down her cheeks.

"Did he seem to you like he was upset about anything? Had something happened?" Mr. Haswell asked.

"Well, maybe a little upset. Maybe he was feeling pressure about football and grades and everything," Donald said.

"Anything in particular?" Mr. Haswell asked.

"Not really," Donald said.

Donald stared down at his cleats. Although he had decided it was possible Teddy had committed suicide that night, he could not actually remember any specific times when Teddy seemed sad.

"Donald, the Academy sent us Teddy's things, and we went through them all yesterday," Mr. Haswell said. "We hadn't realized Teddy kept journals."

"Did you know Teddy had a diary?" Mrs. Haswell asked.

"A journal, not a diary," Mr. Haswell said.

"No, I didn't know," Donald said, wondering what the difference was between a journal and a diary.

Donald had seen Teddy writing in a notebook plenty of times, but he had never asked what he was doing. He certainly would not have pegged Teddy as the kind of guy who kept a diary—or a journal, for that matter.

"He didn't write in it every day, but he did write something the day he died," Mrs. Haswell said. "It said you two were going to do something in Jessup Hall, and he hoped he wouldn't get into too much trouble. What were you going to do, Donald?"

Donald swallowed hard. He was an excellent liar, but he did his best work when he had some time to prepare. When he had to make up lies on the spot, it could be hard to keep his story straight.

"Oh, we were just going to pull a prank or something on some other guys. I don't even really remember," Donald said.

"You were going to pull a prank in Jessup Hall?" Mrs. Haswell asked.

She looked very serious and was not crying anymore. It was unfair that she was asking questions one after the other. She was not giving him any time to think.

"Yeah, in the library. The library's in Jessup Hall. We were going to take some guy's book or something."

"And you did that? You took another cadet's book?" Mrs. Haswell asked.

"No, we changed our minds. We decided just to study. You know, because the Westport game is coming up, we didn't want to get in any trouble."

"So you boys decided not to pull a prank and instead my son killed himself," Mrs. Haswell said, her voice rising sharply. "That doesn't make any sense to me, Donald. Why would Teddy be too worried about the Westport game to take a book, but be willing to jump off the roof?"

Donald felt like the sofa was getting smaller and smaller and he was being pressed from both sides. He wanted to get up, but there was no place to go, since he could not just leave the office without permission. He wished Teddy's mother would realize that if she asked her questions more slowly, he would be able to come up with better answers.

"Marjorie, please. Donald's also suffering from Teddy's loss," Mr. Haswell said.

"Of course, and I'm so sorry to bring this all up, Donald," Mrs. Haswell said in a suddenly softer tone. "We just want to know what happened. There's nothing in his diary about him feeling depressed or wanting to commit suicide. Nothing at all. So we are just trying to piece together what could have happened that night."

"We asked Colonel Overstreet to leave so you wouldn't have to worry about getting into any trouble if you and Teddy were up to something that could get you demerits," Mr. Haswell added. "We just want to know the truth. I promise we won't say anything to the colonel, if that's what you're worried about."

Donald knew the weak link in the chain of reasoning that Teddy committed suicide was that his best friend had never seemed particularly depressed. If he were going to survive this inquisition from Teddy's parents, Donald realized he needed to sow some seeds of doubt about Teddy's seemingly upbeat disposition.

"I think maybe Teddy was the kind of guy who didn't like to talk about it when he felt sad. He was kind of the Gary Cooper, strong-but-silent type, you know," Donald said. "He almost never said anything about his feelings."

Donald stopped for a second to see how this newly invented theory about Teddy's stoicism was being received by Teddy's parents. They looked intrigued, so he kept going.

"Maybe he wouldn't even write anything about being sad in his diary. He was a captain of the football team, you know. He probably thought if he admitted he was depressed, it would be like he was weak or something."

"But you think he was depressed?" Mrs. Haswell asked.

"I think yeah, maybe," Donald said.

"And you don't think this prank, taking a book or whatever it was from the library, had anything to do with Teddy's death?" Mr. Haswell asked.

"No, we changed our minds about that," Donald said. "I guess Teddy just didn't have time to update his journal about us changing our minds, you know, since he died and all."

Just as Donald finished speaking, Colonel Overstreet's secretary, Mrs. Kreitzenbach, opened the office door and peeked in. She was a tiny woman with a remarkably high bouffant hairdo, and her hair appeared in the doorway a few seconds before her face.

"Sorry to disturb your conversation, but the colonel asked me to make sure Donald didn't stay too long. He's needed at football practice," Mrs. Kreitzenbach said.

Donald jumped up from the couch before Teddy's parents could say anything. He was feeling proud of himself. The information about Teddy's diary had thrown him for a loop at first, but then it was like he had used mind control to shift the conversation. But he did not want to test his powers by staying any longer.

"Okay, sorry I can't talk anymore now," Donald said, practically running toward the office door.

"Just one more thing," Mr. Haswell said before Donald had managed to get to the door. "We can't find Teddy's watch. He wasn't wearing it, and it wasn't in the stuff the Academy sent us. Have you seen it? It's a family heirloom, so we really hope to find it."

Donald knew exactly where Teddy's watch—a gold Omega Seamaster—was at that moment. It was inside a sock in Donald's storage locker. Just before the custodians had arrived to pack up Teddy's things, Donald had found the watch in Teddy's desk drawer. He had decided to take it as a reminder of his best friend. He was sure Teddy would have wanted him to have it.

"I'll be sure to keep my eye out for it, sir," Donald said before racing out of the office.

6

Thursday, October 10, 1963 (4:15 p.m.)

JERRY STAHL WAS ENJOYING HIS SUDDEN POPULARITY AT
the Academy. Ever since he'd found Teddy's body on Jessup
Quadrangle, the other cadets had wanted to hear about his
gruesome discovery. Just seeing a dead body would have
been enough to interest his classmates. That the body he had
found belonged to a fellow cadet who was also the school's
star quarterback made him the toast of campus.

He had repeated the story so many times that the embel-
lishments had started to add up. His account now included
stepping in Teddy's blood and then turning the body over and
seeing Teddy's lifeless eyes staring up at him. Although these
dramatic moments always elicited a strong reaction, neither
had occurred. Jerry had never gotten within ten feet of Teddy.
He had noticed the body as he was walking back to the library,
and then he ran to Jessup Cafeteria, where he knew it was faculty poker night, to get help.

Jerry was now setting up Jessup Auditorium for the fall
dance along with the other members of the Academy's spirit

club. The dance was held every year jointly with the Parker School, the all-girls boarding school that was just five miles from the Academy. It was always held the day after the big football game against Westport Country Day.

The fall dance was an important tradition at the Academy. Other than the commencement ball in May, the fall dance was the only time girls were allowed on campus. The mission of the Academy was to produce disciplined and educated young gentlemen, and part of becoming a gentleman was learning how to treat a young lady at a dance.

The fall dance was particularly critical for the fourth-year cadets, because the commencement ball six months later was only for graduating cadets and required a date to attend. For many fourth-year cadets, the fall dance was their only chance to speak to a girl all year. If a boy struck out entirely there, he might need to resort to bringing a cousin or a friend's sister to the commencement ball.

Jerry had joined the spirit club specifically to get a leg up on finding a date. Every year, during the week before the fall dance, the members of the spirit club got to take a field trip to Parker to plan the event. They met for one hour, under very close supervision of faculty from both schools, with Parker's social events committee. It was commonly believed at the Academy that all the most beautiful girls at Parker joined the social events committee. Therefore, membership in the spirit club meant getting to meet the cream of the girls' school before all the rest of the cadets.

Just as Jerry had hoped, there had been a beautiful girl on Parker's social committee. To make it even better, she had sat across from him during the planning session. Her name was Cindy Grubb. She was tall, but not too much taller than Jerry, with long blond hair and blue eyes. Although they had only spoken for a few minutes before the meeting began, Jerry was sure he had made a good impression. It turned out they had a lot in common. During their brief chat, they discovered they both liked Paul Anka, which Jerry took as a good sign for their future relationship.

Jerry had been surprised to see a familiar face at the meeting. Dorothy Rodgers, from his hometown in Queens, had been there. He had forgotten she went to Parker. They had gone to elementary and middle school together in Kew Gardens, and Dorothy had been the smartest kid in every class since first grade. Donald used to say he was smarter than Dorothy and could get just as good grades as her if he tried, but Jerry knew that was not true. Dorothy's brain just seemed to work at a different speed than everybody else's.

Although Dorothy was friendly to him, Jerry was relieved she went and sat on the other end of the table. She had always intimidated him. Her mouth moved a mile a minute and, for some reason, the faster she spoke, the more tongue-tied he always became. He was sure he would not make a good impression on Cindy if Dorothy were sitting nearby.

Having established a connection with Cindy at the meeting, Jerry was planning to look for her as soon as the Parker girls arrived for the dance. He wanted to stake his claim before any of the more popular boys had a chance to notice her. If the conversation went well, he would ask her right then and there to the commencement ball in May. With luck, he would have Cindy locked down as his date for the ball before the fall dance had even really started.

Jerry was up on a ladder, taping fake palm fronds made of butcher paper onto a Jessup Auditorium wall. The Academy generally prohibited cadets from putting up any kind of decorations, in the barracks or elsewhere. The previous headmaster believed decorations could lead to "homosexual thoughts." Even for the big game against Westport Country Day, the cadets were not allowed to hang any signs at the football field.

However, at the strong urging of Miss Parker, the Parker School's headmistress, they were permitted to select a theme for the fall dance and put up a modest amount of decorations. At the meeting, they had agreed on a South Pacific theme for this year's dance. Colonel Overstreet, who had served in the South Pacific during World War II, thought that was a horrible theme choice and initially vetoed it. His main memory of the South Pacific was virulent dysentery. But he relented after Miss Parker reminded him about the Rodgers and Hammerstein musical. She had sung a few bars of "I'm Gonna Wash That Man Right Outa My Hair" to trigger his memory.

The spirit club interpreted the South Pacific theme to mean they should tape one butcher paper palm tree to each of the four walls of Jessup Auditorium. They thought that the trees, along with serving Hawaiian Punch at the snack table, would create a sufficiently tropical environment for the dance.

Jerry had put up a few palm fronds when he realized he did not have enough masking tape to finish the job. He looked down at his fellow spirit club member, Glen Eberhardt, who was steadying the ladder.

"Got any more tape?" Jerry asked.

"Nope," Glen replied.

"Anyone got tape?" Jerry yelled in the direction of the six other club members, who were together in the middle of the auditorium working on cutting out and painting palm trees from two large rolls of brown butcher paper.

There was no response, and Jerry decided it was not worth asking again. He left his handful of paper palm fronds on the top rung of the ladder and quickly climbed down.

"I'll go over to the library and ask Mrs. Dumb Cannon for tape," Jerry said to Glen.

As Jerry was leaving Jessup Auditorium, he noticed Donald in his practice uniform following Colonel Overstreet into Jessup Hall. He guessed Donald might have gotten into trouble at practice. It reminded Jerry of being back in third grade at Kew Gardens Elementary and watching Donald being marched by their teacher, Mrs. Naughton, to the principal's office, which used to happen at least once a month.

Back then, Donald had been Jerry's best friend, and Jerry had assumed it would stay that way when they both went to the Academy. But almost as soon as they got on campus, Donald did not seem to want to spend any time with him. He was always with his football and baseball team buddies, especially Teddy Haswell. Even when they were back in Queens for the summer, where their parents only lived a few blocks apart, he rarely saw Donald anymore.

Jerry missed being Donald's best friend. Donald had a way of making even everyday sorts of things feel special. Since as far back as Jerry could remember, Donald had always had this unique confidence that whatever he was doing was absolutely the right and perfect thing to do at that moment. That made Jerry feel lucky just to be doing it with him. Even if they were just taking turns kicking a rock down Jamaica Avenue, Donald could make Jerry feel like there was nothing better in this world that two guys could be doing right then than kicking that rock.

Being Donald's best friend certainly came with challenges. He was stubborn about everything, and if he did not get his way, he could be demeaning and cruel. But Jerry quickly learned just to let Donald call all the shots. As long as he did that, there was something magical about being Donald's best friend.

Jerry went into Jessup Hall and found Mrs. Duncannon at her usual spot at the library's front desk. It was his first time back in the library since that night.

"Jerry, how are you?" Mrs. Duncannon asked.

"I'm okay, Mrs. Duncannon. Do you have any tape we could use for decorating the auditorium?"

He was not sure if Mrs. Duncannon had heard him. She just kept staring at him with an extremely sympathetic look on her face.

"Any tape, Mrs. Duncannon?" he asked again.

"Oh, Jerry, how horrible it must have been to find a classmate like that," Mrs. Duncannon said, ignoring his request. "Were you and Teddy friends?"

Jerry looked at Mrs. Duncannon's desk and could see there was a large tape dispenser right in front of her. In fact, it was within inches of her right hand. But she did not make a move for it.

"I guess we were friends," Jerry said.

"But you didn't see him jump, did you?" Mrs. Duncannon asked.

"No, I don't know when he jumped. I just found the body."

"Did you know right away it was Teddy?" Mrs. Duncannon asked.

Jerry was about to tell his latest version of the story, in which he had turned over the body and seen Teddy's eyes, wide open and lifeless, but he wondered if he could get in trouble for saying he had touched the body. Maybe turning over a dead person before the police arrived was against the law. He decided when he was speaking to adults, he should stick just to what had really happened.

"No, I didn't know it was Teddy at first," Jerry said. "He was lying facedown."

"Such a tragedy," Mrs. Duncannon said.

"To tell you the truth, at first I thought it was Fu Manchu."

Mrs. Duncannon looked confused. He guessed she might not know Stanley's nickname.

"I mean Stanley. I thought it was Stanley Wong," Jerry said.

"Why in the world would you think a body you found on the quadrangle would be Stanley Wong?" Mrs. Duncannon asked.

"Well, just because about ten minutes before that I saw Stanley standing on the roof."

That night, Jerry had left the library to get his trigonometry textbook from his room. As he was walking through Jessup Quadrangle on his way to the barracks, he had noticed someone moving around on the roof of Jessup Hall. There was a large light on the roof to make the building visible to pilots landing at Newark Airport nearby, and when the person walked near that light, Jerry saw clearly it was Stanley.

"You're sure it was Stanley on the roof?" Mrs. Duncannon asked.

"Yeah. You know Stanley doesn't really look much like other guys around here," Jerry said.

Mrs. Duncannon looked confused again. Jerry wondered if she was unaware of a fact that was well-known among the cadets. Ever since a bunch of kids were trapped and killed in a stairwell during a school fire in Staten Island last year, the Academy had been leaving all their stairwell exit doors unlocked from the inside.

"Was he alone up there?" Mrs. Duncannon asked.

"I didn't see anybody else," Jerry said.

He could not understand why Mrs. Duncannon was so interested in Stanley. It was not as if Stanley had committed suicide.

"So, Mrs. Duncannon, I should really get back to the auditorium. Can I borrow your tape?"

Jerry was relieved that Mrs. Duncannon finally reached for the tape dispenser on her desk. She picked it up and handed it to him.

"Jerry, did you tell anyone else you saw Stanley on the roof of Jessup Hall that night?"

Jerry thought for a few seconds. He had told the story of finding Teddy's body so many times in the past week, it was not easy to remember all the details he had shared with different people.

"I don't think so," Jerry said.

7

Thursday, October 10, 1963 (7:03 p.m.)

"So, THE TOPIC TONIGHT IS WHO DO WE THINK WILL be the Republican nominee in the presidential election next year," Dorothy Rodgers said.

She was standing in front of the six members of the Parker School's current events club, who were sitting around the long conference table in the school's activities room. The current events club met every Thursday night at 7:00 p.m. for an hour.

Dorothy had come up with the club last year. She had written its charter and was the club's president. She was also its acting treasurer ever since Diane Lewis had resigned last month.

The topic that had caused Diane to quit was the anti-miscegenation laws that existed in many states. Dorothy considered herself a fierce advocate for civil rights, and she had picked that topic so she could go on record that she considered those laws repugnant. As usual, Dorothy spoke first and most of the other club members simply agreed with her. Only Diane took the other side, arguing it would be too confusing to let blacks and whites get married, because their children would not know which race they were. After a while, Diane decided Dorothy was falsely implying she was a racist. She stood up, announced she was resigning from the club effective immediately, and stormed out.

Since no one else was willing to replace Diane as treasurer, Dorothy became acting treasurer, taking on the responsibility for the club's small snack budget. Dorothy decided it would be a good idea to avoid controversial topics for a while. If the club lost any more members, it could lose its right to use the activities room.

"What do people think?" Dorothy asked the club. "Any ideas for nominees?"

"Do we really have to talk about that? It's so boring," Lizzie Matthews said. "Everybody knows Kennedy's going to win again. Let's talk about something else."

"Excuse me, Lizzie," Dorothy said. "But, as you know, under the club's charter, the president sets the main topic for the night. If you want to propose a secondary topic, you can do that, but only after at least half the club members attending the meeting have spoken on the main topic."

Lizzie always tried to steer the discussion toward more trivial topics like movies or school gossip, and Dorothy was tired of constantly needing to fight to keep the club compliant with its charter. In fact, Dorothy was tired of the club altogether. She was busy enough being president of five other school clubs, and she had only started the current events club to strengthen her college applications. Since she had received an early admission letter from Wellesley the week before, the club had already served its purpose.

She only wanted to keep the club going for her friend Cindy Grubb. Cindy was too shy to speak in class. The club was the one place Dorothy had ever seen Cindy express an opinion in front of a group.

"Cindy, do you have any ideas you want to share?" Dorothy asked.

"You mean about the presidential election or about whether we should talk about something else?"

"About possible Republican nominees," Dorothy said.

"I don't really know. Maybe Nixon? Can he run again?"

"He can, but Nixon's already said he's done running for office. Don't you remember he said that after he lost for California governor?"

Dorothy stressed *he can* to sound positive about Cindy's answer. She knew Cindy might stay quiet for the rest of the night if she felt like she had said something dumb.

"Oh, okay. Well, I'm not sure then," Cindy said, looking down at the table.

"See, I told you this topic is boring," Lizzie said. "Who cares about Republicans anyway? They should just let Kennedy be president for life."

"I agree," Mary Mills, Lizzie's best friend, added. "Let's talk about something else."

"Like how about why Cindy spent so much time at the social events committee meeting talking to that one guy from the Academy," Lizzie said.

Dorothy considered whether to squash this second attempt by Lizzie to hijack the agenda, but she decided to let it go this time. Maybe a little time spent gossiping would be good for club morale.

"What are you talking about?" Cindy asked.

"That guy you were sitting across from," Lizzie said. "He was getting all googly-eyed talking to you."

"No, he wasn't!" Cindy protested.

"Yes, he was. He looked like he was falling in love with you right then and there in the meeting," Lizzie said.

"You guys must be talking about Jerry Stahl. He's from my hometown," Dorothy said.

"What's he like? Is he good-looking?" Mary asked.

Dorothy only ever thought of Jerry in relation to his best friend from back in Kew Gardens, Donald. And she could not stand Donald. He was the kind of boy who never had anything valuable to say, but thought he would seem smarter if he spoke louder than everyone else. Jerry was just a miniature Donald wannabe. It had never even crossed her mind to consider whether he was good-looking.

"Umm . . . I don't think so," Dorothy said after pondering the question for a few seconds. "He's kind of short and has bad skin."

"You guys are so gross!" Cindy said. "I didn't like that guy. He's, like, four inches shorter than me! It felt like talking to one of my stupid little brother's friends."

"Well, Sal Mineo's short and he's good-looking," Mary said.

"Yeah, and I read that Tony Curtis is only, like, five-foot-six," Lizzie said.

"Okay," Dorothy said, wanting to get the club back on track before Lizzie and Mary could think of any more short actors. "I think we should get back to the main topic now. What about Governor Rockefeller? Does anyone think he could be the Republican nominee?"

"Well, maybe he could get nominated just because he's rich," Cindy offered hesitantly.

Lizzie and Mary groaned to express their displeasure that the gossip session had been cut short. Dorothy took a long breath, closed her eyes, and told herself that soon she would be far away from these silly Parker girls and with other women just like her at Wellesley.

8

Friday, October 11, 1963 (3:45 p.m.)

Stanley Wong had been a voracious reader ever since he was three years old. That was when he had shocked his mother by picking up *The Tale of Peter Rabbit* off the nursery floor and then reading the first paragraph out loud to her. This intellectual feat was so unprecedented in the Wong family that many of his relatives in Hong Kong did not believe it. They suspected his mother had made up the story.

There was some reason for their skepticism, as it was a common practice in the Wong family for parents to exaggerate wildly about their children's accomplishments. One of Stanley's aunts had claimed that his cousin was a violin prodigy for years until the family learned the boy had quit the violin after only a few lessons. But in Stanley's case, the story was true.

After reading that first paragraph about Mrs. Rabbit instructing her children not to go into Mr. McGregor's garden, there was no stopping Stanley. He was almost never seen again without a book in his hands. By the time he left for the New

Jersey Military Academy, he had devoured much of the collection in the Hong Kong Central Library.

Stanley also read most of the books, in Chinese and English, in his family's own library. That was no small feat, since his grandfather, in addition to building one of the most powerful criminal enterprises in South China, had been a renowned bibliophile. He had used a significant portion of his ill-gotten gains to build up one of the largest book collections in Canton. Luckily for Stanley, his grandfather had managed to move that collection to Hong Kong one step ahead of the Chinese authorities confiscating it.

According to family legend, Stanley's grandfather had offended an army general by taking too much of his money one night at the mahjong table. Tipped off that as revenge the general was about to have him arrested, his grandfather had decided to make a run for it. He had only a few hours to pack all the things he could onto a junk and sail for Hong Kong. Finally, with a battalion of soldiers reported to be closing in on the dock, his grandfather needed to choose between loading fifteen crates of high-quality opium or his precious book collection. He chose the books.

His grandfather's book collection ended up filling ten floor-to-ceiling bookcases in one of the largest rooms in Stanley's house. Stanley had spent countless hours in that room, methodically reading his way through the collection. Whenever he ran into an English word or Chinese character he did not know, he would run to his mother and demand she stop whatever she was doing and explain it to him.

When he got to the Academy, Stanley had been excited at first to learn the cadets would be reading novels in English class. At his school in Hong Kong, English class just meant endless memorization of vocabulary and English grammar rules.

But Stanley quickly realized that most of his fellow cadets did not share his love of literature. Their lack of interest in reading, combined with the English faculty's low expectations, meant the cadets read very few books. Usually the teachers assigned a chapter a week, so it took months for the class to finish a single novel. During their entire first year, the only book the cadets had been expected to read was *A Tale of Two Cities*, and they still had several chapters left when the school year ended.

Since Stanley usually finished a book the weekend after it was handed out in class, he decided to supplement his English classes with his own private literature study. Mrs. Duncannon soon noticed how much time Stanley spent in the library wandering around the shelves looking for books, and by his second year they had worked out an arrangement. Every week, Mrs. Duncannon would choose a novel for Stanley to read, and the next week they would get together to discuss it.

Mrs. Duncannon mainly stuck to the classics, and Stanley had read many of the books already. He had gone through the Hong Kong library's English fiction section alphabetically by author, making it all the way to *M*. So only authors with last names late in the alphabet were completely unfamiliar to him. But Stanley never let on if he had read a book before. He thought that would be rude, and besides he wanted the chance to discuss each book with Mrs. Duncannon.

That first year, Mrs. Duncannon fed him a steady diet of nineteenth-century English novels like *Jane Eyre*, *Wuthering Heights*, and *Oliver Twist*. No matter how thick the book or difficult the prose, Stanley showed up at the library in one week, ready for his private tutorial. The next year, Mrs. Duncannon focused on classic American literature, like *The Last of the Mohicans*, *Uncle Tom's Cabin*, and *The Old Man and the Sea*.

One week, she assigned him *The Catcher in the Rye*. She made Stanley promise to keep the book hidden, because it was banned by the Academy's board. A few years ago, the board had instructed Colonel Overstreet to confiscate all of the copies from the library. But, when the colonel, glum-faced and clearly uncomfortable, came to her to carry out the board's order, she had given him only two of her three copies. She had hidden the other one in a desk drawer. Mrs. Duncannon said the board thought the story was sympathetic to Communism, but she disagreed, and she wanted Stanley to decide for himself.

Stanley's view of Communism came from his grandfather, who always said the only people in China more corrupt and bloodthirsty than the Nationalists were the Communists. One time he told a seven-year-old Stanley that the Nationalists would have put him in prison if they had ever caught him, but the Communists would have chopped him up and made New Year's dumplings out of him. That gruesome image had been impossible for Stanley to get out of his head for weeks.

Based on Stanley's understanding of Communism, *The Catcher in the Rye* had nothing to do with it. In fact, he had been disappointed when he finished the book. He thought the story would have been more interesting with a few bloodthirsty Communist characters.

For his last year, Mrs. Duncannon decided they would concentrate on Russian authors. Since she knew his English class would spend most of the year struggling through *Crime and Punishment*, she suggested Stanley develop a sense of the Russian literary context for that book. Stanley liked that idea. He had always been fascinated by the Russian immigrants who had come to Hong Kong after World War II. Even on the coldest days of winter, he would see Russians strolling through Hong Kong Park in light summer clothes, as if they were oblivious to the icy winds coming off Hong Kong Harbour. His most recent assignment from Mrs. Duncannon was *The Brothers Karamazov*.

As usual, Mrs. Duncannon was at her desk in front when Stanley came into the library. Her desk was perfectly organized as always, with a neat stack of books on one side and a notebook and pen on the other. It was Stanley's first time back in the library since that night.

When Mrs. Duncannon saw him, she stood up and smiled so broadly, her eyes seemed to close for a second. She took a few steps toward him, and Stanley was worried she was planning to hug him. Luckily, she did not get too close. His status at the school was low enough already. The last thing he needed was a rumor going around that he had been hugged by the librarian.

"Stanley, I was so worried about you!" Mrs. Duncannon said.

"I'm sorry," Stanley said.

"No, I wasn't blaming you," Mrs. Duncannon said. "I was just worried because I saw you that night being helped out of the building by Lieutenant Drake. You looked so weak, I was really scared for you."

"Okay, well, sorry," Stanley said, not sure what else he was supposed to say.

"What did Dr. Jamison say? Does he think it could happen again?" Mrs. Duncannon asked.

"I'm pretty sure it won't," Stanley said.

Stanley could not wait for people to stop asking him about his seizure. He was tired of needing to lie, and he just wanted his life to go back to normal. Talking to Mrs. Duncannon about a book on a Friday afternoon was part of his normal routine, so he had been looking forward to this trip to the library.

"Can we talk about the book?" Stanley asked, taking his copy of *The Brothers Karamazov* out of his jacket pocket.

"You finished it?" Mrs. Duncannon asked. "How did you possibly have time with everything that happened?"

"I had a lot of free time in the infirmary," Stanley said.

When he was brought into the infirmary, Dr. Jamison, the school doctor, had told Stanley that he suspected epilepsy, which he guessed might be a common affliction among the Chinese. The doctor hadn't let Stanley study, to avoid any chance that reading might trigger his possibly epileptic brain. Fortunately for Stanley, his copy of *The Brothers Karamazov* was in his jacket pocket when he was brought in, and he was able to read all night after Dr. Jamison went home.

"You're such a fast reader, Stanley. And sure, I would like to talk about the book," Mrs. Duncannon said. "You know I always have this time reserved for you."

Mrs. Duncannon opened the top drawer on her desk and pulled out a paperback copy of *The Brothers Karamazov*. He was impressed she knew exactly where her copy would be, even though she had not been expecting him. He followed Mrs. Duncannon to the small private study room on the other side of the library.

The study room, which was just big enough for a small wooden table and four chairs, was the only one of its type in the library. Mrs. Duncannon once told Stanley that she had researched the history of Jessup Hall and learned that when the library served as a convent chapel, the study room had been a punishment area for nuns who broke any rules. If a nun got caught falling asleep during Mass or talking during silent hours, she would have to take her prayers in that room, away from all the others.

In its current incarnation, the room was always empty. Stanley was not sure if Mrs. Duncannon knew why the cadets suddenly stopped using it a few years before, but he did. When they were second-year cadets, Donald had seen two of their classmates coming out of the study room and had started a rumor that they had gone in there to make out with each other. After that, the study room had been known among cadets as the "fag closet." Even going in there alone would have been dangerous for a cadet's reputation.

Mrs. Duncannon sat down at the study room table. As always, Stanley left the door halfway open just to play it safe and avoid any rumors starting about him and the librarian.

"So, did you like the story? Are you a big Dostoevsky fan now?" Mrs. Duncannon asked.

"Yeah, it was really good," Stanley said, sitting across the table from Mrs. Duncannon.

During those two nights in the infirmary, Stanley had not been able to put the book down. The complex family dynamics reminded him of his father's stories about the Ho Fong Triad. As his father described it, the triad was full of people with hidden agendas, secret alliances, and patricidal thoughts, just like the members of the Karamazov family.

But it was the long passages about guilt and the powerful compulsion to confess that had kept Stanley reading until morning. In the story, one of the brothers, Dmitri, feels responsible for his father's murder by his half brother, and the guilt drives him mad. It was the same fate as Raskolnikov in *Crime and Punishment*. Stanley thought that Russia must be a very scary place. It seemed that doing something wrong there always doomed people to losing their minds.

All alone in the infirmary in the middle of the night, Stanley had started to imagine Dostoevsky was somehow speaking directly to him. Like he was pushing Stanley to confess about that night and save his sanity. Stanley would sweat through his thin Academy pajamas and toss and turn in the sheets whenever he tried to put the book down and sleep for a while. Dostoevsky's characters were just lucky they did not have to live under the Ho Fong Triad's code of silence. These Russians, with their intensely guilty consciences, would never make it in a triad, Stanley thought.

"Major Clark said the theme of *Crime and Punishment* is that if you do something wrong and you don't confess, you can go crazy," Stanley said.

"Well, yes, I think Dostoevsky was very interested in what a guilty conscience can do to someone," Mrs. Duncannon said.

"Do you think it's true?" Stanley asked.

"Do I think Major Clark's right about that being a theme in *Crime and Punishment?*"

"No, do you think it's true if you know something and you don't confess, you will go crazy?" Stanley asked.

"Well, I think guilt is certainly a very powerful emotion," Mrs. Duncannon said. "Of course, I've never killed anyone, but I do know how hard it can be to keep a big secret. I think people all have a powerful desire to confess and be forgiven."

"So it's like the honor code says," Stanley said.

"How's that?" Mrs. Duncannon asked.

"The Academy honor code. It says you should always confess if you violate a rule or you know someone else who did. Maybe that's in the honor code so cadets don't go crazy," Stanley said.

"You know, I've never thought about it that way exactly," Mrs. Duncannon said.

"I think Dostoevsky was a very smart guy," Stanley said.

"I agree," Mrs. Duncannon said. "But, Stanley, is there something you want to tell me? You can talk to me about anything, you know. We don't just have to talk about books."

"No, nothing in particular," Stanley said. "But can we talk more about the book?"

9

Friday, October 11, 1963 (6:05 p.m.)

CADETS AT THE NEW JERSEY MILITARY ACADEMY sometimes wondered why their main football rival was Westport Country Day, a school that was more than seventy miles away, in Westport, Connecticut. They also wondered why they never played the General Hayes School for Boys, the only other military boarding school in New Jersey, which was less than twenty miles away, in Morristown. The answers to these questions went back to the founding of their school.

The New Jersey Military Academy was established in 1933 by New Jersey horse-racing magnate Randolph Jessup. Randolph was not an educator by nature. Rather, he founded the Academy out of necessity after his son, Randolph Jessup Jr., was kicked out of Summit High School for attacking his freshman English teacher with a grammar manual, a hardbound edition. Randolph decided that his overly rambunctious son could benefit from a strict military education. He had his secretary investigate military schools, and her research revealed that the only one within a reasonable driving distance of his house was the General Hayes School for Boys.

That school had been founded thirteen years before by General Lucius P. Hayes. General Hayes served for almost one month in France during the First World War before he contracted a particularly aggressive case of trench foot and needed to be evacuated to London. During his very brief time on the battlefield, General Hayes observed that his young officers, many of whom had gone to elite private schools like Andover, Exeter, and Choate, lacked the personal discipline and grit needed to lead men at war effectively. Upon his retirement from the army, General Hayes resolved to start a school that would instill those characteristics in future generations of upstanding boys of good breeding.

The General Hayes School for Boys was exactly the kind of institution Randolph believed could make a man out of his wayward son. Unfortunately for Randolph, however, General Hayes explicitly had enshrined "high character" in the school's charter as its primary admissions criteria. The school had a firm policy of not admitting students who had a history of assaulting teachers, and even an offer of a very large financial gift was not enough to get Randolph Jr. admitted.

When it became clear that the General Hayes School for Boys was determined to keep Randolph Jr. out no matter what Randolph offered them, he decided to create his own school. He bought an empty, former convent building from the Archdiocese of Newark, which was available for a very good price due to its proximity to the newly opened Newark Airport. He renamed the convent building Jessup Hall and hired a collection of retired military men as teachers and administrators. With that, the New Jersey Military Academy was born.

The General Hayes School objected immediately to the name of Jessup's new school, because General Hayes used the phrase "New Jersey's Military Academy" in its own marketing. In fact, the school's emblem consisted of a pair of crossed Revolutionary War–era muskets over a Roman legion–style shield with the slogan "New Jersey's Military Academy" underneath. Their lawyer believed that, given its marketing and emblem, the General Hayes School for Boys held an implicit trademark on the name "New Jersey Military Academy."

Randolph's lawyer advised him just to pick another name for his new school, suggesting that surely Newark Military Academy would be just as good. But Randolph was not the type of man to run from a fight. After the General Hayes School had insulted him by rejecting his son, he was not about to back down.

Ultimately, the dispute went to the New Jersey state courts. Randolph worked his connections in the state Capitol in Trenton to ensure the case was assigned to a judge who owed a considerable amount of money to one of his racetracks. The judge ruled succinctly that *New Jersey's* and *New Jersey* are different words. That decision, which would famously become known as the "Apostrophe S Case" to generations of law students studying for the New Jersey state bar exam, meant that the General Hayes School had no right to prevent the New Jersey Military Academy from using that name.

The General Hayes School felt so aggrieved by the judge's decision, its board of trustees decided they wanted nothing to do with Randolph's new school. They even wrote into the school's bylaws that they would never engage with the New Jersey Military Academy in "any sporting or academic contest" unless Randolph's school changed its name. As a result, the Academy needed to find a different sporting rival.

They found one the next year when they were invited to Connecticut to play football against the also newly established Westport Country Day. Westport's coach was a West Point graduate, and he invited the Academy to play, thinking a team of highly disciplined cadets would set a good example for his own players.

The New Jersey Military Academy lost that first game to Westport 45–3 in a cold, driving rain. The Academy's players were in an angry mood as they lined up to get on the school's bus for the long ride back to Newark. Randolph Jessup Jr. was particularly upset. He had been kicked out of the game during the first quarter for biting the Westport quarterback's arm after a tackle and had spent the rest of the game angrily pacing the sidelines.

Randolph Jr. snuck away from the rest of the team as they boarded their bus and waited next to the door to the Westport locker room. He had decided to vent his frustration by sucker punching the first person who came through that door.

It turned out the unlucky person was Reverend Jonathan Brady, Westport's eighty-five-year-old chaplain. Reverend Brady had just finished leading the team through its customary postgame prayer. As he walked out the locker room door, Randolph Jr. dropped him with one vicious punch to the bridge of his nose and then ran back to join his teammates on the bus.

By the time the Westport players had found Reverend Brady lying in the locker room doorway, his face covered in blood, and realized what had happened, the Academy's bus was already heading toward the school's main gate. Westport players ran toward the bus, but they could not stop it from going through the gate and speeding away down Westport Avenue. That one incident cemented Westport as the Academy's football rival.

The game against Westport was always the biggest one of the season, but this year the game was especially important because both teams were going into it with identical 3–0 records. Never before had they met for a game with both teams sporting undefeated records.

As Coach Mulrooney expected, Westport protested the field conditions before the game even started. Such protests were common at the New Jersey Military Academy, since there was a small hill in the middle of Jessup Field. Although it was only a few feet high, the hill was made more noticeable by the fact that the Academy's groundskeeper avoided it when he chalked the field, resulting in a fifty-yard line that stopped on one side of the hill and resumed twenty feet away on the other side. Predictably, the presence of the hill on the field frequently led to protests from the opposing team.

The hill had appeared a few years before, after the Academy's board of trustees had approved an upgrade to Jessup Field. Randolph Jessup Jr., who was by then the school's chairman of the board, owed his accountant a considerable amount of money at the time for getting him through a difficult tax audit. In exchange for canceling some of that debt, Randolph Jr. awarded his accountant's nephew the Jessup Field contract. Although Randolph Jr. was told the nephew had some landscaping experience, and even owned his own backhoe, it turned out football fields were not his expertise.

Despite the odd appearance the hill gave to a field that bore his family name, Randolph Jr. made it a point of principle to refuse to let the board of trustees pay to have it repaired. He believed the hill might give the Academy players an advantage since they would be familiar with it, whereas opposing players might trip and fall. In any case, Randolph Jr. felt that since hills on the field were not explicitly prohibited by any New Jersey high school athletic association regulations, there was no need for the Academy to spend money to remove it.

For this game, Westport's protest proved to be wholly unnecessary. It turned out that the hill at midfield did not impact the outcome, because almost the whole game was played on the Academy's side of it.

The death of the Academy's star quarterback had destroyed the competitive balance between the two teams. Since Teddy Haswell had been the team's quarterback for each of the past four seasons, they lacked an experienced player to take his place. The Academy's backup quarterback, Lou Douglas, was only five-foot-five and 138 pounds and had never played a single down during his entire time on the team. He had been named Teddy's backup just because he was the only other player who could memorize all of Coach Mulrooney's playbook.

With Lou leading the offense for the first time, the Academy was being destroyed by Westport. For a short time during the first half, their stout defense kept them in the game, but as Lou turned the ball over again and again, even the defensive players lost heart and gave up.

It was clear that the New Jersey Military Academy was going to lose the game badly, and Donald absolutely hated to lose. What made losing this game even more painful for Donald was that his father was in the crowd. Every year, his father only came to the game against Westport. He said since Donald played on the offensive line and did the same thing on every play (block the boy in front of him), seeing one game a year was plenty.

Donald felt proud that his father was given a seat of honor at Jessup Field, halfway up the bleachers on the fifty-yard line and right next to Randolph Jessup Jr. Randolph Jr. was recognizable to all the cadets, because he made a speech to the student body on the first day of every school year. The speech never varied much year to year and always included the words "a military education is like having a steel rod implanted in your loins that you'll carry with you for the rest of your life." That line had required a generation of cadets to try their best to stifle their laughter.

By the time they were in their fourth year, cadets had heard the same speech four times, and most of them mercilessly mocked it. Jokes about having steel rods in their pants never went out of fashion at the Academy. Donald pretended to laugh along with everybody else, but he couldn't help but admire Randolph Jr. The Jessup name was on virtually every part of the campus. He also found the steel rod line inspiring every time. It made him feel like he was a superhero with special powers from his steel implants.

Donald would have loved to impress his father and Randolph Jr. It was unfair he was on the losing team since, unlike Lou Douglas, he had been doing his job well. All game long, he had been lined up against Westport's all-state defensive end, Bill "the Bear" Baranowski, and the Bear had not once gotten by him. Lou might have fumbled the ball eight times over the course of the game, but it was never because of the Bear. Still, every time he glanced up into the stands, Donald felt like he could sense his father's disappointment. That, together with the physical pounding he was taking from blocking the Bear, had put Donald in a foul mood.

With three minutes left in the fourth quarter, Westport was ahead 31–0. The Academy had just gotten the ball, and they were hoping to run out the clock so the game could mercifully come to an end.

On first down, Lou handed the ball off to Lenny Thomas, who ran straight into the line and was taken down for a one-yard loss. Donald fell on top of the Bear during the play. As he tried to get up, the Bear grabbed the front of Donald's jersey and pulled him back to the turf.

"If we score again, you guys all gonna commit suicide like your quarterback?" the Bear asked with a sarcastic laugh as one of his teammates helped him up.

Donald slowly got up and walked back to his team's huddle, steaming mad. How dare the Bear taunt him, he thought. Westport may be winning by a large score, but the Bear had very little to do with that. Donald had controlled him all game.

In the huddle, Lou called for the same play again, another straight-ahead run by Lenny Thomas. Donald had something else in mind. He wanted the team to run a play that would give him a better angle to attack the Bear. The Bear had to learn Donald was not someone he could taunt and get away with it.

"No, let's roll out to the left this time," Donald said.

"Coach wants us just to run out the clock," Lou said, looking over toward Coach Mulrooney, on the sidelines.

"Just one play, let's all go left," Donald said. "That jerkwater Baranowski was making fun of Teddy, and I'm gonna teach him a lesson."

Donald looked over at the Westport huddle. He could not hear what they were saying, but he could see the Bear was still laughing. Donald was not going to let an opponent get away with laughing at him. His team might be losing, but Donald was not a loser.

"Everybody agree? We're running left?" Donald asked.

"Come on, Lou. Let's do this for Teddy," Joey Bortz, the team's rotund center, said.

"Okay," Lou said, looking again nervously toward the sidelines. "Roll out option to the left, for Teddy," Lou said before clapping his hands to end the huddle.

As the two teams got into position on the line of scrimmage, the Bear sneered at Donald and spit through the face mask of his helmet. An impressively large glob of spit landed right next to one of Donald's cleats. Donald already had his plan to bring down the Bear. The giant spitball just removed any doubt he would go through with it.

The play started with Joey snapping the ball to Lou, who ran to the left, with Lenny Thomas running next to him. Donald, together with the rest of the offensive line, also ran to the left to protect them. Lou had called an option play, which meant he could decide to keep the ball and run himself or he could hand it off to Lenny.

Donald was only watching the Bear. He knew that the Bear, who had been prevented all game from getting to Lou, was desperate to bring down the Academy's miniature quarterback at least once.

Donald slowed down just enough to give the Bear space to get through the offensive line. As Donald anticipated, the Bear rushed through the opening he had been given and headed straight toward Lou, who was now slowing down as he approached the sideline. Donald followed behind the Bear and launched himself at full speed, shoulder first, into the back of the Bear's knees. There was a loud cracking noise followed by a truly bearlike howl of pain from the Bear. He crumpled to the ground as Lou ran out of bounds for another one-yard loss.

While the Bear lay on the turf, holding his leg and screaming obscenities, his Westport teammates started yelling and pushing the nearest Academy player. A Westport defensive lineman almost twice Lou Douglas's size shoved Lou as he tried to come back in bounds, and that was enough for Lou to reach his breaking point. All game long, he had been tackled and thrown to the ground and had the ball ripped out of his hands, and he was not willing to take any more physical abuse. As soon as the Westport lineman turned around, Lou jumped on his back and began pounding the top of the lineman's helmet with his fists.

The Westport player, with Lou attached to his back and his helmet pushed down so far by Lou's blows that it covered his eyes, stumbled over and fell on top of the Bear. The Bear howled in pain even louder than before, and the couple of Westport players who had been doing their best to attend to him now tried to dislodge Lou from their teammate's back. Donald ran over to help Lou, and, with that, a wild, bench-clearing fight broke out between the teams. Within minutes, large groups of players were fighting all over the field as referees and coaches helplessly blew their whistles.

10

Friday, October 11, 1963 (6:46 p.m.)

THE GAME NEVER RESUMED AFTER THE FIGHT. IT TOOK twenty minutes for the two teams to be separated, and then a group of referees, coaches, and school administrators met in the center of the field and decided there was no need to play out the remaining two and a half minutes. The situation was deemed too volatile for the Westport players to stay on campus and change in the locker room. So, still in their pads and sweaty, grass-stained uniforms, they boarded their school bus to be driven straight back to Connecticut. The only Westport player not on the bus was Bill "the Bear" Baranowski, who was loaded carefully into the back seat of a Westport coach's Chevy Impala and driven to the emergency room at Newark General Hospital.

The Academy's tradition after the Westport game was to allow the players off campus for two hours to have dinner with their parents. Coach Mulrooney argued strongly for canceling that tradition this year as a disciplinary measure, but he was overruled by Colonel Overstreet. The colonel decided the risk of angering so many parents outweighed the disciplinary imperative.

In the locker room, the players were showering and getting dressed as quickly as possible. They wanted more time with their parents. They also hoped to get out of the locker room before Coach Mulrooney decided to come back and give them another postgame harangue for suffering their worst loss to Westport since 1934.

The cadets had to wear their Academy dress uniforms to go off campus with their parents. The only part of the uniform they had to leave behind was the sword. The swords were ceremonial and not sharp enough to be used as real weapons. But they hadn't been allowed off school grounds since a cadet had threatened a Newark taxi driver with his to try to get out of paying a fare.

Donald was sitting at the end of a locker room bench, fumbling with the two long rows of silver buttons that went up the front of his jacket. He knew he looked dashing in his uniform, but he hated putting it on because he always had trouble with the buttons. Donald was convinced the button holes on his jacket were smaller than on all the other cadets' jackets.

Donald wanted to get away from all the losers in the locker room as soon as he could. The problem with team sports, Donald thought, was there were no scores given to individual players. He had won that day as a player, and it was unfair that his performance was not recognized in some way. Once he had managed to button his jacket, he threw his wet towel and dirty uniform into the big laundry hamper near the door and walked out of the locker room.

He knew the football team parents would all be waiting, as usual, in the lobby of Jessup Hall. He hoped to find his father quickly and go straight to Nunzio's. Nunzio's was only a few miles from campus and was known for having the best steaks in Newark. Donald was sure they'd go there, because his father considered it the only decent restaurant south of Manhattan and north of Philadelphia. Donald just wanted to dig into a New York strip and forget about the game.

When Donald got to Jessup Hall, he saw his father holding court in the middle of a group of six or seven other parents. Donald was not surprised. His father built and managed apartment buildings all around the outer boroughs of New York, and he was perpetually on the lookout for prospective investors and tenants.

Donald sometimes wished his father could be more selective with his marketing efforts. His family's real estate empire was built on a foundation of cheap one- and two-bedroom apartments in the outer boroughs. It was not like he had an inventory of top-end apartments in gleaming Manhattan skyscrapers. All he owned were small units in run-of-the-mill buildings in out-of-the-way locations far from the center of everything that was exciting about New York City. Donald was sure no one standing around his father in Jessup Hall would be interested in places like that.

He knew his father was not to blame for the quality of his real estate portfolio. It was not like he had been born with a Chrysler Building–size silver spoon in his mouth like the Rockefellers or the Dursts, the families who owned big chunks of Manhattan. His father had inherited land from Donald's grandfather in less desirable sections of Queens, so naturally that was where he had started to build, filling some of the most remote parts of that borough with one-bath, eat-in kitchen units.

Donald felt disloyal just having those thoughts. His father was one of the best businessmen in the world. He knew everything there was to know about negotiation, financing, and marketing. But he was satisfied with what he had, an outer-borough real estate business that had never built a building higher than twenty stories.

His father noticed him as he came through the front door of Jessup Hall. He waved at Donald to come over.

"Donald worked on the project last summer," his father announced to the group around him. "He knows the quality of that building."

Donald knew his father must be talking about Coney Island Estates, his newest project. Donald had spent a week at the site over the summer, just before the building opened, so he could learn about installing finishes, like floor tiles and bathroom fixtures.

"Oh yeah, great fixtures in that building. Highest quality," Donald said.

"And tell them about the flooring, Donald," his father said.

"The units all have Armstrong vinyl asbestos floor tiles," Donald said, proud he could still recall the brand name even though he hadn't thought about Coney Island Estates for months.

"You have to see these tiles," his father added. "They're beautiful and hardier than anything else on the market today. Plus, they're completely fireproof. You could hold a blowtorch to these tiles and all they'll do is slowly melt, so you know there's never going to be a fire in one of those kitchens! Usually you would need to pay a lot extra for a tile packed with that much asbestos, but I know a guy who got me a great deal."

Donald wished his father would stop. He was sure none of his classmates' parents were in the market for a small rental on the outer edge of an outer borough.

"So if you know anybody looking to live in a great new building by the water, tell them to give me a call," Donald's father said, putting his arm around Donald's shoulders and walking away from the group. He led Donald to a quiet area near the entrance to the library.

"That sure was a tough game today. You boys really missed Teddy," his father said.

"But did you see how I dominated that guy? And he's all-state in Connecticut," Donald said.

"Well, not much point blocking if your team doesn't have a quarterback anyway," his father replied.

Donald knew he should have expected a reaction like that, since his father didn't really know anything about football. In fact, his father wasn't interested in any sports. It had been his Great-Uncle Johan who had pushed him to play football. Johan had immigrated to the United States in his twenties, and he became fascinated by the sport. He said it reminded him of the way America took on the Nazis: "They huddled and planned and waited, and then bam, attacked all at once!"

"Sorry your mother couldn't come," his father said. "But you know how she is about keeping to her schedule."

"It's okay," Donald said.

He hadn't expected to see his mother at the game. Since the day his parents had dropped him off at the Academy as a freshman cadet, she had never been back to the campus. He knew she would never come to a football game, since they were all played on Fridays. Friday afternoons were reserved for her "bridge game" (which is what his mother called having cocktails with her sister).

"I have bad news, Donald," his father went on. "I need to get back to the city for a business dinner. I won't be able to take you out tonight, I'm afraid."

Donald was crushed. He had been thinking about Nunzio's since halftime. He felt like a plate of perfectly well-done steak was being ripped out of his hands and thrown in the garbage right in front of him.

"That's okay. I understand. It's business," Donald said.

"Exactly, son. It's business."

11

Friday, October 11, 1963 (7:05 p.m.)

Nunzio's had operated out of the same nondescript brick building on Green Street in Newark since 1948. For most of its existence, it had catered mainly to a loyal group of regulars from the neighborhood. That had all changed a few years before when Nunzio slipped a reporter from the *Newark Star-Ledger* a hundred bucks to run a false story that Frankie Valli took his mother to eat there at least once a week. After that, the restaurant's clientele expanded dramatically by scores of Four Seasons fans who came in hope of seeing their favorite singer. Soon Nunzio's was one of the most popular restaurants in Newark.

To commemorate the reason for his success, Nunzio hung a framed photograph of Frankie Valli on a wall near the restaurant's front door, right next to a framed copy of the *Newark Star-Ledger* article. He also invested some of his Frankie Valli wealth in white tablecloths, gold-rimmed dishware, and fancy Italian wall sconces adorned with cherubic angels.

The night of the big game, Rosemary Duncannon and Natalie Coleman were having dinner at Nunzio's. They were seated at a table for two along the back wall, directly under one of the gold sconces. As always, Natalie had claimed the seat facing the dining room.

When they had first started working at the Academy, they rarely went out to dinner together in Newark, and certainly never to a place as close to campus as Nunzio's. They were afraid their relationship would be discovered. If it had been, they both could have been fired, since homosexuality was strictly prohibited by the Academy's code of conduct.

Over time, they realized they were worrying for no reason. The idea that a lesbian couple was working at the Academy was so far beyond the imagination of the men who ran the school, there was no risk of them being found out. Everyone assumed Mrs. Duncannon was a widow who shared a house with Natalie so they could split expenses. Natalie sometimes joked they could be seen kissing passionately in Jessup Quadrangle, and still none of the men at the Academy would ever guess they were a couple.

As usual, Natalie had gone to the game that day. She loved football, having grown up listening to New York Giants games on the radio with her father. She liked to say if she had not met Rosemary, she probably would be married now to Frank Gifford, the Giants star running back. Since Rosemary didn't share that interest, Natalie always went to the games alone.

Over their Nunzio's special appetizer salads of iceberg lettuce, red onion, and tomato, Natalie had been telling Rosemary all about the game. She had just started to describe the fight when she suddenly noticed Colonel Overstreet was across the room, sitting by himself at a table for two.

"Guess who's here," Natalie said.

"Oh my God! Is it Frankie Valli?" Rosemary said.

"No, sorry. It's just Colonel Overstreet."

"Who's he with?" Rosemary asked, starting to turn in the direction Natalie was looking.

"Wait, don't turn around. He just looked over here," Natalie said. "Anyway, he's alone."

"You know, I told the colonel today about Stanley Wong being on the roof that night," Rosemary said.

Natalie had heard about Stanley from Rosemary the previous evening. In fact, Rosemary had recounted for her the whole conversation with Jerry Stahl. It had been one of the many recent nights Rosemary had wanted to spend talking about Teddy Haswell's death, and it was becoming harder for Natalie to feign interest. She was as sad as anyone that a cadet had died, but she worried Rosemary had become obsessed with figuring out exactly what had happened that night. Some things were just unknowable, Natalie thought, and one of those things was the inner workings of a teenager's mind.

"How did the colonel take the news about Stanley?" Natalie asked.

"Well, he didn't look very happy," Rosemary said. "And then I told him Donald was also running around somewhere in Jessup Hall at the same time. He didn't look happy about that news either."

"I told you the colonel wouldn't want to hear anything about this," Natalie said.

"I know," Rosemary said. "And then he told me it was my responsibility to keep students from going upstairs at night. But I'm not sure how I can be expected to control the whole building. I'm not even supposed to leave the library."

"You should tell him you need more help in the library then," Natalie said.

"I do need more help, but you know how tight the colonel is with the library budget."

As Rosemary was speaking, Natalie noticed a man who looked familiar walking into the restaurant. He was in his sixties, she guessed, and he was with a tall blond woman who had to be almost forty years younger. As she watched the couple walk to their table for two, it suddenly dawned on her who the man was. It was Donald's father. She had met him when he brought Donald to the Academy for an admission interview.

"Speaking of Donald, his father just walked in. He's over there," Natalie said, pointing to the right.

Rosemary turned in that direction. When she looked back, Natalie was smiling.

"For some reason, I don't think that's Donald's mother," Rosemary said.

"She's too young to be anybody's mother," Natalie said.

12

Friday, October 11, 1963 (7:07 p.m.)

COLONEL FRANK OVERSTREET HAD RETIRED AFTER twenty-four years in the United States Army with a large colonel's pension, supplemented by additional monthly payments he received from having been injured both in the Pacific during World War II (where he lost a toe) and in Korea (where he lost most of the hearing in his left ear). However, he also retired with significant legal obligations to support two ex-wives and four children in the United States, as well as a moral obligation to send money occasionally to the son he had secretly fathered in Korea.

Because of all these obligations, Frank could not afford simply to put his nine-toed feet up and enjoy a peaceful retirement. He had needed to find work, and the headmaster position at the New Jersey Military Academy had seemed like a perfect post-retirement job. He would be able to continue doing what he liked most about the army, molding young men into soldiers, while not having to work too hard and still having time for golf. Most important, he would be able to make his monthly alimony and child support payments. Both of his ex-wives had hired the same divorce lawyer, a real shark in Trenton named Emile Ledbetter, and whenever those checks were late by even a day, Ledbetter would threaten him with collection agents.

The job was available because the previous headmaster, also a retired army colonel, had been terminated for "mental exhaustion." That was the official reason given by the Academy's board of trustees after he was caught in an Atlantic City hotel room with a cadet. Frank had a Korean War battalion connection with a retired brigadier general on the board who got him an interview. After the school's bad experience with its last headmaster, who was a lifelong bachelor, the fact that Frank had been divorced twice turned out to be a point in his favor, and he got the job.

During his five years as headmaster, Frank had come to judge his job performance based on the number of calls he received each week from parents of cadets. Zero calls signified an extremely successful week and anything over five calls meant he was doing poorly. By that standard, this week was one of his worst ever. Since Teddy Haswell's body had been found in Jessup Quadrangle, parents had been calling almost every hour. At first, he took all the calls, but the last few days he had been getting his secretary, Mrs. Kreitzenbach, to make excuses for him.

Although Frank felt awful that any cadet, and especially one as impressive and well-rounded as Teddy Haswell, should die, he had been relieved when the Newark police and army investigator had determined it was suicide. A student suicide would be a black mark on his record to be sure, but he felt confident he could survive one suicide as headmaster. It would clearly be viewed as an isolated incident. Given Teddy's success as a student and an athlete, he could not be expected to have seen it coming. In fact, if he had been asked which one of his cadets was most likely to commit suicide, he would have picked Dicky Daniels, not Teddy.

All things considered, therefore, Frank felt a student killing himself was a sad but manageable event. On the other hand, a fatal accident would cause him much more trouble. That could suggest a school that was out of control, where all the cadets were potentially at risk. An incident like that could set off an avalanche of parents pulling their students out of school, and no headmaster could survive something like that.

Unfortunately for Frank, it was seeming increasingly possible that the tidy explanation that Teddy had killed himself might not be accurate. Teddy's parents were convinced their son died because Donald and Teddy were involved in some kind of dangerous prank in Jessup Hall. They had found something about that in Teddy's diary. Then it seemed Donald had confirmed it when they talked to him yesterday, even though he had expressly instructed Donald to stay quiet. Teddy's parents were threatening to go straight to the board of trustees to demand the school conduct its own investigation if Frank did not take any action.

On top of that, the school librarian had approached him this morning with more bad news. Not only did she confirm Donald was on the loose in Jessup Hall around the time Teddy died, but also that Stanley Wong was, for some reason, on the building's roof. This information was surely going to damage him with the school's board. They'd hired a retired colonel to maintain strict discipline on campus, not so cadets could run amok in Jessup Hall after hours.

Now he was waiting at Nunzio's to have dinner with Randolph Jessup Jr. They ate together every year after the

Westport game. It was not by Frank's choice, but rather a tradition he had inherited from the previous headmaster.

As far as Frank was concerned, Randolph Jr. was a pompous blowhard. He seemed to think his opinions were more valuable than other people's just because he was rich. Frank could not stand that attitude, especially since he knew all of Randolph Jr.'s money had come from his father. Along with inheriting the Academy, he ran the same horse-track empire his father had built.

Frank also thought Randolph Jr. was a coward. Although he was about the same age as Frank, he had never served in the military. Frank had asked him one time why he was not in the war, and Randolph Jr. had explained how he was excused from service because he had thin ankles. Hearing Randolph Jr. say that through Frank's one remaining good ear, the colonel had to muster all of his self-control not to hit him in the face.

Given his dislike for Randolph Jr., Frank did not look forward to these dinners even when everything was going well at the school. After the week the school had just gone through, which had begun with a cadet's death on Monday and had ended with a horrible loss to Westport followed by a fight on Friday, he was truly dreading it. He knew Randolph Jr. was going to be in an even more critical mood than usual. Frank would also have to explain to Randolph Jr. the need to open an investigation into Teddy's death. He was convinced Teddy's parents were not going to give up on that demand.

The one characteristic of Randolph Jr. that Frank appreciated was that he always came late to these dinners. Waiting for him to arrive, Frank was peacefully enjoying an extra-dry martini and looking around Nunzio's crowded dining room. Several tables away, he saw Natalie from the admissions office sitting with the librarian, Mrs. Duncannon. He usually felt sorry for those two women. Neither of them had been able to find a husband, so they were forced to share a house just to make ends meet.

But that night he was too angry with Mrs. Duncannon to feel any sympathy for her. It was clear she was not at all doing her job of keeping tabs on the cadets' use of Jessup Hall after hours. He decided when the smoke all cleared from this incident, he would make a faculty member stay each night to monitor the building. He could not make that change yet, because if he acted too soon after the incident, it would look like an admission that leaving Jessup Hall solely in Mrs. Duncannon's hands was a mistake.

The restaurant door opened, and Frank watched Donald's father walk in, followed by a busty young blond woman in a tight dress. As sexy as the girl looked in that dress, having just mailed alimony checks to his two ex-wives, Frank was not sure if he was more envious of Donald's father or worried for him. It was certainly high-risk for him to bring a date like that to a restaurant so close to his son's school. Other parents likely would be eating at Nunzio's that night, and who knows what information could get back to Donald's mother.

A few minutes later, the door opened again and Randolph Jr. walked in. Nunzio, who had just returned to the front of the restaurant from seating Donald's father and his date, greeted Randolph Jr. warmly, like an old friend. Then Nunzio said something that made Randolph Jr. laugh so long and so loudly that it stopped conversations all around the restaurant. It was typical Randolph Jr., Frank thought, making sure everyone in the room knew he had arrived.

Randolph Jr. first made a quick trip around the restaurant to shake hands with a few other customers he knew before he joined Frank at his table. They ordered steaks and talked for a while about the game. Not surprisingly, Randolph Jr. was angry about the loss and thought Coach Mulrooney should be fired immediately. But his anger seemed to be largely counterbalanced by satisfaction with the fact that Donald had sent one of the Westport players to the hospital and that a fight had ensued. He thought it showed the cadets still had some of the same pride and team spirit he'd had when he'd played for the Academy.

When there was nothing more to be said on the topic of football, Frank decided it was time to talk about Teddy. He would need Randolph Jr. to be on board with any plan for an investigation. Frank first told Randolph Jr. what he had learned from Teddy's parents and Mrs. Duncannon.

"But I thought the police already decided it was a suicide, and the army agreed, right?" Randolph Jr. asked.

"That's true, but they didn't have this information about other cadets being in the building at the same time. I only learned about all that today," Frank said, lying slightly about the timing.

"You want to ask the police to come back?"

Frank certainly did not want the police back on campus. Before, when it seemed like a clear case of suicide, they had barely spent an hour at the school, they had not spoken to any cadets, and nothing had ended up in the papers. But if they were to come back and open a full investigation, there was no telling what could happen. The police reporters from the *Newark Star-Ledger* and the *New York Herald-Tribune* could hear something and start poking around. If parents were reading about an incident at the school in their morning papers and hearing their sons were being interviewed by the police, his days as headmaster would surely be numbered.

"No. I think we need to handle this quietly and in-house," Frank said. "As far as I can tell, the Haswells just want to know what exactly happened with their son. They haven't said anything about the police."

"Good, that's what I was thinking," Randolph Jr. said.

"So I'll set up a faculty panel to investigate and we'll try to get this finished as soon as possible," Frank said.

"A faculty and board panel, you mean. I should be part of the investigation," Randolph Jr. said.

"Of course," Frank said.

Frank had not expected Randolph Jr. to want to be personally involved, but he liked the idea. As unpleasant as it was to spend any time with Randolph Jr., if he were on the panel, it might keep him from second-guessing him later.

"You said Donald and the Chinese kid were with Teddy that night, right?" Randolph Jr. asked.

"Maybe. We don't know if they were all together, just that they were all in Jessup Hall at the same time," Frank said.

"But you said the Chinese kid was on the damn roof!" Randolph Jr. said. "Maybe he pushed our quarterback off?"

"I don't know for sure he was on the roof. Just that another cadet thinks he might have seen him up there."

"Well, my money's on the Chinese kid being the culprit here in any case."

Frank realized he may have shared too much information with Randolph Jr. He had not intended the investigation to be about finding someone to blame. He just wanted it to determine whether Teddy's death had been a suicide or an accident.

"I don't think there's any culprit here at all. We just want to find out if those boys know anything that can help us figure out what happened," Frank said.

"Come on, Frank, it's gotta be the Chinese kid. You were in Korea. You know you can't trust those people," Randolph Jr. said. "My dad would roll over in his grave if he knew there was a cadet named Wong at the Academy."

"Stanley Wong happens to be the top student in the fourth-year class," Frank said, angry that Randolph Jr. kept calling him Frank instead of Colonel. "And he's competing for us in a very prestigious science competition."

"Well, that's great. Our football team is lousy, but at least we have a boy named Wong representing the Academy at a science fair," Randolph Jr. said mockingly.

"I just thought you should know that Stanley Wong is a model cadet," Frank said.

13

Saturday, October 12, 1963 (6:58 p.m.)

EVERY YEAR ON THE MORNING OF THE FALL DANCE, THE Academy made all the cadets go on a five-mile training run in fatigues and combat boots. The theory was that if the boys were tired, their testosterone would be held in check during the dance. Football players who were injured in the big game against Westport did not have to join the run, so Donald claimed he had sprained his ankle during the fourth quarter.

Donald had wondered if Coach Mulrooney would be suspicious of his injury, since it was the fourth consecutive year he'd claimed to be too hurt to join the run. To his relief, the coach had not seemed concerned in the least. When Donald reported his sprained ankle, Coach Mulrooney just grunted a barely audible acknowledgment and scribbled Donald's name down on his injury list.

Donald was well rested and his hormones were fully raging by the time the fall dance began. He had not spoken to a girl since the start of the fall semester. In his excitement, he was among the first group of eager cadets to arrive at Jessup Auditorium.

The girls from the Parker School had already arrived on their school bus. They were standing in several large groups on one side of the auditorium, laughing, smoothing their long dresses, and whispering to each other as the cadets filtered in through the main door. The cadets wore their Academy dress uniforms, but without the swords and hats. The army orchestra from Fort Dix was warming up on the stage.

Donald sauntered into the auditorium next to his friends Joey Bortz, from the football team, and Tommy Callahan, from the baseball team. Joey had gained at least five inches and thirty pounds during his four years at the Academy, but his parents had not sprung for a new dress uniform since he was a freshman. His jacket was stretched so tightly across his torso, it looked like one sneeze or sudden movement might cause the jacket to split open and the buttons to go flying off in every direction.

"Damn, Bortz, you look like a Polish sausage in that jacket," Tommy said.

"What do you want me to do?" Joey said.

"I don't care how cheap your parents are, Bortz, you gotta get out of here. You're making us look bad," Donald said. "Me and JFK have to get to work."

Donald had nicknamed Tommy "JFK" because, like the president, he was a copper-haired Irish Catholic from Boston. Befriending a Catholic had been his father's idea. Donald's father was sure the country was going to have a Kennedy as president for sixteen straight years, eight for John and then another eight for his brother Bobby.

Since they'd be facing such a prolonged period of Catholic domination, his father told Donald to make friends with as many Catholics as he could. That instruction had surprised Donald, since before then all he could remember ever hearing his father say about Catholics was that they drink too much. But he never wanted to disappoint his father. Since the Catholic cadets in his class could be counted on one hand, his choice had been limited. Tommy was the one Donald had targeted to be his friend.

"Look at that dolly over there in the pink," Donald said, gesturing toward a group of eight or nine girls, half of whom were wearing pink dresses.

"Which one?" Tommy asked.

"The blonde with the nice bazoombas, of course," Donald said. "I think I'm going to talk to her."

Donald knew there was no time to waste identifying the prettiest girl there. The fall dance was only ninety minutes long, and no extension had been given on the usual barracks curfew. He also did not want to take too long picking out his target, because soon all the other cadets would arrive, and the competition would become more intense.

"Yeah, she's okay, but how about that dolly over there talking to Jerry? She's super pretty," Tommy said, nodding to a group standing near the stage.

Donald turned and saw Jerry Stahl talking to a blond girl in a pale yellow dress and a short brunette who looked familiar. Donald decided immediately the blonde was the most beautiful girl at the dance. Even under the auditorium's harsh fluorescent lights, her hair glowed like pure gold to Donald's eyes. His father always said blondes made the best wives because they were bad at keeping secrets from their husbands. It would be hard for someone to be any blonder than this girl.

Donald knew Jerry didn't stand a chance with a girl like that. Standing next to her, Jerry looked like her awkward kid brother, since she was at least three or four inches taller than him.

"Good eye, JFK," Donald said. "I'm going over there to relieve Jerry of duty."

Donald smoothed down his blond hair, locked his face into what he considered to be his most winning smile, and walked straight toward the beautiful blonde. He was sure she would be happy to see a guy like him come over after having to endure talking with a pip-squeak like Jerry.

"Hey, pal, who are your friends?" Donald said, putting a hand on Jerry's shoulder as he came up next to him.

Donald's father had taught him that in any kind of negotiation, it helps to initiate physical contact. A sudden touch can disarm the other man and weaken his resolve.

"This is Cindy Grubb," Jerry said, looking pained by Donald's sudden arrival. "And, of course, you know Dorothy."

Donald suddenly realized why the short brunette looked so familiar. It was Dorothy Rodgers, who had grown up with him and Jerry in Kew Gardens. He forgot she went to Parker.

Considering they had been classmates since the age of seven, he should have recognized her right away. But he had never seen Dorothy dressed up and wearing makeup before. She was the kind of girl who did not care enough about boys to try to look nice.

"Hi, Donald," Dorothy said.

"Hi, Dorothy, how have you been?" Donald asked.

"Other than worrying about the nuclear annihilation of the planet, I've been fine," Dorothy said. "How about you?"

"Okay, I guess," Donald said.

He wondered if Dorothy was trying to embarrass him in front of her friend. Did she want to make it seem like Donald was not smart enough to worry about nuclear war? He was an officer in the Junior ROTC, so of course he understood all there was to understand about nuclear war. Certainly, he knew much more about it than just some civilian like Dorothy. And why did she feel the need to show off her vocabulary like that? Donald knew plenty of big words also. He knew some very long and impressive words, like *radioactive isotopes*. But he would never use them at a dance. Dances were supposed to be for fun.

It reminded Donald why he never liked Dorothy. She always thought she was the smartest kid in class, even smarter than all the boys. He realized he should just ignore her and focus all of his attention on the blonde.

"So, what's your name again?" Donald asked Cindy.

"Cindy Grubb."

"Cindy Grubb. That's a beautiful name," Donald said.

"Thanks!" Cindy said, smiling sweetly.

"Oh please," Dorothy said in a mocking tone of voice. "That's the best line you can think of, Donald?"

"What kind of name is that?" Donald asked Cindy, ignoring Dorothy.

"It's short for Cynthia."

"No, I mean your last name," Donald said.

"Oh, I think Grubb's a German name," Cindy said.

"So your family's from Germany?" Donald asked.

"I guess so."

"Well, this is a fascinating conversation, but I'm going to go," Dorothy said. "Nice to see you guys again, and I'll catch up with you later, Cindy, okay?"

"Okay," Cindy said.

Donald was glad that ignoring Dorothy had worked to get her to leave. She had always been an unpleasant person, and even just her being there was making it difficult for him to concentrate on impressing Cindy.

"My family's German too," Jerry said hopefully as Dorothy walked off to join a group of mainly pink dress–wearing girls nearby.

Donald was impressed by Jerry's pluck. Although he was clearly out of his depth with Cindy, he hadn't yet given up. He realized he needed to put Jerry in his place before he got carried away with too much hope. To accentuate how much taller he was than Jerry, Donald stood up as straight as he could. Then he smoothed his hair again, not wanting to take any chance it might have moved out of place.

"My family's from Sweden," Donald lied.

In fact, Donald's paternal grandfather, Friedrich, had emigrated to New York from Bavaria around the turn of the century. However, after the Nazis destroyed the brand value of German heritage in the United States, Donald's father had decided the family should no longer be German. It was bad for business, particularly considering all the Jewish tenants he had in his apartment buildings. For the last twenty years, Donald's family had been of Scandinavian descent instead.

Donald resented his father for changing the family's nationality. He had heard many stories growing up of his proud Bavarian roots from Great-Uncle Johan, who was Friedrich's younger brother. Johan also held a low opinion of Donald's fake heritage. He told Donald even ordinary Bavarian families lived in ornate stone-and-timber houses at least three stories tall that were like palaces compared to the mud-walled, thatched-roofed huts that the Swedes sat shivering in through the winter. For the good of the business, Donald conceded to his father's wishes to be Swedish, but whenever he repeated that lie, he could hear Johan's voice: *In Europe, no one pretends to be Swedish!*

"That's so interesting," Cindy said. "I've never met anyone from Sweden before."

"I think my last name, Stahl, means 'steel' in German," Jerry said. "My grandma says we got the name Stahl because our family made armor for knights back in the old days. That's pretty neat, right?"

Donald knew Cindy was not even listening to Jerry. She was looking only at him now. He was not surprised, since he was well aware of how handsome he looked in his dress uniform. When his mother had seen a picture of him in uniform in his yearbook, she said he looked just like a young Burt Lancaster.

The Fort Dix army orchestra started to play its first song of the night, an instrumental version of the "Tennessee Waltz." The music spurred a few of the bolder cadets to bravely cross the auditorium and ask the Parker girls to dance. Since Donald hated dancing, he wanted to make sure Cindy wouldn't be expecting him to ask her out onto the dance floor.

"I hurt my ankle yesterday in the football game," Donald lied. "So I can't dance."

"It's okay," Cindy said, flashing Donald another sweet smile. "I don't like dancing that much anyway."

"Let's get some punch then, Cindy," Donald said, using her name so Jerry would know the invitation was not also meant for him.

Leaving Jerry behind, he led Cindy to the snack table, which was stocked with rows of small Dixie cups filled with Hawaiian Punch. As they walked across the auditorium, Donald scanned the groups of Parker girls one more time to be sure Cindy really was the prettiest one there. Although her chest was disappointing up close, Donald felt confident she was indeed the best-looking girl at the fall dance. No doubt, her bust would fill out in time. She had sparkling blue eyes and dimples so big, Donald wondered if he could fit an M&M's candy inside one without it falling out.

Over Hawaiian Punch, Donald told Cindy about the fight with Westport. Without mentioning the score of the game, he focused on how he had disabled Westport's star defensive lineman. She laughed at all the right places in his story and did not seem upset in the least that Donald had intentionally smashed into the back of an opponent's knees. By the time they had finished their cups of punch, Donald had closed the deal: Cindy would be his date to the commencement ball.

14

Sunday, October 13, 1963 (10:25 a.m.)

THE MEMORIAL SERVICE FOR TEDDY HASWELL WAS held in Jessup Chapel, which was one of the four gray stone buildings that surrounded Jessup Quadrangle. The other three—Jessup Hall, Jessup Auditorium, and Jessup Cafeteria—were all older. Jessup Chapel had been built in 1955 after the school's founder, Randolph Jessup, died, largely with money from Randolph's estate.

Were he able to look down from Heaven, Randolph surely would have been surprised to see that money from his estate had gone to building a chapel at the Academy, since he did not actually leave any funds for that purpose in his last will and testament. In fact, he had left no money at all to the Academy, believing he had done enough for the school while he was alive. But he did bequeath half a million dollars to his longtime mistress, Theresa Davis.

That money never made it to Theresa. Enraged by her late husband's generosity to his mistress, Randolph's widow took the trustee of the estate to court. She managed to have the bequest overturned on the grounds that gifts given in exchange for illicit sexual services violated the moral turpitude provision of the New Jersey State Constitution.

The court ruled that the half a million dollars Randolph had intended for Theresa instead should go to a morally upstanding purpose. Ultimately, the trustee of the estate decided that building a house of worship at the Academy would be most in keeping with the spirit of both Randolph Jessup's life and the court's order.

The completion of Jessup Chapel created a proper quadrangle at the Academy. Before then, the area in the center of campus had been planted with grass and was known as Jessup Lawn. Once the lawn was surrounded by buildings on all four sides, it was renamed Jessup Quadrangle. Phil Owens, the Academy's groundskeeper, convinced the board of trustees that it would be difficult to keep grass in the quadrangle green because it would be shaded for much of the day by the four buildings. Although many of the trustees suspected Phil just wanted less mowing to do, they agreed to tear up the grass and replace it with large granite tiles.

While the exterior of Jessup Chapel was done in gray stone, the interior was designed in a minimalist Episcopalian style, with twenty rows of simple wooden pews leading to a largely unadorned altar and pulpit. Although it was consecrated as an Episcopal church, as a US Army–affiliated institution, the Academy had a formal rule against religious discrimination. Therefore, the chapel was open to students of all Protestant denominations, from Lutherans to Presbyterians.

At first, Frank Overstreet had planned Teddy's memorial for Jessup Auditorium. He was worried Jessup Chapel would not be an appropriate venue, since Teddy had committed suicide. Dick Roberts, the Academy's chaplain, had convinced him otherwise.

Dick was Frank's good friend, having served in the same platoon in Korea. After the war, he had gone to divinity school at Rutgers on a GI Bill scholarship. Frank knew that ever since their platoon had made the terrible mistake of confusing a school in Incheon for a Chinese army hideout, his friend Dick had been racked with intense, and sometimes uncontrollable, feelings of guilt. Occasionally Frank would smell alcohol on Dick's breath, which he knew meant Dick had fallen back into one of his dark moods. Dick had channeled those feelings into an intense study of the Protestant theology of forgiveness. He had read everything he could find on the subject, from John Wesley to Albert Camus.

At Rutgers, Dick had even written his master thesis on the relative forgivable-ness of various sins. He made a list of eighty separate sins, from murder to masturbation, and assigned each one a forgivability rating from one to ten (with ten being the least forgivable). Through his research, Dick had determined that suicide fell on the highly forgivable part of the overall sin spectrum, rating it only a three. He saw no reason to have the memorial anywhere other than Jessup Chapel.

Teddy's memorial was held just after the Academy's regular Sunday morning church service. As he did at the start of all cadet assemblies, Frank had begun the memorial by setting out the ground rules and the punishments for violations of those rules. Cadets were required to sit up straight, pay attention, not speak unless called upon, and not fall asleep. Failing to comply with any of the first three rules would earn a cadet one demerit, and falling asleep would be punished with two demerits.

Frank then called up Chaplain Roberts, who read from the Book of Isaiah. After the Chaplain's scripture reading, Coach

Mulrooney eulogized Teddy by describing how he possessed the eleven traits of a great quarterback, with one trait corresponding to each of the letters of the word *QUARTERBACK*. Frank had given him five minutes to speak.

The coach started with *Q* for "quiet dignity," and after ten minutes he was only at the second *A* (which was for "attitude"). Frank considered cutting the coach's eulogy short, but by then he was curious to learn what the *K* would stand for, guessing it might be "kindhearted." By the time Coach Mulrooney finally concluded with *K* ("knack for the unexpected"), fifteen minutes had passed and the memorial was behind schedule.

After that, it was Donald's turn to speak. Since this was his first cadet memorial, Frank had called an old army buddy who was headmaster of a military school in North Carolina to find out who should speak on behalf of the students. His buddy had suggested having the top-ranking cadet in the Junior ROTC do it. But, in the Academy's case, Teddy was the top-ranking cadet. Frank decided on Donald, since he had been Teddy's roommate.

As Donald passed him on his way to the pulpit, Frank whispered to Donald that he should speak for at most two minutes. Frank could see the cadets were already getting fidgety, and he wanted to end the service soon before he would have to start handing out demerits.

Donald nodded. He climbed the three pulpit steps, took a piece of paper out of his pocket, unfolded it, and put it on the lectern. Then he tapped the top of the microphone several times, sending a piercing screech of feedback through the chapel's sound system.

"Good morning, fellow cadets," Donald began, reading from the paper he had put on the lectern. "I'm Donald, but you guys all know me already. Or at least you should know me.

If you don't, that would be pretty sad, because I'm one of the top-ranking cadets in this school, and I'm also a starter on the football and baseball teams. Teddy Haswell was my roommate, and he was a great, great guy. My dad always says the world is full of a few winners and a lot of losers, and Teddy was definitely one of the winners. Teddy and I were also really good friends. In fact, we were probably the two best friends at this school. So of course it's a big-time tragedy for me personally that Teddy decided to jump off the roof of Jessup Hall. I don't know why he did that. Believe me, I have no idea, since I wasn't there and don't know anything about it. But what I do know is that I really miss Teddy a lot. Since that night, many people have told me that I've been very brave through this tragedy, and that's true. They all ask me how I can be so brave, and I'll tell you the reason. It's because I know Teddy had such great faith in me. Teddy always told me he was sure I would be a great success in life and probably very, very rich. I mean, a lot of people have told me that, but when your best friend says something like that, it's special. So, now, when I leave the Academy and go on and succeed in my life, I like to believe Teddy will be looking down on me from Heaven, happy that his prediction came true. That thought is what helps me be brave in the face of this tragedy, and maybe it can help all of you also."

Donald smiled and then abruptly turned and walked down from the pulpit. The cadets were quiet for several seconds, seemingly unsure if the speech was over. Then a few briefly applauded. Frank had heard many eulogies by young men for other young men at army funerals, but never one quite like that before.

15

Sunday, October 13, 1963 (5:38 p.m.)

DONALD WAS NOT SURE WHY HE HAD TAKEN TEDDY'S watch. It had been a purely impulsive decision. Since he was not planning to wear it or sell it, the only value the watch had was sentimental. It had played a part in them becoming close friends.

Donald had heard the story of the watch from Teddy and knew it was a Haswell family heirloom. Teddy's father had worn it during the Korean War, and since he had survived the war, he considered it a good luck charm. The watch face was scratched in many places, because his father had spent the war specifically in Honolulu, managing an army supply depot a few hundred yards from Waikiki Beach. He frequently spent his afternoons surfing and sunbathing at the beach, and the watch had taken a beating from all the sand and saltwater it had been exposed to during his war years. But, since it still kept good time, he had given it to his son to wear at the Academy.

One day early in their freshman year, Teddy couldn't find the watch in his locker after football practice. He looked for it all around the locker room, and when his search there came up empty, he ran back out to Jessup Field and methodically walked every inch of it. It was as if the watch had just disappeared.

The upperclassmen on the football team mocked Teddy's frantic search. One senior, Bob Gunderson, performed an exaggerated pantomime of Teddy looking for his watch, complete with him wiping away imaginary tears. At the Academy, an accusation of crying was about as damaging a charge as could be leveled against a cadet. Criers at a military school had a status similar to snitches in a prison. Donald knew Teddy was no crier and had not shed any tears that day.

Donald already had his own reason for hating Bob. He had mocked Donald for having the worst time on the team in the fifty-yard dash. Donald deeply resented the accusation that he was slow, since he considered himself to be deceptively fast over shorter and longer distances. It just so happened that fifty yards was the worst distance for him. Bob went so far as to try to get the rest of the team to call him "Slowpoke Donald," which Donald, an expert in nicknames, knew was both unfair and very uncreative. Although that feeble attempt at a nickname had not caught on, Donald never forgave Bob.

A few weeks after the watch went missing, Donald was in the school's infirmary. He had faked appendicitis to get out of a pop quiz in English class. Dr. Jamison didn't find any evidence of an inflamed appendix, but since it was Donald's second faked appendicitis of the semester, the doctor told him to wait outside his office while he did some research on what else could be causing Donald's mysterious recurring pain. Tired of waiting for a diagnosis he knew would be meaningless, Donald was about to leave when Bob Gunderson walked into the infirmary.

As soon as Bob realized Donald was there, he covered his wrist, but he was not fast enough. Donald had already noticed the gold watch Bob was wearing looked an awful lot like Teddy's missing Omega Seamaster.

At that moment, Donald didn't say anything. Making an allegation of theft against an upperclassman was dangerous. He could have spent the rest of his freshmen year doing push-ups on Bob's orders.

So Donald decided to wait to get a better look at the watch when it was not attached to Bob's wrist. That opportunity arose a few days later when the fourth-year cadets were having their class picture taken in Jessup Quadrangle. Knowing the fourth-year halls in the barracks would be empty, Donald snuck into Bob's room and searched for Teddy's watch. He found it eventually in Bob's storage locker, tucked in among his underwear.

Teddy was delighted to be reunited with the watch that had seen his father through an extended deployment in Hawaii. After Donald explained how he got it, Teddy decided he would challenge Bob to a fight. But Donald convinced him that would be self-defeating. Bob was the best offensive lineman on the team, so Teddy would be making an enemy of someone responsible for protecting him on the field. He also pointed out there was a good chance Teddy would lose the fight. Like all boys from Staten Island at the Academy, Bob had a reputation for being a tough guy. They decided to say nothing to anyone and just let Bob wonder how the watch had found its way back to Teddy.

The incident of the lost-and-found watch had made Donald and Teddy even closer friends. Donald was remembering that now as he sat on his bed fiddling with his own cheap Japanese-made watch. He was pulling hard on the watch's winding mechanism, to see how much force it could take before it would break off, when he heard a single knock on his door. Without waiting to be invited, Lenny Thomas, the starting running back on the football team, came into his room, carrying an envelope. Lenny's room was three doors down the hall.

"Can you believe how bad Lou is as quarterback?" Lenny said.

Since the game on Friday, most of the conversations among the football players had begun this same way. Snide comments about Lou had replaced "hello" as the most common way they greeted each other.

"I know, Lou's a complete disaster," Donald said. "A lot of the guys think I should play quarterback."

"Who thinks that?"

Donald hadn't actually heard that sentiment expressed by anyone. But he used to be a good quarterback during pickup games after school in the playground at Kew Gardens Elementary. If the other guys on the team had seen those games, he was sure they would want him to play quarterback instead of Lou.

"A lot of guys," Donald said.

"I guess I just don't know any of them," Lenny said with a laugh. "Anyway, Donnie got a letter meant for you."

Lenny handed the envelope to Donald. Donald and Lenny's roommate, Donnie Thorn, sometimes got each other's mail because their names were so similar.

Getting mail was not usually very exciting for Donald, because the only person who ever wrote to him was his youngest sister, Elizabeth. She would update him on boring topics from home, like what dumb things their little brother, Robert, had done or what pets she wished she had but could not, because of their father's strict no-pet policy. But this time Donald felt a rush of excitement when he saw the return address on the envelope.

It was a letter from Janet Riverstone, the most beautiful girl in his hometown of Kew Gardens. They had been in the same school together from third grade, when Janet's family had moved from Forest Hills. Donald had had a crush on Janet from the first time he saw her come into Mrs. Naughton's third-grade classroom, with her big brown eyes and her beautiful blond hair done in a braided ponytail.

Donald had not been the only boy who had appreciated Janet's appeal. She was always the most sought-after girl at every school dance. Donald had managed to slow-dance with Janet once (to "Earth Angel" by the Penguins), and it had been the highlight of his time in seventh grade.

Since coming to the Academy, Donald had spent many nights dreaming about her. After he'd read *The Great Gatsby* in English class, he had decided Janet was his Daisy Buchanan—the girl who was meant for him. He had arranged to meet her a few times back in Queens over the summer, together with other friends, and, whenever he did, he always made sure to wear his very best shirt. He hoped she would notice. Donald had considered asking her out for real, but then he had heard through mutual friends she was dating Ricky Dunstan.

Ricky Dunstan was the James Dean of Kew Gardens. He had a real leather jacket and had been smoking since seventh grade. There were rumors he carried a switchblade in his jacket, and people said he always wore his hair in a high pompadour to cover a scar he had gotten when some Italian kids broke a beer bottle over his head during a fight. Donald had not been surprised Janet would be with a guy like that.

"Janet Riverstone," Lenny said. "Sounds like a real doll."

Donald resented hearing Janet's beautiful name come out of Lenny's stupid mouth. He did not want to waste any more time. Janet had never written to him before, and he wanted some privacy to see what she had to say.

"Scram, Lenny. And close the door on your way out."

"Jeez, okay."

Lenny walked out of the room, leaving the door wide open behind him. Donald decided it was not worth the effort to get up and close it. He ripped open the envelope and read the letter, which was written in very curly handwriting on a piece of pink stationary. Then he reread it.

Janet Riverstone, the former "it girl" of Kew Gardens Middle School and still quite possibly the most beautiful girl in central Queens, wanted Donald to know she was interested in him, and she had hoped all summer Donald would ask her out. Donald couldn't believe it at first. He checked the envelope to make sure Lenny wasn't playing a cruel trick on him, but he realized he was just being paranoid. Lenny could not possibly know there was a girl named Janet Riverstone in his hometown.

Donald quickly came up with a list of reasons why Janet would want him over Ricky Dunstan. For one thing, Donald's family was much richer than Ricky's. Also, Donald was taller and smarter and was a much better football and baseball player. The more he thought about it, the crazier it seemed he ever thought Janet would prefer Ricky over him. Ricky might be cool, in a greaser kind of way, and Donald had to admit Ricky did have a very nice head of hair, but he was really no match for Donald as a prospective boyfriend.

Donald imagined how jealous the other cadets would be when he showed up at the commencement ball in May with a girl like Janet as his date. She was stunning, and her name made her sound rich and classy. It seemed like she was from the kind of family where a butler with an English accent would answer phone calls by saying "Riverstone residence." In truth, Janet's father ran Riverstone Plumbing on Hillside Avenue. But the only person at the Academy who would know she was a plumber's daughter was Jerry Stahl, and Donald could keep Jerry from saying anything.

A full ten minutes passed—during which he read Janet's letter three more times—before Donald remembered he had asked Cindy Grubb to be his date to the commencement ball less than twenty-four hours before. He would have to deal with that complication later. For now he was enjoying daydreaming about Janet.

16

Monday, October 14, 1963 (9:21 a.m.)

"I UNDERSTAND YOU THREE BOYS WERE IN JESSUP HALL at the same time as Teddy," Colonel Frank Overstreet said, tapping a pencil on his desk.

Donald, Stanley, and Jerry sat in chairs across from him. He had wanted to speak with the cadets who were most likely to have information about what had happened that night, so he had asked Mrs. Kreitzenbach to collect those three from their morning classes and bring them upstairs.

"We're going to conduct an investigation into Teddy's death," Frank continued. "There'll be a hearing, and all three of you will be asked to answer some questions."

Frank paused and looked at the boys, who were shifting anxiously in their chairs. One by one, he stared directly into each of their eyes with the most intense glare he could muster. That was the technique he always used to get information from young soldiers and cadets who might be reluctant to volunteer it. He found that silence, combined with direct eye contact with a colonel, was sometimes all that was needed to elicit the truth.

"I didn't actually touch the body! I said I did, but it wasn't true," Jerry blurted out. "I just found Teddy's body. I never turned him over, sir."

Frank was pleased that his glare had worked on at least one of the boys. But whether Jerry touched the body or not seemed like a secondary issue. He did not want to get bogged down with that now.

"Thank you for that admission, Jerry," Frank said. "Does anyone else have anything to say? If there's something you want to get off your chest, this would be the time to tell me."

"Colonel, could I get in trouble for saying I touched the body?" Jerry asked.

"Probably not," Frank said. "But we can discuss that later."

"I also never stepped in any blood, sir," Jerry added.

"Jerry, we will talk later about your handling of the body," Frank said. "Right now, I am more interested if any of you boys know what Teddy was doing that night, before he died."

None of the boys spoke. Frank tried another round of probing stares.

"Stanley, is there anything you want to ask me about the investigation?" Frank asked.

"The police already decided Teddy killed himself, right, Colonel?" Stanley asked.

"That's right," Frank said.

"So you think the police were wrong, Colonel?" Stanley asked.

"Well, no. I certainly don't expect we'll come to a different conclusion from the police. They're the experts, after all," Frank said. "But we owe it to Teddy to do our own investigation."

"Thank you, sir," Stanley said.

"How about you, Donald? Any questions?" Frank asked.

"Is that statue real gold, sir?" Donald asked, pointing at the Buddha statue on Frank's desk.

Frank had bought the Buddha at a trinket shop in Tokyo on his way home from Korea. It had only cost the equivalent of about fifty US cents. Frank guessed it was brass covered in thick gold paint, but he felt no need to explain that to a cadet.

"I mean questions about the investigation," Frank said.

"No, Colonel," Donald said. "I don't have any questions, because I didn't see Teddy that night except in the library. I shouldn't even be here, sir."

"You're here, Donald, because I want you to be here, and you will answer questions at the hearing for the same reason. Do you understand, cadet?"

"Yes, Colonel," Donald muttered.

It was cadets like Donald that reminded Frank how different a military school was from the actual military. If a soldier had mouthed off to Frank like that when he was on active duty, there would have been real consequences. But as headmaster of a military school, Frank understood his main responsibility was to keep the tuition checks coming in every semester. He could never really discipline the cadets, because every Saturday they were given a chance to call home and complain to their parents.

Recently, those reminders of how different his current job was from his army days had started to depress and anger Frank. It had caused him real physical pain to give Donald all As for the semester. In the real army, a guy wouldn't get any extra benefits just because his buddy next to him in the foxhole got his head blown off. But the Academy's board had required him to reward Donald with good grades for his roommate's suicide.

When he had informed Donald about that, Frank had felt as if the words were choking him.

"I'll let each of your parents know we're holding a hearing," Frank said. "They'll be allowed to attend, if they like."

"Our parents, sir?" Jerry asked, sounding frightened.

"Yes, Jerry. This is a very serious matter, and your parents need to know this is going on," Frank said.

Frank scanned the faces of the boys in front of him. Stanley was looking out the window, Donald was still staring at the Buddha statue, and Jerry looked so frightened, Frank worried he might burst out crying. It seemed there would be no valuable admissions or questions from the boys today.

"All right, cadets. I'll let you know when the hearing is scheduled," Frank said. "Now go back to class."

17

Monday, October 14, 1963
(9:54 a.m./9:54 p.m. Hong Kong time)

SITTING ON A SOFA IN ARTHUR WONG'S LIVING ROOM, Deputy Governor of the British Crown Colony of Hong Kong, Sir James Hogg-Warren, looked extremely uncomfortable. In fact, Arthur thought he looked like he would rather have been anywhere else in the world at that moment. He was sweating profusely and nervously crossing and uncrossing his legs.

Sir James's presence on the sofa was the result of a plan Arthur had hatched several months before. Arthur needed the colonial government's approval for a new business venture, and, as much as the government claimed to support entrepreneurial activity in the colony, they did not willingly extend that support to the triads. A triad leader needed to come up with a very special incentive to get a well-placed official like the deputy governor to visit his home.

The particular incentive Arthur had used was a thick envelope of photographs that had been delivered to Sir James's office in Government House the previous day. The photographs depicted Sir James naked and in a variety of sexual positions, some conventional and others quite exotic, with a young male member of the Ho Fong Triad named Edson Chang. In the envelope, Arthur had also included a note listing the parties who would receive copies of the pictures if Sir James did not pay Arthur a visit the following day at 9:30 p.m. That list included the governor; the British Foreign Office; Sir James's wife, Margaret; and his mother, the Countess of Scunthorpe.

Arthur's plan had taken several months to come to fruition. He had originally placed a different Ho Fong Triad member into Government House, a young woman named Evangeline Ho. Evangeline was a part-time model and actress who Arthur felt sure would be able to attract Sir James's attention. However, after six weeks of unsuccessfully trying to elicit his interest, Evangeline decided she had been assigned an impossible task. She was confident a young man would have a better chance of success with the deputy governor.

Based on Evangeline's advice, Arthur had her replaced in Government House with Edson Chang. Edson was also a part-time actor, and had played "young man with bamboo pole" in a popular local movie called *The Beggar King*, which had been financed by the Ho Fong Triad. Within a few weeks of Edson replacing Evangeline, Arthur had started to receive compromising photographs of Sir James that showed him thoroughly enjoying Edson's company in a central business district hotel room. Once he felt he had a sufficiently comprehensive set of pictures that clearly captured Sir James's face as well as other incriminating body parts, Arthur had the envelope delivered to Government House and dropped on Sir James's grand mahogany desk.

The business venture for which Sir James's help was needed had been brewing in Arthur's head for many years. He wanted to build a new horse-racing track in the colony. Arthur had already found a piece of land on the western side of Hong Kong Island that he thought would be a perfect location. It was flat, which was not easy to find on the mountainous island, and close enough to the heavily populated downtown to attract plenty of gamblers. But the land, like all of Hong Kong Island, was the property of the British Crown. Arthur was sure the British would never agree to lease it to him to build a racetrack unless he had support from the very top of the government.

Building a racetrack would be the fulfillment of a long-held dream of the Ho Fong Triad that predated Arthur's time as Dragon Head. They had jealously eyed Hong Kong's one existing racetrack in Happy Valley since Arthur's father had first set foot in the colony in 1924. Horse-racing tracks were like a triad gold mine, being places where many of their most important lines of business intersected. Gambling, of course, was the primary revenue source from horse racing, but gamblers on a losing streak also generated multiple other business opportunities, from loan-sharking to extortion to opium sales. Considering all these possible revenue sources, for a triad, a racetrack was the most profitable kind of property there was per square inch.

Unfortunately for the Ho Fong Triad, the Happy Valley racetrack had existed since the middle of the previous century, and it had been firmly under the control of the Shing Yee and Lucky 88 Triads long before Arthur's family had ever come to Hong Kong. Since those two triads were not inclined to share any of their Happy Valley racetrack business with Arthur, he had decided his only option to get into the horse-racing industry was to build his own racetrack. Arthur knew the Shing Yee and Lucky 88 Triads would not welcome the competition and would do everything they could to stop him. If he had the deputy governor on his side, his chance of succeeding would go up dramatically.

As Arthur had expected, Sir James had arrived at his house at exactly the appointed time. The British officials who ran Hong Kong were nothing if not punctual. Arthur had one of his men escort Sir James into the living room and leave him for twenty minutes to stew. He wanted to make sure the deputy governor understood Arthur was in full control of the discussion to come, including when it would begin.

Sir James was shifting anxiously on the sofa when Arthur finally came into the living room and sat down on a chair across from him. He could see Sir James's almost bald head was glistening under a thick layer of sweat.

"I understand my assistant offered you jasmine tea already," Arthur said. "Are you sure you don't want any? I have a very special tea from the Fujian province in China. I promise you won't find jasmine tea like this anywhere else in Hong Kong. It's perfectly balanced."

"I don't want any tea, and there's no need to pretend this is a social call," Sir James said. "You summoned me here. Now tell me what you want, Mr. Wong."

Arthur was encouraged by the anger in Sir James's voice. If he could rattle the deputy governor just by offering him special Fujian tea, he felt confident he could get what he wanted. In Arthur's experience, angry people did not make good negotiators.

"You're the deputy governor of the colony, and I'm just a local businessman. I hardly have the power to summon you. I asked you to come here because I have a business proposition I wanted to discuss with you."

"Mr. Wong, if you were a legitimate businessman, and this were a real business discussion, we would be having it in my office in Government House. You wouldn't have needed to send me those horrid pictures."

Arthur was surprised by Sir James's choice of words. The photographs were certainly very graphic, but not horrid. In fact, Arthur thought the photographer had done a remarkably good job. For extortion pictures, they were nicely lit and had a rather artistic quality.

"I'm very sorry if those photographs offended your sensibilities," Arthur said. "But I was concerned you wouldn't agree to meet me unless I gave you a compelling reason."

As Arthur was speaking, his housekeeper, Mrs. Chao, came into the living room carrying a tray with a blue-and-white porcelain teapot and two small tea cups. She put down the pot and both cups on a small side table next to Arthur's chair and then left the room.

"You're sure you don't want to try this tea?" Arthur asked.

"No, thank you, Mr. Wong, and please get to the point. I want to get home to my wife as soon as possible."

"Of course, I would never want you to disappoint your wife," Arthur said, pouring himself a cup of Fujian jasmine tea. "My point is very simple. I want to build a horse-racing track in Hong Kong. I found the right piece of property for it, and I need your help getting a lease of that land."

"Hong Kong already has a horse-racing track in Happy Valley," Sir James said.

"Yes, but I want to build a competitor to the Happy Valley racetrack," Arthur said as his home phone started to ring. "I understand you Englishmen believe very much in the economic benefits of competition. Adam Smith and all that. Isn't that right?"

"Adam Smith was Scottish," Sir James said.

"Oh, I didn't realize there was any difference. Anyway, I think when you see the economics of what we are proposing, you'll understand how competition in this case can be very good for both of us."

One of Arthur's first lieutenants came into the room while he was talking. He was called Three Fingers Chiu for anatomical reasons related to a time he had been held captive by the Shing Yee Triad. The nickname also helped distinguish him from Arthur's two other lieutenants named Chiu.

"What is it?" Arthur asked in Cantonese.

"There is someone calling from your son's school in America," Three Fingers Chiu responded.

During Stanley's four years at the New Jersey Military Academy, the school had only called Arthur once before. That was after his tuition payment was late, because he had sent the cash with a shiftless cousin who had stopped for three weeks in San Francisco to drink heavily on his way to the Academy. Since Arthur knew he was up-to-date with the tuition payments, he worried Stanley might be hurt or in serious trouble.

"I am sorry, but I need to take a call," Arthur said to Sir James. "I will ask my lawyer, Solicitor Chan, to come in now and explain our business proposition for the racetrack."

Arthur walked out of the living room, through the dining room, and into his office. One of his lieutenants handed him the phone. On the other end of the line was Colonel Overstreet.

Over a very scratchy telephone line, the colonel told Arthur about Teddy Haswell's suicide. He said the school would be holding a hearing next week about the death to be sure all the relevant facts were known ("just for good measure," as the colonel had put it). He also said Stanley would be required to testify at that hearing because he had been in the same building when the incident happened. Finally, the colonel said that while he knew it was probably impossible, given how far away he was in Hong Kong, Arthur was invited to attend the hearing. Arthur had just listened without asking any questions.

Arthur thanked the colonel for his call, put the phone down, and went straight upstairs to his bedroom. He took down an old leather suitcase from a closet shelf and began to pack. He knew Solicitor Chan could handle the rest of the discussion going on downstairs in his living room with the deputy governor. His lawyer was going to explain to Sir James that in addition to destroying the photographs, they were going to put him on a payment plan that would be triggered when certain milestones in building the racetrack were met.

He was not sure when the next flight in the direction of the United States would be leaving Hong Kong Airport. But, since the journey to Newark would take at least two days, he wanted to get to the airport as soon as he could. If Stanley was being made to testify in an investigation in America, Arthur was going to be there. In his line of work, all investigations were taken seriously, and the outcomes were never left to chance.

18

Monday, October 14, 1963 (5:02 p.m.)

THAT MORNING, AS THEY WERE LEAVING COLONEL Overstreet's office, Donald told Stanley and Jerry to meet him in the Jessup Field bleachers at 5:00 p.m. He wanted to make sure they had their stories straight about what had happened that night.

As long as they stuck together, Donald was sure the investigation would blow over. Colonel Overstreet had already lost one cadet that semester. He would not want to lose any more through expulsion. But Donald could not take any chances. He needed to impress on Stanley and Jerry that they should protect each other, and that the best way to do that was to follow his lead.

Donald had picked Jessup Field for the meeting because after practice he knew there would be no one around to overhear their conversation. He also thought that, as a football player, he would have home-field advantage there. Jerry and Stanley were both too small and weak to play any varsity sports. If he met them wearing football pads on Jessup Field, he was sure his dominant position in their threesome would be obvious.

That day, practice finished a few minutes early. After losing Teddy and then being destroyed by Westport, Coach Mulrooney seemed to accept that the season was a lost cause. He had not worked the team very hard and left out the wind sprints that he usually put them through at the end of practice. If they were not going to win anyway, Donald wished the coach would just cancel the rest of their games.

As his teammates headed to the locker room, Donald, still dressed in his sweat-soaked practice uniform, walked over to the bleachers and took a seat halfway up. He was killing time kicking the wooden bench below him with his cleats to see if he could crack it when he spotted Jerry walking around the edge of the field.

Watching Jerry walk toward the bleachers, Donald thought he looked so "Kew Gardens," he felt embarrassed for him. Donald might be from the same town, but he knew whenever he went into Manhattan, he could easily pass as a local. Not Jerry. He looked like a guy who belonged in Queens, Donald thought.

In terms of status at the Academy, if Teddy had been an A+ roommate, Jerry would barely merit a C. He was neither an athlete nor a top student nor a leader in the Junior ROTC, whereas Teddy had been all three. But with an investigation looming, he would make a very useful ally. Donald had decided to ensure Jerry's loyalty by offering him the empty bed in his room.

"Hey, pal, how'd you like to move into my room?" Donald asked as Jerry climbed up the bleacher steps toward him.

"What do you mean?" Jerry asked.

"Well, you know I need a new roommate now. I thought maybe you'd want to move in with me," Donald said.

Jerry sat down next to him. Donald knew Jerry's roommate was Eddie "the Windbreaker" McClellan. Donald had given him the nickname the Windbreaker because three years before, during freshman gym class, he had farted loudly doing a deep knee bend. Rooming with Donald would be a huge step-up in status for Jerry.

"I'm sure you'd be glad to get away from the Windbreaker," Donald said.

"Eddie's really not bad," Jerry said. "Did you know his father's a pilot?"

"Come on, wouldn't you rather live with me? Two old buddies from Queens back together again? Imagine all the fun we could have," Donald said.

"You think I'd be allowed to change rooms?" Jerry asked.

"I checked already, and all you need to do is file a room-transfer application with Mrs. Kreitzenbach," Donald said.

"Okay, sure. I'll look into it," Jerry said.

Donald was disappointed, since he had been expecting a more effusive reaction. Probably the generosity of his offer had just taken Jerry by surprise, he decided. Being Donald's roommate would make Jerry a somebody for once at the Academy. Once Jerry had time to absorb the magnitude of this opportunity, Donald was sure his old friend would be extremely grateful to him.

"So, I hear you're taking Cindy Grubb to the commencement ball," Jerry said.

"Yeah, she's pretty, right? You got to admit, I've always had a great eye for girls," Donald said.

"She's really pretty. I was thinking about asking her to the ball myself, but I guess you beat me to it," Jerry said.

"Oh, I didn't realize you liked her like that," Donald said.

Donald had seen firsthand how interested Jerry was in Cindy at the fall dance. But he was surprised Jerry would think she was a real possibility for him as a date. She was far out of his league, and he thought Jerry would be better off focusing on more realistic options. Jerry had plenty of female cousins in Queens he could ask to go with him to the dance.

But at least that explained why Jerry had not been more excited about his roommate offer, Donald thought. Even though Jerry obviously never had a shot with a girl like Cindy, he'd somehow gotten it into his head that Donald had stolen her from him.

Donald thought it would only make Jerry more upset if he told him he might not take Cindy after all. She was the most beautiful girl at the fall dance, but she couldn't hold a candle to Janet Riverstone. Janet had been his dream girl since third grade. He was looking for a way to change the subject when Stanley appeared on the edge of the football field, walking toward them.

"There's Fu Manchu," Donald said, pointing at Stanley.

"You know, I understand why the colonel wants you and Fu Manchu at the hearing, but why me? I just found the body," Jerry said.

"What are you talking about, Jerry? Why would I know anything?"

"I just mean you guys were roommates, so you spent a lot of time together," Jerry said.

"So what? Just because we were roommates, I'm supposed to know why Teddy committed suicide? That's the dumbest thing I've ever heard," Donald said.

"Well, you were best friends, too," Jerry said.

"Yeah, we were best friends. So? That makes me some kind of expert on what was going on in his head? Are you crazy, Jerry? You can't just go saying crazy things like that and think you can get away with it," Donald said.

"Jeez, Donald, sorry. I didn't mean anything by it," Jerry said.

"You better not have meant anything by it. And you better never say anything like that again," Donald said.

If Jerry thought Donald might know something about Teddy's death, maybe other guys at the school did too. Donald had to nip any talk like that in the bud before it got out of hand. But Donald realized it was too late to stress the point any further now, because Stanley had already reached the bleachers. He did not want Stanley to see any discord between him and Jerry. Stanley would feel more pressure to stay in line if he saw them as a united front.

Stanley walked up the bleacher steps and sat down next to Jerry without saying a word. His scowl made it clear he was unhappy to be there.

"Jerry and I were just agreeing there's no reason why I should be involved in this investigation," Donald said.

"You were agreeing? It didn't sound that way from the field. I thought you guys were fighting about something," Stanley said.

"Nope, we were agreeing," Donald said.

"Well, what about me? There's no reason I should be part of this either," Stanley said. "I didn't even know Teddy died until the next day."

"Well, you were on the roof that night," Jerry said.

"What?" Donald and Stanley asked in unison.

"I mean, that's probably why the colonel wants you at the hearing, since you were on the roof. Maybe he thinks you saw something," Jerry said.

"What are you talking about?" Stanley asked.

"Yeah, what are you talking about?" Donald repeated after Stanley.

"I saw you up on the roof of Jessup Hall just, like, ten minutes before I found Teddy's body," Jerry said.

"And you told the colonel about that?" Donald asked.

"No, but I told Mrs. Dumb Cannon. Maybe she told the colonel," Jerry said.

"Fu Manchu, you were on the roof the same time Teddy fell? That sounds very suspicious," Donald said.

Donald could not believe his luck. He felt like all his concerns about that night had been on a plane, and he had just gotten word that plane had gone down over the ocean and there were no survivors. If Stanley had been on the roof, any suspicion would fall on him, not Donald. Also, if Stanley was a prime suspect, anything he said to try to incriminate Donald would carry less weight.

"You think it's suspicious, Donald? Really? Why did you say Teddy fell? That sounds suspicious to me," Stanley said.

"What are you talking about?" Donald asked.

"Just now. You said I was on the roof when Teddy fell. I thought Teddy jumped; he didn't fall. Why do you think Teddy fell?"

"Teddy fell or jumped. How should I know? I wasn't on the roof like you," Donald said.

"And why would you tell Mrs. Duncannon you saw me, Jerry? You guys are no good at keeping secrets," Stanley said.

As much as Donald was enjoying seeing Stanley squirm, he had to keep in mind the purpose for this meeting. He wanted to make sure nobody would squeal at the hearing. If Stanley felt other guys were freely talking about that night, he might decide there was no reason to keep his own mouth shut.

"Fu Manchu's right," Donald said. "That was really stupid, Jerry. From now on, we don't say anything to anybody about that night."

"Yeah, but I said that to Mrs. Dumb Cannon before I knew about any investigation. I didn't think it was a big deal," Jerry said.

"How could you think that's not a big deal? If that's not a big deal, maybe I know some things that aren't a big deal also that I should start telling people," Stanley said.

"Come on, Fu Manchu, Jerry made a stupid mistake, but we're all friends here and we're cadets," Donald said. "You know that under the Academy's honor code, we can't ever tell each other's secrets."

"That's not what the honor code says," Stanley said.

"Yeah, that doesn't sound right," Jerry said.

"In fact, it's the exact opposite. Have you ever read the honor code, Donald? Section Four says if you know another cadet has violated a rule, you should turn him in immediately," Stanley said.

"Yeah, that sounds more correct," Jerry said.

"Anyway, you know what I mean. Cadets shouldn't rat on each other. Maybe it's not in the honor code, but that's just common sense," Donald said, angry at himself for even mentioning the honor code.

"Why were you on the roof anyway?" Jerry asked.

"It's none of your business, but I like to watch the planes land at the airport. It reminds me of where I live. In Hong Kong, my family's house is on a hill, and I can see the planes land across the harbor at the airport," Stanley said.

"So you go up on the roof a lot?" Donald asked.

Stanley's face suddenly changed back to a scowl. He stood up and started to walk down the bleachers. The last thing Donald wanted was for this conversation to end with Stanley storming off, but he was not sure how to stop him.

"I don't trust you guys," Stanley said without turning around.

"Come on, pal," Donald said.

Stanley stopped and looked back at Donald and Jerry. His face was red, and he looked like he might charge back up the bleachers and attack them. At least he would probably attack Jerry first, since he was smaller, Donald thought.

"We're not pals," Stanley said. "You think my pals call me Fu Manchu?"

Donald had not meant that nickname to be insulting. It was just his way of pointing out that Stanley and Fu Manchu were both Chinese. He thought Stanley should understand something as obvious as that, but right now he just needed Stanley to calm down.

"Come on, I give nicknames to all my friends. If you don't like that one, I'll change it," Donald said.

"Don't forget, Donald, I looked out Lieutenant Drake's office window that night!" Stanley said before turning around and continuing down the bleachers.

19

Tuesday, October 15, 1963 (2:56 p.m.)

ROSEMARY DUNCANNON STARTED SLEEPING SOUNDLY
again after she'd told Colonel Overstreet everything she
knew about the night Teddy had died. She had done all she
could. It was now up to the colonel to decide what to do with
that information.

Insomnia had caused her to fall behind on her special project at work. She had decided some years ago that the library
would benefit from more specialized resources befitting the
Academy's status as the second-oldest military school in New
Jersey. So she had taken it on herself to compile an index of
every major battle in history, annotated with a short description, and a list of the resources on that battle that were available
in the library. Although she hadn't yet told anyone about her
project, she knew it would be an important part of the legacy
she would leave behind when she eventually retired.

Her index already covered the period from the Spartan
siege of Athens in 404 BC up to the Battle of Bunker Hill in
1775. She still had almost two hundred years of history left

and she was aware there were some gaps (she had not been able to find any information about battles in Asia, Africa, or Latin America), but she was pleased with her progress so far. Each battle included in the now twenty-page document was the result of several days of research, squeezed in among all of her other duties.

While she was having trouble sleeping, she had been too exhausted during the day to work on the index. But now, after several good nights of sleep, she was looking forward to getting back to it. She had just started work on the Battle of Quebec when she saw the extremely rare sight of Colonel Overstreet entering the library. Rosemary went over to greet him by the front desk.

"Good afternoon, Colonel," Rosemary said.

"Same to you, Mrs. Duncannon. I hope I'm not disturbing anything important?"

"Not at all. What can I do for you, Colonel?"

During his five years at the Academy, she could only remember seeing Colonel Overstreet in the library twice before. Once when he came to confiscate the copies of *The Catcher in the Rye*, and another time when he asked Rosemary to wrap a birthday gift for his first son by his second ex-wife, because his usual gift-wrapper, Mrs. Kreitzenbach, was out sick. This time, he didn't appear to have a gift, but she noticed he was carrying a yellow Western Union telegram.

"Actually, it's related to our conversation last Friday," Colonel Overstreet said.

"About Teddy?"

"Yes, with all the new information that's come to light recently, I've decided the Academy should hold an investigation into Teddy's death," Colonel Overstreet said. "Now, obviously, we don't expect to find anything different from the police and the army, but we owe it to Teddy to be thorough."

"I'm sure that will be a great relief to Teddy's family," Rosemary said.

"We're setting up an investigation panel, and I'd like you to be on it, Mrs. Duncannon."

"But I already shared with you everything I know," Rosemary said.

"That's understood, Mrs. Duncannon. I am not expecting you to have all the answers. Just to be one of the panel members."

Rosemary was glad there would be an investigation, but she had just started to sleep well again. She could envision her insomnia returning if she was made to be part of an investigation.

"I'm just not sure that's something librarians should do," Rosemary said. "I mean, I don't have any type of training for that."

"Let me be frank then, Mrs. Duncannon. We just need a civilian member. That's what it says in my army handbook," Colonel Overstreet said. "I'm confident you have all the skills needed to do that. So I can count on you then, Mrs. Duncannon, right?"

"Of course," Rosemary said, realizing there was no way out. "You can count on me, Colonel."

"Thank you, Mrs. Duncannon. I'm sure you'll do a great job as a civilian."

"And does that relate to the investigation, Colonel?" Rosemary said, pointing to the telegram in his hand.

"No, actually, it's good news for a change. It just came in from Morgan Chemical," Colonel Overstreet said. "Stanley Wong's a finalist in their chemistry competition."

"That's wonderful," Rosemary said.

"I wanted to give Stanley the good news myself," Colonel Overstreet said. "Mrs. Kreitzenbach thought if I was in the library, I'd be able to catch him after last period."

Rosemary looked at the clock above the library's front desk. She thought the last period of the day should have just ended and, sure enough, a few seconds later she heard the first voices and footsteps coming from the descending herd of cadets.

She stood next to Colonel Overstreet, watching the cadets come down and flow out the main door of Jessup Hall. She saw Stanley walking down next to Dicky Daniels and pointed him out to the colonel.

"Stanley!" Colonel Overstreet yelled. "Come over here for a minute."

Stanley walked slowly over to where Rosemary and the colonel were standing in front of the library. Rosemary imagined it must be scary for a cadet to hear his name yelled out by the headmaster.

"I have good news for you, Stanley. Morgan Chemical's picked you as a finalist for their chemistry prize," Colonel Overstreet said, ceremoniously handing Stanley the telegram.

"Thanks, Colonel," Stanley said.

"That means you have a one-in-ten chance of winning the thousand-dollar scholarship, Stanley," Colonel Overstreet said. "Think about that. One thousand dollars. When I was your age, if I won ten dollars, that would've seemed like a big prize. I'm sure your parents will be very proud."

"Okay, sir," Stanley said, offering the telegram back to Colonel Overstreet.

"Oh no, Stanley. You can keep that," the colonel said. "And you're invited to the award ceremony in New York on

Thursday. I've decided the Academy will pick up the tab for your train ticket."

"Thank you, sir," Stanley said.

"I am very happy for you, Stanley," Rosemary said. "I know how hard you worked on your project."

Rosemary noticed Donald stop at the bottom of the stairwell and glare at them angrily. His expression gave Rosemary the shivers. She quickly looked away and went back into the library.

20

Tuesday, October 15, 1963 (7:05 p.m.)

DONALD AND TEDDY HAD RUN A SECRET POKER GAME IN their room in the barracks almost every week since they were third-year cadets. The game was always on Tuesday night from 7:00 p.m. to 8:55 p.m., allowing the players five minutes to get back to their own rooms by the Academy's 9:00 p.m. curfew.

To make space for the game, they moved their beds against one wall and then pushed their desks together in the center of the room to serve as a makeshift poker table. All the players they invited had to bring their own chairs.

The game was originally Teddy's idea. He loved poker, having learned the game from his grandfather, who used to take Teddy with him to play at the VFW lodge in Trenton. Donald, on the other hand, hated poker. He thought it was a fundamentally unfair game, since the best players might not get the best cards. But he jumped at the idea of running a game as soon as Teddy mentioned it.

Donald's father had preached to him since he was young that there was no more profitable position in all the world than to be the house at a casino. "The house always wins" would certainly have made a top five list of his father's favorite maxims, and it would have been the only one on that list that did not involve real estate.

He had learned from his father that, specifically when it came to poker, the house always won by taking a percentage of every pot, called the "rake." For their game, Teddy and Donald set the rake at 10 percent. Since a typical pot was around forty cents, and the boys played roughly twenty-five hands of poker per hour, over the course of a good night Teddy and Donald could take in about two dollars from the rake.

On top of that, they generated additional income by selling bottles of Coke to the players. Branching out into beverages had been Donald's idea. The Cokes were sourced at a price of ten cents per bottle from a vending machine in the faculty lounge, which was in the basement of Jessup Hall. Only cadets on the Academy's honor roll could use that vending machine and only on Friday and Saturday evenings. Since most semesters neither Donald nor Teddy made the honor roll, they employed some of the smarter cadets to work as their Coke suppliers.

They would give each of their suppliers a dime to buy a bottle and a nickel as a commission, and then sell the Cokes to the poker players for a quarter. If they had six players who were all drinking one bottle of Coke per hour, that meant an additional one dollar and twenty cents of income in a night just from the Coke business.

They knew they were taking a big risk running the game. If they were ever caught, they assumed that, at best, they would be spending many Saturday afternoons doing marching punishment in Jessup Quadrangle, and, at worst, they would be expelled. But, to mitigate that risk, Donald paid a freshman a quarter to stand in the hallway outside their room all night to warn them if anyone was coming. As long as their lookout did his job properly, they were confident they would be able to hide the cards, money, and Coke bottles before a faculty member could get in the room.

Teddy played in the game, but Donald never did, since he did not want to put any of his earnings for the night at risk. Instead, Donald's self-appointed roles were to calculate the rake on each pot, pressure the players to buy Cokes, and provide running commentary on the game, which mainly involved mocking the players who were losing.

Donald had canceled the game the previous Tuesday, since it had not been even twenty-four hours since Teddy had died. He felt playing poker so soon after that would have been disrespectful. But now, with a full week having passed since Teddy's death, Donald decided it was time for the game to resume. With Teddy gone, it had occurred to Donald that he would no longer have to share the profits.

He had invited his regulars, who were Tommy Callahan (his designated Catholic friend from the baseball team), Joey Bortz, Lou Douglas, Lenny Thomas (from the football team), and Tim Jessup, the grandnephew of the school's founder. That night, for the first time ever, Donald also invited Jerry Stahl.

All the players other than Jerry had arrived and were playing the first hand. Donald, as usual, was sitting on his bed and commenting on the game.

"Looks like Loser Lou is trying to bluff," Donald said after Lou Douglas raised the pot by a nickel.

"Shut up, Donald. I told you not to call me that," Lou said angrily.

"Don't blame me," Donald said. "It's like they say, if the shoe fits."

Since their freshman year, Donald's nickname for Lou had been "Louis Armstrong." But he had changed it to "Loser Lou" after the loss to Westport.

"Donald's got a point," Lenny Thomas said, throwing his own nickel into the pot.

"Did you guys hear another one of those monks set himself on fire in Vietnam?" Tommy Callahan asked.

"No way, another one? I don't believe it," Donald said.

Donald vividly remembered seeing the picture over the summer on the front page of the *New York Times*: a Buddhist monk who had covered himself in gasoline, burning on a Saigon street. It was the first time Donald had ever heard of a Buddhist monk or of a country called Vietnam.

"There's no way these guys are seriously barbecuing themselves like that," Tim Jessup said. "I don't believe it. Nobody would do that to themselves."

"What do you mean you don't believe it? I saw the picture with my own eyes in the *New York Times*," Donald said.

"Just because something's in the paper, doesn't mean it's real," Tim said. "They can fake pictures, you know. That could've just been a store mannequin that was dressed up to look like some Vietnam guy. My dad says the commies can fake anything."

"Really? You think so?" Lou asked.

Donald was sure Tim was wrong. He had seen the exact same photograph on the news with Walter Cronkite. There was no way both the *New York Times* and Walter Cronkite would be lying.

Billy Barton, the freshman Donald paid to keep watch in the hall, opened the door and stuck his head in. Billy was barely five feet tall and looked like he could still be in elementary school. The players all grabbed for their cards and coins, assuming Billy was about to warn them that a faculty member was on the way.

"Sir, there's some guy out here who says he's playing tonight," Billy said to Donald.

"Who is it?" Donald asked.

"It's me, Jerry!" Donald heard Jerry yell from out in the hall.

"It's okay, Billy, let him in," Donald said.

Billy opened the door all the way, and Jerry walked in carrying his desk chair, a big smile on his face. Donald could tell from that smile that Jerry understood what an honor it was for him to get an invitation to Donald's poker night. The other players were either jocks or Tim Jessup, who did not play sports but was like Academy royalty anyway since his family had started the school. Donald was sure Jerry had never spent time with such a popular crowd.

"Who's that little kid?" Jerry asked as he found some space between Tommy and Lenny to put down his chair.

"That's Billy. He's a freshman who works for me," Donald said.

"Billy's from my hometown," Lou said.

"Yeah, they're both from Munchkinland," Donald said, causing everyone in the room, except Lou, to crack up laughing.

"Shut up!" Lou shouted, which only made the laughter become louder.

Donald had invited Jerry to talk about a plan he had in mind. He decided they should have that conversation now before Jerry lost any money and got in a bad mood.

"Jerry, before you start playing, I need to talk to you for a minute," Donald said, getting up from his bed and walking toward the door.

Jerry stood up and followed Donald out into the hall. From his post a few feet away from the door, Billy saluted Donald.

"Thanks a lot for inviting me to play tonight," Jerry said.

"Sure thing, pal," Donald said.

Donald closed the door to his room and motioned for Jerry to follow him down the hall. He stopped next to the door to the custodian's closet, since no one would be able to overhear them there.

"We might have a problem with Fu Manchu. You saw how weird he was acting yesterday in the bleachers," Donald said.

"I think he's just mad we call him Fu Manchu all the time," Jerry said.

"It's more than that. I think he may be looking to squeal on us."

"Squeal on us," Jerry said. "What does Fu Manchu have to squeal about?"

"Who knows? But he was up on the roof that night at the same time as Teddy, and he claims now not to know anything. He's obviously lying. He could make up something just to get the heat off him," Donald said.

"What do you think Fu Manchu meant about looking out Lieutenant Drake's window?" Jerry asked.

"I have no idea." Donald said.

Donald knew it was best not to tell Jerry about what he and Teddy had been up to that night in Jessup Hall. He was not sure Jerry could handle any more information. Jerry had been very rattled in Colonel Overstreet's office just trying to describe how he'd found the body. Any more details about that night would surely overwhelm him. In any case, if Teddy had committed suicide, it hardly mattered whether he had jumped from the roof or from the ledge outside Lieutenant Drake's office.

"It just seems really weird that Fu Manchu would make stuff up about us," Jerry said. "He's the smartest kid at the school, and all the teachers love him. What does he have to worry about?"

"That's exactly why he would make stuff up. Believe me, he doesn't want to risk getting into any trouble now," Donald said. "You think he'll still get into some fancy college if he gets expelled from the Academy?"

"I don't know—I guess you could be right," Jerry said.

"I was already worried and then I saw him talking to the colonel after class today. He's probably already started lying about us. We can't waste any more time," Donald said.

"Waste any time before what?" Jerry asked.

"Before we find a way to shut him up, of course."

"You have something in mind?" Jerry asked.

"We need some leverage over him. Something we can use to make sure Fu Manchu stays quiet," Donald said. "I know exactly how to do that, but I need to make sure we're in this together."

"Yeah, sure," Jerry said.

"Because if you're not willing to work together with me on this, then it will be every man for himself at the hearing, if you know what I mean," Donald said.

Jerry looked worried, just as Donald had hoped. If Jerry felt safe and secure, he would never go along with Donald's plan.

"Sure, let's work together," Jerry said. "What's your plan?"

"Teddy's watch was some kind of family heirloom. If that watch turned up in Fu Manchu's room, and I suggested to some people that Teddy thought Fu Manchu took it, that would not look good for Fu Manchu, right?"

"You mean you want to make it look like Teddy and Fu Manchu were fighting over a watch?" Jerry asked.

"Not necessarily," Donald said. "You know, I just want to suggest it's possible that was happening."

"But how are we going to get his watch anyway?" Jerry asked. "Didn't his parents take all his stuff?"

Donald took Jerry's response so far as a very good sign. He had just laid out a plan to plant something in Stanley's room, and Jerry had not yet raised any fundamental objection to the idea. He was just asking technical questions.

"Teddy left his watch with me," Donald said.

"So, how's the watch going to be found in Fu Manchu's room?"

"You're gonna put it there," Donald said.

Jerry did not speak and his facial expression went from worried to petrified. Donald remembered seeing that exact look on Jerry's face once before. It was back in fifth grade when Donald had spilled grape juice all over Jerry's mother's favorite carpet. He had wanted to scare Jerry, but not this much. Before Donald could come up with something more reassuring to say, the door to Donald's room opened, and Lou stepped halfway out into the hall.

"Hey, guys, is Jerry gonna play or what?" Lou yelled to them.

"We'll be back in a second!" Donald yelled back.

Donald knew his regulars were eager to get a crack at playing with Jerry. Since he was a first-timer in the game, they were expecting to be able to get a couple of dollars off him over the course of the night.

"See, you're a popular guy now," Donald said, turning back to Jerry.

"Why do I need to put the watch in Fu Manchu's room?" Jerry asked.

"Well, it can't be me. I already went to Fu Manchu's room once to talk to him about that night. If someone saw me back there again, it would look really suspicious, right?"

"I guess so," Jerry said.

"So if we're in this together and it can't be me, that leaves you, right?" Donald said. "Anyway, if you really want to be my roommate, this is the kind of thing roommates do for each other."

"What do you mean, if I want to be your roommate? I already filed the room-transfer application like you told me to," Jerry said.

"Well, yeah, sure, okay," Donald stammered. "But, you know, nothing's final until it's final, right?"

Jerry was quiet again. Donald decided not to press him any further that night. He just needed to give Jerry some time to think, and then he was sure Jerry would come around.

"Anyway, think about it. We should get back to the game. You're gonna have a great time tonight, pal," Donald said.

"Okay," Jerry said, still looking very worried.

21

Wednesday, October 16, 1963 (12:01 p.m.)

"What do you mean she won't sign the agreement?" Donald's father, Fred, yelled into his office phone.

He was speaking to his lawyer, Bernie Delk, from his office on Jamaica Avenue in Queens. Fred had a wide circle of social acquaintances, and whenever he decided to add a new young woman to that circle, he would ask Bernie to send the woman one of his confidentiality agreements.

The agreement was very straightforward. Party A (Fred) would agree to pay Party B (the woman) two thousand dollars in exchange for Party B agreeing never to disclose any private information she learned about or from Party A during the course of their social acquaintance. There were also a few other provisions, such as one in which Party B would waive her right to ask Party A ever to take a paternity test. Usually Fred's new female social acquaintances would sign the agreement as soon as they received it and would be spending the two thousand dollars within a week.

However, as Bernie had been explaining to Fred over the phone, Fred's newest acquaintance, Linda Delvecchio, was refusing to sign the agreement. In fact, she had written the word *INSULTING* on the first page of the agreement in large red letters and sent it back to Bernie's office by bicycle messenger. In Bernie's professional opinion, that emphatic response suggested she was not open to negotiation.

Fred did not feel comfortable maintaining a social acquaintanceship with a woman for more than a few dates without this agreement in place. His lenders, investors, and tenants expected him to be an upstanding member of the community, and he could not risk any information getting out that might suggest otherwise.

Given such great concern for his reputation, Fred had always told Bernie he would just stop seeing anyone who refused to sign the agreement. But in this case he was not ready to give up on Linda just yet. He'd had a wonderful time with her on their first date in Newark after Donald's football game and was already anxious to see her again.

"Tell her I'll go up to twenty-five hundred, but not a penny more than that," Fred said.

"Okay, I'll try that," Bernie replied. "But I'm not sure that will make the offer any less insulting."

"Just get it done, Bernie!" Fred said before slamming down the phone for dramatic effect.

Fred looked at his watch and cursed loudly when he saw it was 12:01 p.m. He had gotten distracted by the unexpected call from Bernie, and he was now going to be a few minutes late for his lunch with Harold Ruck, the president of Queens Savings Bank. He knew it was too much to hope Harold would be running late also. Harold was the kind of banker who always kept exactly to a schedule. He was also the type who would hold a customer's lateness against him.

Fred grabbed his suit jacket off the back of his chair and ran out of his office. As he passed his secretary in the outer office, she reminded him unhelpfully that he was late for his lunch. At the elevator bank, Fred pressed five or six times in rapid succession on the down button, until, with no elevator in sight, he gave up and hurried down the five flights of stairs to the lobby. Reaching the first floor sweating and out of breath, Fred hoped an empty yellow cab might be waiting, by some miracle, near the front door of his building. It turned out no cab was there, so Fred ran the three blocks down Jamaica Avenue to Belle's Steakhouse.

Belle's was one of the oldest steakhouses in Queens. The walls were covered with framed pictures of the owner, Belle, shaking hands in front of her restaurant with all kinds of New York dignitaries, from Mayor La Guardia to Joe DiMaggio to Vito Genovese. It was well known up and down Jamaica Avenue that for an important business lunch, there was no better place than Belle's. People said if the walls of Belle's could talk, they would be able to tell the secret of every major property deal, political trade-off, and mob hit that had happened in the borough over the last thirty years.

As Fred had expected, Harold was already at the restaurant, looking impatient and sitting in a red leather upholstered booth near the front. Fred quickly wiped the sweat from running three blocks off his upper lip and tried as best he could to reposition his hair back into place. He then put on his most confident-looking smile and walked over to greet Harold.

Of all the lunches he could be late for, this was not one of them. Not only was Harold a stickler for punctuality, but Queens Savings Bank was Fred's most important lender. He used to have similarly strong relationships with Kings County Bank and Trust and the Bank of Massapequa, but recent cash-flow problems that had led to defaults on his Coney Island Estate project had put an end to those relationships. Now, without the continued support of Queens Savings Bank, Fred's real estate business would quickly come to a halt.

"Great to see you, Harold," Fred said, giving Harold a handshake so firm, both of their hands turned white during the shake and then red upon release.

"I'm afraid I don't have much time today, Fred. Even if you had been on time, I only had forty-five minutes," Harold said.

Fred slid into the booth next to Harold. He hoped Harold would not keep up the jabs about his being late. Fred resented bankers who thought they always had the upper hand just because they were supplying most of the money for his projects. He was the real estate visionary who was redesigning New York's outer boroughs. Bankers were just interchangeable cogs in the financial machine. Although kowtowing to bankers from time to time was part of Fred's job, it always infuriated him.

"Well, let's get the menus and order then," Fred said.

"Since you were late, I already ordered the flank steak for both of us."

"Perfect! Flank steak sounds delicious," Fred said.

He hoped his disappointment had not come through in his voice. All morning long he had been salivating over the thought of having one of Belle's special pork chops.

"I hope you don't mind if I get straight down to business, Fred," Harold said. "You know after the problems we had on the Coney Island Estates project, my board's now very concerned about all the exposure we have to your partnerships."

Fred was tired of being reminded about the Coney Island Estates project. It was his biggest project ever, and it was supposed to have been the launchpad for Fred to enter the upper echelon of outer-borough real estate developers. But the project had run into problems when it turned out the top two floors of the ten-story tower would throw a synagogue nearby into permanent shade. For months, the synagogue's rabbi and his aggressive team of Brooklyn lawyers had held up the development in court.

To get the project out of litigation, Fred had finally agreed to chop the top two floors off the plans. While that solved one problem, it had created another, because the construction loans Fred had taken out on the project mandated Coney Island Estates would have two hundred units. Since the plans already called for the building to take up the whole lot, there was no way to make the building wider. To squeeze in the required number of units, Fred's architect decided, after going through many possible alternatives, that their best option was to reduce the size of the kitchens by fifty percent and eliminate the tenant parking lot.

The delays caused by the synagogue's lawsuit, combined with the difficulty of renting apartments with tiny kitchens and no parking, resulted in Fred violating numerous construction loan covenants and falling way behind on his payments. The banks that had funded the project all had been at Fred's throat for months demanding their loans be repaid. Fred was not personally liable for any of it, since, as with all his projects, he had set up a limited liability partnership to own the building. But if he lost the support of his bankers over this, he would be out of the real estate development business going forward. Debt was the lifeblood of his company.

"As I've been saying for months, Harold, if you'll just lend me another fifty thousand, we can spruce up the building enough to get it fully rented," Fred said. "Then we can finally put Coney Island Estates behind us both."

"We're still thinking about what to do specifically with Coney Island Estates," Harold said. "But the issue is bigger than that, Fred. Now you want us to finance the project in Flushing also. The board wants me to revisit the bank's entire relationship with you. They are very concerned."

"Believe me, Harold. Flushing Towers is going to be a landmark development for Queens. Queens Savings Bank doesn't want to miss out on that one."

Fred could feel a trickle of sweat making its way down his long right sideburn, but he did not want to call attention to the fact that he was sweating by wiping it away. He absolutely needed Harold's support with Flushing Towers. The project was meant to be an important part of the legacy he would leave for his children. It was going to be two apartment towers of the highest quality overlooking Flushing Cemetery, where his father, Friedrich, was buried. Building Flushing Towers would be a seminal event of his reign as patriarch of the family. It would be a way of honoring his father (Friedrich would enjoy eternal rest in the cool shade of Flushing Towers) while also assuring his children's future wealth.

Fred idolized Friedrich, who had arrived virtually penniless at Ellis Island from Bavaria at the age of only sixteen with a dream to strike it rich in the new world and buy property. After several years of moving from job to job, searching for the right business to make his fortune, Friedrich eventually purchased a failing English pub in the East Village of Manhattan called the Impressionable Dwarf from a bankrupt Englishman who advised him that just selling drinks was no way to strike it rich in America.

Friedrich soon agreed with that assessment, and decided to diversify the Impressionable Dwarf's business away from just alcohol, turning it into a bar, brothel, and German sausage house, all in one. The first and only business of its kind in New York. As the money began to roll in from this unique combination of services, Friedrich redecorated the place with heavy emphasis on red velvet and gold leaf, recalling the style of grand cafés he had seen in his native Bavaria. With its slogan "Come for the Best Ladies, Stay for the Wurst," the Impressionable Dwarf became a huge success. Friedrich was soon rich enough to get married. He decided it would be unseemly to start a family as a brothel owner, so he sold the Impressionable Dwarf to his younger brother, Johan, who had just arrived from the old country, and Friedrich bought a house for himself and his new wife in Flushing, Queens. Fred was born shortly thereafter.

At that time, Flushing was still more like a sleepy country town than the bustling metropolis it would become. Friedrich had never given up his dream of making money in property, and he started purchasing undervalued parcels of empty land around Queens. His plan had been to someday develop those parcels into opulent buildings like the ones he remembered from the Old Town in Munich. But Friedrich never got to see that plan come to fruition.

One day in 1918, while the Spanish flu was raging throughout New York, Friedrich had insisted, despite the pleading of Fred's mother, to go into Manhattan to attend the annual dinner of the German Businessmen's Association of Greater New York. Two weeks later Friedrich died of the flu. It was up to Fred to complete the family legacy. He would take the parcels of land Friedrich had purchased, and build a property-development business. But he needed the continued support of Queen's Savings Bank to do that.

"We're no longer comfortable with the amount of equity you have in your partnerships, Fred," Harold said. "It's just too low."

"But, Harold," Fred pleaded, "I've been operating the same way for years. You know my projects always make money for the bank in the end."

"I'm sorry, Fred," Harold said. "To maintain our relationship, we need to see you bring in substantial new equity investors to your projects. Fresh money."

Having significant outside investors in his projects would mean less money going into Fred's pocket at the end of the day. It would also mean more people he would need to answer to if there were construction delays or squabbles with subcontractors. And those always occurred.

But Harold's comment had not come as a surprise. Fred knew he had gotten away this far using partnerships with much less capital than was typical for apartment projects in the city. If playing in the New York outer-borough real estate big leagues meant he would now need more investors, so be it. And he already had one such investor in mind. Randolph Jessup Jr. Fred had spent most of Donald's last football game working on Randolph Jr., and he thought he was almost ready to reel him in.

"No need to worry at all, Harold. I have a big new investor ready to sign on any day now."

22

Wednesday, October 16, 1963 (3:01 p.m.)

AFTER HIS CONVERSATION IN THE BARRACKS HALLWAY with Donald, Jerry Stahl had not been able to concentrate on the poker game. He finished the game up by two bucks, the most of anyone. Given how bad the other players were, he should have won almost every hand. Lou Douglas did not even seem to know the basic rules of the game. He had thought he had won a hand with two pair, even though Lenny had three tens and Jerry had thrown down a flush.

After the game, Jerry had not been able to sleep for most of the night. He just lay in his bed, listening to Eddie's heavy breathing and thinking about Donald's request.

In the morning, Jerry pulled himself out of bed and went to class, feeling exhausted and still struggling with whether to agree to Donald's plan. Finally, during his third-period trigonometry class, he had made up his mind. He decided he could not go through with it.

As much as he wanted to be Donald's friend again, it just felt too wrong to sneak Teddy's watch into Stanley's room. If that really was the only way to keep Stanley from lying about them, Donald would just have to plant the watch himself. And if refusing to do it meant Donald would not want him anymore as a roommate, he could accept that. Eddie really was not such a bad roommate, Jerry thought. Despite the Windbreaker nickname Donald had given Eddie, he did not even fart that much in the room.

Jerry's last class of the day was chemistry with Major Burnside. He tried to follow the major's lecture on the difference between ionic and covalent bonds, but he couldn't concentrate. Jerry just kept going over in his mind what he would say to Donald and imagining how Donald was going to react.

As soon as Major Burnside excused the class, Jerry raced down the stairwell. He did not know what class Donald had last period, but since all of the school's classrooms were in Jessup Hall, if Jerry got downstairs quickly, he would be sure to catch Donald on his way out of the building.

Jerry waited outside the main door until he saw Donald come out, talking to Joey Bortz. Unlike the other cadets, who were all streaming out of Jessup Hall carrying textbooks, notepads, and pencils, Jerry noticed Donald was not holding anything at all.

"Donald, can we talk for a minute?" Jerry asked.

"Sure, pal," Donald said.

The stream of cadets leaving Jessup Hall went down the front steps of the building and then veered sharply to the right in the direction of the barracks. Jerry and Donald walked in the opposite direction to a quiet spot in Jessup Quadrangle where they could speak without being overheard.

"Did you get a note about the hearing?" Jerry asked.

During his fifth-period English class, Colonel Overstreet's secretary had handed him a typewritten note that the hearing about Teddy would be on Monday, and Jerry was required to attend.

"Yeah, I got one," Donald replied. "Obviously this means we need to work fast."

"Yeah, about that," Jerry said as he felt his heart rate going up and his palms getting sweaty. "I need to tell you something."

"What is it, pal?"

"I don't think I can put the watch in Fu Manchu's room," Jerry said. "It just doesn't feel right to me. Fu Manchu's never done anything bad like that to me."

Jerry was relieved to get those words out of his mouth, but now he waited nervously for Donald's reaction. He knew how much Donald hated to be disappointed. In fifth grade, Donald had smashed a glass vase at his house just because his mother told him he couldn't watch *The Lone Ranger*. This would be an even bigger disappointment.

"We need to do this, Jerry," Donald said, sounding surprisingly calm. "Maybe Fu Manchu hasn't done anything to you yet, but I know he's gonna try to blame Teddy's death on us."

"But I don't get it," Jerry said. "How can we be blamed?"

"Think about it, Jerry. Fu Manchu was on the roof. He's gonna get in trouble for sure unless he finds other people to blame," Donald said. "Believe me, he'll lie about us to stay out of trouble, because he doesn't want to lose out on going to Harvard."

"Actually I think he wants to go to MIT," Jerry said.

Jerry saw Donald's face redden. He wished he had just let the Harvard remark pass, since he knew how much Donald hated being corrected.

"Believe me, Jerry," Donald said. "The school wants someone to blame, and it's going to be us or Stanley."

"But Teddy committed suicide. Why does anyone need to be blamed?"

"Because Teddy's dead, Jerry! It doesn't matter what the truth is. The school needs someone to pay for that," Donald said.

Jerry had assumed that the worst that could happen at the hearing was he would receive a few demerits for lying about touching the body. But the way Donald made it sound, it was practically going to be a criminal trial. Jerry was getting more worried by the second.

"You really think one of us could get in big trouble?" Jerry asked.

"Of course we could," Donald said. "But really this is about loyalty, Jerry. I would take a bullet for my roommate. If you're not even willing to do something as small as this, I don't know what to say."

Jerry could feel his will weakening. For the last three years, he had hoped to become friends with Donald again, and now he finally had that chance.

"I want to help," Jerry said. "I really do. It just doesn't feel right."

"Jerry, we've been friends since first grade. What has Fu Manchu ever done for you?"

"That's true," Jerry said, happy to hear Donald call him a friend.

"Oh, and I forgot to mention last night, if you do this for me, I'll ask Cindy Grubb to go to the commencement ball with you instead of me."

Jerry could not believe what Donald was offering to do. After Donald had stolen Cindy away from him at the fall dance, he had sulked the rest of the night. He had not even tried to line up a date for the commencement ball, because he was too upset about losing Cindy after they had developed such a strong connection.

"Seriously? You would do that for me?" Jerry asked.

"Of course I'll do that for you, pal," Donald said. "I'll write Cindy a letter tonight and tell her all about what a great guy you are. Once she reads what I have to say about you, I'm sure she'll want to go with you."

Jerry remembered Cindy's perfect smile and sensed that his resolve to resist Donald was not going to last. He knew how wrong it would be to set up Stanley, but what he wanted most in the world was to take Cindy Grubb to the commencement ball.

"Maybe you're right about Fu Manchu," Jerry said.

"I am right, and you're a good man, Jerry," Donald said. "I know I can count on you to do the right thing."

Donald's choice of words caused Jerry to feel a final, fleeting stab of guilt. Jerry knew he was not doing the right thing. He would be violating at least three sections of the Academy's honor code just to win back an old friend and get a date with a beautiful girl. Then he pictured himself in his dress uniform walking into Jessup Auditorium with Cindy Grubb on his arm, surrounded by his envious classmates, and the last of his moral qualms melted away.

"Okay, so how do I get the watch into Fu Manchu's room?" Jerry asked.

23

Thursday, October 17, 1963 (9:05 a.m.)

WHEN ROSEMARY DUNCANNON WAS ELEVEN YEARS OLD, her father was a successful stockbroker in the Newark office of Brown Brothers. She lived with her parents and two younger sisters in a large five-bedroom house in Millburn, New Jersey, within walking distance of Taylor Park. She was a straight-A student at Millburn Elementary School and was the winner, two years running, of the school's penmanship award.

The only significant problem she faced that year, other than an extended bout of tonsillitis, was that, no matter how hard she tried, she could not get Henry Wright to notice her. Henry was a quiet and studious boy who had the most unusual eyes she had ever seen. They were an intense blue gray, with a small ring around the center almost the color of robin's eggs. Rosemary decided his eyes must be an indication of a deep and soulful character. His family had moved to Millburn the year before from Wilmington, Delaware, which made Henry the most well-traveled kid in the sixth grade.

After months of daydreaming about Henry, she finally confided her feelings about him to her best friend, Irma Clarke, after first swearing her to secrecy. Irma pushed Rosemary to say something to Henry, but she was scared. She had barely said ten words to Henry since he'd moved to Millburn.

After several weeks of seeing no progress made in her best friend's relationship, Irma decided to take matters into her own hands. During recess, she snuck back into the classroom and left a note in Henry's desk. It said there was a girl in class who liked him, and if he wanted to find out who it was, he should come to the duck pond in Taylor Park at four thirty that afternoon.

Without saying anything to Rosemary about the note, Irma made sure they were standing by the duck pond at the appointed time. Sure enough, after a few minutes of watching the ducks, she saw Henry coming down the path toward them. Irma told Rosemary she was going to use the toilet next to the bandstand and then come right back. She ran up the path and, as she was passing Henry, stopped for a second and whispered to him, "It's Rosemary."

Rosemary and Henry ended up talking for thirty minutes by the pond, which was the most thrilling half hour of her life up to that point. After some very nervous small talk, they had swapped life stories.

He had played baseball and had a lot of friends in Wilmington, but then his older brother had gotten in some trouble at school, and his parents decided they needed a fresh start. So they moved to Millburn, where his father got a job at his uncle's appliance repair shop. Although Rosemary did not have anything in her background nearly as exotic as having lived in Delaware, she talked about her family and how bratty her two younger sisters were. By the end of their conversation,

Rosemary and Henry agreed they were now boyfriend and girlfriend.

That night, Rosemary wondered how her life would change now that she had a boyfriend. As it turned out, it changed dramatically, if only for two days. During those days, Rosemary held hands with Henry at recess and sat next to him in the lunchroom. As soon as school ended, they met at the gate and walked together to Taylor Park, where they sat on one of the long wooden benches by the flower garden and talked mainly about how happy they were with their relationship. Although she knew her parents would expect her at least to finish high school before she got married, Rosemary wondered if Henry might someday be her husband.

Then, after those two blissful days, everything changed. On the third day, Rosemary ran up to Henry when she saw him outside school in the morning, but he was cold and distant. He barely muttered good morning to her before walking away. Then he ignored her at recess and in the lunchroom and was nowhere to be found when she looked for him by the gate after school. Rosemary could not imagine what she had done wrong.

After several more days of Henry barely looking in her direction, Rosemary finally got up the courage to ask him what was wrong. She caught him in the corridor one day just after school ended, and they went together to a quiet spot near the school library.

Henry told her that Roger Turnbull, and the three other boys who followed him everywhere, had surrounded Henry in the boys' bathroom a few days ago. Roger informed him that boys in the sixth grade were not allowed to have girlfriends without his permission. If he saw Henry with Rosemary again, there would be serious consequences.

Henry was clearly frightened, and Rosemary understood why. She had gone to school with Roger since kindergarten and knew well what a bully he was. He had started out in the first grade just pulling girls' hair and grabbing books and pencils away from other boys. By sixth grade, now reinforced by his makeshift gang, Roger was ruling over Millburn Elementary School like a cruel feudal lord. His power at the school was, in many ways, much greater than that of the headmaster or any of the teachers. Roger and his gang could make a classmate's life truly miserable.

Rosemary felt awful that she had caused Henry to cross Roger, but she confessed that she still wanted to see him. Henry felt the same way. He was not ready to give up on their relationship.

They agreed that while they were at school they would ignore each other. Then, after school, they would meet at the duck pond in Taylor Park. Rosemary assured Henry that she and Irma had been going to the duck pond since fourth grade, and they almost never saw any of their classmates there.

The plan seemed to work perfectly. Every afternoon, they each would take a different route from school to Taylor Park, and then sit together by the duck pond for an hour. Sometimes they would even hold hands. It turned out keeping the relationship a secret made her romance with Henry even more exciting.

Then one morning it all fell apart. Rosemary remembered that it had rained heavily the night before and it was still raining when she and Irma walked to school. Just as they went through the school gate, Rosemary suddenly felt a strong push from behind that caused her to lose her balance and fall face-first into a big dirty puddle of rainwater. Soaking wet and starting to cry, she looked up at who had pushed her and saw Henry standing there. Roger and his three henchmen were behind him, laughing their heads off.

Rosemary only spoke to Henry one more time after that. He apologized and explained that one of Roger's gang had spotted them together in the park. Roger had threatened to beat him up every day after school unless he proved he was not dating Rosemary. Rosemary listened, but she had already made up her mind, as she was lying in that puddle, that she was done with Henry.

During high school, Henry and his family moved back to Delaware and Roger dropped out to enlist in the army. She heard later that Roger had joined the Millburn police. She almost never thought about either one of them again. The last time she told that story was many years ago when she and Natalie were first dating. They had swapped stories about their experiences with boys before they realized they were gay.

Rosemary suddenly remembered that story as she watched Donald put a letter into the Jessup Hall lobby mailbox from her seat at the library's front desk. She realized why she'd had such a reflexive dislike for Donald ever since he was a freshman cadet.

Donald was a bully with the same predatory look in his eyes as Roger. They both were boys who were always trying to take advantage of someone else's weakness. No wonder she could never stand Donald. He was the Academy's Roger Turnbull.

If Donald was a Roger, maybe Teddy was a Henry Wright. A sweet and caring boy who simply could not stand up to a bully. And maybe not being able to stand up for himself was the reason Teddy had died. Rosemary was more convinced than ever that Donald knew what had happened that night in Jessup Hall. She wondered if this meant her insomnia would be returning.

24

Thursday, October 17, 1963 (2:06 p.m.)

THE NEW JERSEY MILITARY ACADEMY AND THE PARKER School were only five miles apart and were on the same route for postman Milton Washington. If not for that, Donald's letter to Cindy Grubb never would have been delivered. All Donald had written on the envelope, in his cramped and almost illegible script, was Cindy's name, Parker, and Newark. But that was enough information for Milton. He was used to carrying letters between the two schools, particularly just after the Academy's fall dance.

Milton had picked up Donald's letter from the Academy's mailbox in Jessup Hall at 10:05 a.m. on Thursday, canceled the postage by hand in his truck, and delivered it to the Parker mailroom fifty minutes later. Just after lunch, Cindy saw the letter in her mailbox and felt her pulse start to race. Although Donald had not written his return address on the envelope, Cindy could tell from the very poor quality of the handwriting that the letter was from a boy.

She sat on a bench outside the mailroom, opened the envelope, and slid out the letter. It was written in pencil on a piece of paper that clearly had been roughly yanked out of a spiral notebook. Cindy's eyes first went straight to the bottom of the page, and she was excited to see it was from Donald, as she had been hoping.

Then she read the letter. It confused her at first, and she had to read it through from beginning to end one more time before she felt she understood. It seemed Donald was saying he did not want to take her to the commencement ball, and instead he was recommending she go with his friend Jerry Stahl.

Cindy had never received a letter like this one from a boy before. In her experience, letters from boys usually said flattering things that made her feel good about herself, like that she was beautiful and funny and smart. This was the first time a boy had been so mean to her, and her emotions quickly swung from surprise to anger. How dare Donald think he could not only reject her, but pass her off to his friend?

Although Cindy's first instinct was to rip up the letter and throw it in the nearest trash can, she decided it would be better to keep it, just in case Donald ever had second thoughts and tried to ask her out again. Then she could pull out this offensive note and throw it in his face. So she folded up the letter and put it in her book bag.

A few hours later, Cindy was still upset about the letter when she arrived at her last class of the day, gym with Miss McLemore. Miss McLemore allowed the girls who were having their periods to skip the main class activity and just walk around the school's track. Among the students at the school, the walk of menstruating girls during Miss McLemore's class was known as the "that-time-of-the-month-athon."

Cindy decided to claim she was having her period so she could spend the class focused just on trying to walk off her anger toward Donald. Since the main activity that day was basketball, a particularly unpopular sport among Parker girls, she was joined on the track by about half of the class.

As Cindy started to walk on the track, her friend Dorothy Rodgers came up from behind her. Cindy was a regular in the that-time-of-the-month-athon. But Dorothy almost always participated in gym regardless of her monthly schedule. She wanted to safeguard her perfect grade point average.

"Funny to see you here," Cindy said, smiling.

"Yeah, I just hate basketball," Dorothy said. "And besides, I already did the extra credit project about vitamins, so my A in this class is pretty much guaranteed."

Cindy was amazed Dorothy could still be so diligent about school even though she had already gotten into Wellesley. When Miss McLemore mentioned the extra credit project, Cindy had never given it a second thought. She only needed a C+ average to get into Montclair State, so she certainly was not going to do extra credit just for gym class.

"How about you?" Dorothy asked. "You just hate basketball or it's really that time of the month?"

"Actually, it's funny. I haven't gotten my period all semester. I'm just in a bad mood today, so I didn't feel like playing."

"You know what it can mean if you don't get your period for a long time, right?" Dorothy asked.

Cindy was not sure what Dorothy was talking about, but she did not want to look stupid. She knew how judgmental Dorothy could be.

"Of course I do. But it's nothing physical. I just feel blue today," Cindy said.

"Want to talk about it?" Dorothy asked.

Getting rejected by a boy was not something Cindy was eager to discuss. But she remembered that Dorothy knew Donald from home. If there was anyone at school she could talk to about him, it was Dorothy.

"So, you know Donald at the military academy, right? Didn't you say you grew up with him?"

"Unfortunately. Why?"

"Well, I told you Donald asked me to be his date for the Academy's commencement ball, right?"

"Yeah, you did, and I told you that was a big mistake, because Donald's an idiot. Always has been one and always will be one."

Cindy was not sure if she was more impressed or frightened by the way Dorothy could so freely speak her mind. Cindy's mother had always told her if she could not say anything nice about someone, she should say nothing at all. But Dorothy didn't subscribe to that theory.

"But he seemed really sweet at the dance," Cindy said. "And you have to admit, he's very good-looking."

"I'm sorry, but I don't find guys who are that stupid attractive."

Cindy laughed, and wondered what her mother would think if she ever met Dorothy. Her mother could not stand feminists, and Cindy guessed she would consider Dorothy to be one of those. In fact, she would probably tell her that Dorothy was the kind of girl she should stay away from at school.

"Well, maybe you're right," Cindy said. "Because he sent me a really mean letter today. He said he doesn't want to take me to the commencement ball anymore. Can you believe that? And he only asked me five days ago!"

"Oh, Cindy, I'm so sorry. I'll try not to say I told you so, but I did kind of tell you so."

"How could he change his mind so fast? He's at a boys' school, so who could he have met that's prettier than me in the last five days?"

Dorothy smiled slightly, and Cindy knew it must be hard for her not to gloat. She had warned Cindy that Donald was not as good a guy as he had seemed at the fall dance.

"I told you that Donald's an idiot. He's got a very high opinion of himself and no sense of reality. He could have just seen a picture of a girl in some magazine and decided that's who he wants to take to the ball."

"What do you mean? What girl? Which magazine?"

"No, I don't mean that literally," Dorothy said. "I just mean he's a stupid guy who'll change his mind like the wind. And, I hate to point this out, but if you got the letter today, it means he changed his mind a few days ago. It must take a few days for a letter to get here, right?"

Cindy had not thought about that, but she knew Dorothy was right. Mail between the two schools should take several days. Maybe Donald changed his mind about taking her to the commencement ball right after he had asked her. Maybe he even wrote the letter that same night, she thought.

"He even had the nerve to tell me I should go to the ball with his friend Jerry instead of him," Cindy said. "Can you believe that? As if he thinks he has the power to decide who I'll go with."

"I absolutely can believe it. That's exactly how Donald thinks. And Jerry's always been his puppet. It's been that way since first grade. Jerry follows Donald around like a loyal servant, and sometimes Donald throws him a scrap."

Cindy thought Dorothy might have just called her a "scrap" with that analogy, but she decided to ignore it. She knew Dorothy had her best interests at heart.

"So you don't think I should go with Jerry, right?" Cindy asked.

"Of course not! I think you should stay as far away from Donald and his friends as possible," Dorothy said. "There's no need to waste time on guys like that. They're like dinosaurs. You know, in thirty years or so there won't even be guys like Donald and Jerry around anymore."

"Why? Where will they all go?"

"They'll have evolved," Dorothy said.

"But the dinosaurs never evolved, right?" Cindy asked.

"That's true," Dorothy said. "Maybe they will all just die off instead."

25

Thursday, October 17, 1963 (5:27 p.m.)

JERRY STAHL FOLLOWED DONALD'S INSTRUCTIONS FOR planting the watch exactly. First, he made sure no one else was in the hallway before he went into Stanley's room. Then he walked straight to the storage lockers and opened the one marked Wong. Next, he slid Teddy's watch under the winter coat. Then he closed the locker and left the room. In all, he had spent less than sixty seconds in Stanley's room. No one had seen him going in or coming out. He had executed the plan to perfection.

Back in his own room, he lay down on his bed, feeling queasy and lightheaded. He thought vomiting might help, but the bathroom was too far down in the hall. Jerry decided if he propped his head up a bit, the nausea might pass. So he grabbed the thick copy of *Crime and Punishment* off his desk and put it under his thin Academy pillow.

Eddie was out, so Jerry just lay on his bed with the light off, staring at the ceiling. He had assumed he would feel relief once he'd completed his mission to Stanley's room, but all he felt now was intense guilt.

Jerry was not expecting to feel so much guilt. It was not his first time doing something he knew was wrong. When he was nine, he stole a pack of baseball cards from Woolworths on a dare from Donald, and he felt fine afterward. A few years later, Donald spilled a glass of grape juice in the Stahls' living room (where absolutely no food or drinks were permitted), and Jerry blamed it on his sister. Even when his mom took his sister's bicycle away for a month as punishment, Jerry felt only a tinge of guilt. He didn't want to vomit. He hoped this unfamiliar and unpleasant feeling would pass quickly.

Jerry had picked up the watch from Donald the night before. He was surprised that it was such an ordinary-looking wristwatch. When Donald had said it was a family heirloom, Jerry had pictured an old-fashioned pocket watch on a long gold chain. But this was just a well-used watch like the ones he had seen plenty of men wearing.

Jerry refused to promise Donald exactly when he would go through with the plan. But when he got to chemistry class that day, he felt like fate was telling him to act. Colonel Overstreet had come into the classroom and announced that class was canceled because Major Burnside had taken Stanley Wong to New York for a science fair awards ceremony. If Stanley was not even on campus, Jerry knew he would never have a better opportunity to sneak into his room.

There was a knock on his door. Before Jerry could even say "come in," Donald walked into the room.

"What are you doing? Are you taking a nap?" Donald asked. "Jeez, Jerry. This is no time for napping like you're back in kindergarten. You understand the hearing's soon, right?"

"I'm not napping, Donald. I'm just resting a little," Jerry said.

Donald turned the light on and sat down on Jerry's desk chair. He was wearing a sweat-stained T-shirt. Jerry knew Donald had come straight to his room from football practice.

"Pal, there's no time for resting, either," Donald said. "I heard Fu Manchu's in New York today."

"I know," Jerry said. "I was just in his room."

"Seriously? You did it already?" Donald said, smiling.

"Yep, I did just like we planned."

"I knew I could count on you, Jerry," Donald said. "That's why I always tell people Jerry Stahl's a stand-up guy."

Donald got up from his chair, came over, and extended his hand. Jerry reached out and Donald shook his hand so vigorously that Jerry almost fell off the bed. When Donald finally released Jerry's hand, it was briefly bright red.

"Now I need to do my part and tell Colonel Overstreet," Donald said, heading toward the door.

Jerry had assumed they were just going to threaten Fu Manchu with the watch being found. He had not expected Donald would go straight to Colonel Overstreet with that information.

"You're going to tell the colonel that Teddy's watch is in Fu Manchu's locker?"

"Of course not," Donald said. "How would I know where Teddy's watch is?"

"So what are you going to tell him?"

"I'm just going to tell him that Teddy and Fu Manchu were fighting over a watch," Donald said. "Then it's up to the colonel if he wants to check through Fu Manchu's stuff."

26

Thursday, October 17, 1963 (5:27 p.m.)

STANLEY WONG'S ROOMMATE, DICKY DANIELS, HAD sought out small, confined spaces ever since he was very young. The closer in the walls and ceiling of a place, the more secure he felt in it. Since his parents had made him grow up in a full-size house in Hackensack and had given him his own full-size room, Dicky had become an expert in creating tiny spaces in the middle of larger ones.

He started out in kindergarten using bedsheets hung over chairs to create small areas underneath where he could spend hours flipping through comic books. As he got older, the sheets felt too flimsy to provide a sense of security. At that point he started to spend his free time in his closet. However, since even the closet was too roomy from Dicky's claustrophile perspective, he used cut-up cardboard boxes to build within the closet a tiny chamber just big enough for him to sit in and read using a flashlight.

Dicky's father worried incessantly that his son's very small stature was the result of spending so much time in his "little forts," as his mother called the small spaces he created. As far as his father was aware, generations of Daniels men had been of average height, if not taller. He even had a cousin who was six-foot-four and had played basketball at City College. Since clearly there was no genetic reason for his son's height, he decided the little forts must have stunted his growth.

Over the years, Dicky's father had destroyed, like a marauding giant, countless numbers of the little forts. But his efforts to stimulate his son's growth by denying him small spaces to sit in never had any long-term impact. Like an architect living in an active hurricane zone, Dicky responded to these frequent acts of destruction by developing a building style that allowed the little forts to be easily and quickly rebuilt as soon as the storm had passed.

Dicky's father finally reached his breaking point at his son's annual physical when he was fourteen. His father didn't usually go to Dicky's medical appointments, but he went that year so he could consult with Dicky's pediatrician, Dr. Lazlo, on his theory of a link between the little forts and Dicky's size. Dr. Lazlo thought the theory, scientifically speaking, was quite sound. Then, to try to make Dicky's father feel better about his son's height, Dr. Lazlo noted that while Dicky was undoubtedly very small for a New Jersey eighth grader, he would be considered normal size for his age in Japan.

The last thing Dicky's father wanted was a son who would make a typical-size Japanese boy. Dr. Lazlo's misguided attempt at reassurance was all he needed to make up his mind. He was going to send his very small son to the New Jersey Military Academy and see if a military education could make him grow.

Dicky had never really appreciated his life at home in Hackensack until he got to the Academy. Arriving there at age fourteen as a first-year cadet, Dicky had to stop himself from crying in front of the other boys at least three or four times a day. He missed his younger brother, Bobby; his English bulldog, Winston; and his best friend from Hackensack Middle School, Floyd Crane. Most of all, though, he missed his little forts. When he was feeling alone and upset (which was an everyday occurrence during his first semester), Dicky would have given almost anything to be able to retreat to a small, secure place like one of his old closet forts.

On top of all the other stresses and the pain of adjusting to life at the Academy, there was Donald. Dicky had never met anyone like Donald before. Having always been the smallest boy in his class, Dicky had thought he was an expert on bullies. He had certainly encountered many of them at Hackensack Middle School. In Dicky's experience, a bully usually wanted something specific from him, like his Yankees cap or his lunch money or his actual lunch. But Donald was a whole different kind of bully. He seemed to bully just for the sheer joy of it. As if the satisfaction of exerting his power over someone else was all the reason he needed.

Donald had led the group that had stripped Dicky the first time he'd taken a shower in the barracks. Dicky had never used a group shower before, since Hackensack Middle School did not make the boys shower after gym class. He was not sure when and where exactly he was supposed to become naked, so he had walked into the shower room still wearing his gym shorts. When he saw the other boys in the shower room were all naked, he had started to take off his shorts, but he had not moved fast enough. Donald had already spotted Dicky wearing shorts and yelled to Lenny Thomas and Joey Bortz to grab him. Donald saved for himself the prime job of violently yanking off Dicky's shorts and throwing them in a pool of water under one of the showerheads.

Ever since then, Dicky had been known on campus as Shower Shorts. It was not as common a nickname as the one he'd had in middle school ("spaz"), and Dicky guessed some of the cadets who called him Shower Shorts did not even know what it meant. They just understood it was somehow belittling. All things considered, he decided it was not the worst nickname he could have been saddled with by a boy who enjoyed demeaning others as much as Donald did.

Despite missing home, feeling lonely, and having to deal with Donald, Dicky slowly acclimated to academy life. Over time, he no longer even wanted to cry most days. One of the most important coping mechanisms he had discovered was that the small area under his desk made an acceptable little fort. With the desk pushed against the wall, the area under it was closed on three sides.

Every afternoon, Dicky would retreat to the area under his desk to study. On days when Stanley went to the library to study, Dicky could imagine he was completely alone and would feel at peace. He would pretend the barracks had been picked up by a storm like in *The Wizard of Oz* and dropped down in the middle of a massive desert, and he was the only person there, in his little under-desk fort.

The afternoon that Stanley was on his way to New York with Major Burnside for the Morgan Chemical Talent Search awards ceremony, Dicky was, as usual, under his desk. He was trying to focus on chapter eight of *Crime and Punishment* when he realized the sun had started to set. He reached up to turn on the desk light, when he saw the door slowly opening.

Dicky quickly retreated back under his desk. With Stanley gone, he wanted to savor the solitude. He would simply wait for the intruder to leave. Whoever was coming in would think the room was empty and leave right away.

Huddled under his desk, Dicky watched Jerry Stahl enter the room, shut the door behind him, and walk quickly to the storage lockers on the far side of the room. He couldn't see Jerry, but he could hear him opening one of the lockers and then closing it. Then Jerry crept back to the door and opened it slowly. He stuck his head out into the corridor and looked both ways. Then he exited and closed the door. In all, Dicky guessed Jerry had been in the room for less than a minute.

Dicky got out from under his desk and turned on the light. He then went over and opened his storage locker. On quick inspection, it seemed like nothing was missing. If Jerry had taken something, it did not seem to have been from his locker.

27

Thursday, October 17, 1963 (6:30 p.m.)

ALTHOUGH DOROTHY RODGERS WAS THE TOP STUDENT in her chemistry class at Parker, she did not particularly like chemistry. Like all science subjects, chemistry struck her as too cut-and-dried. There was a right answer and all a student had to do was memorize it or figure it out. Although she was happy to find that answer to get a perfect score on a chemistry exam, the process did not excite her.

Dorothy's passion was politics. In her mind, unlike science, politics was all about creativity, ideas, and finding entirely new solutions to ever-changing problems. She looked at what the Kennedy Administration was doing to transform places as diverse as Appalachia and South Vietnam, deploying brainpower and ingenuity to bring change. That kind of work required original thinking. In comparison, seeing how chemicals reacted under a Bunsen burner was boring.

Given her preferences, Dorothy would rather write an essay on the separation of powers than do a chemistry experiment any day of the week. However, there were no competitions for high school students in political science anywhere near as prestigious or lucrative as the Morgan Chemical Talent Search. Morgan Chemical offered the biggest and shiniest prize any student in the New York area could hope to win.

Her feelings about chemistry notwithstanding, Dorothy wanted that prize. Get first place and for the rest of her life she would have *Morgan Chemical winner* on her permanent record. To make it even more special, she would be the first girl to ever win the talent search. She imagined that when she finally died, peacefully in her sleep of natural causes at one hundred years old after a long career in politics, her lengthy obituary would mention that accomplishment from high school. So chemistry had been the focus of the semester for Dorothy.

Dorothy still allowed herself the first forty-five minutes after classes ended every day for her favorite pastime, going to the library and reading the *New York Times* front to back. That was her daily recreation time. After that, she would be in Miss Jenkins's chemistry classroom until dinner working on her project for the Morgan Chemical Talent Search. She was classifying different types of plastic resins by how easily they could be recycled. Her research involved spending countless hours melting down various plastics and seeing which ones resulted in the purest and most easily reusable end product.

Miss Jenkins had suggested that topic. She thought that as plastics became an increasingly common part of American life, they would need to be recycled or they would end up filling every landfill in the country. Morgan Chemical would surely want to know what type of plastic would be easiest to reuse, Miss Jenkins had said.

At first, Dorothy had resisted the idea. She did not think reusing old plastic sounded very exciting. She was also not convinced that Miss Jenkins's opinion was reliable. Miss Jenkins had graduated from Parker ten years before. When she was at the school, she hadn't made the finals of the Morgan Chemical Talent Search. Although Miss Jenkins went on to get a master's degree in chemistry from Radcliffe, Dorothy thought that if she was really such an expert on what Morgan Chemical was looking for, she would have won the competition herself.

Unable to think of a better idea, Dorothy asked her parents, but they didn't have any good suggestions. The best they could come up with was that she could make a papier-mâché model of a volcano with a baking-soda-and-vinegar-based eruption. She knew that would not win first prize in a third-grade science fair, let alone the Morgan Chemical Talent Search. Her friends at school were as useless as her parents, so Dorothy relented and went with Miss Jenkins's suggestion.

After Dorothy typed up her findings on plastic recycling and sent them in to Morgan Chemical, she tried her hardest not to think about the contest. That was difficult, since she was constantly reminded of her project by the acrid smell of burning plastic that had permeated all her school uniforms. But she tried to forget about it nonetheless. She knew no girl from Parker had ever reached the finals. Besides, she didn't even like chemistry. It was crazy to think she could win.

All that effort to keep her expectations low went out the window on Tuesday when Miss Parker handed her a telegram from Morgan Chemical informing her that she was one of the ten finalists. She was so excited, she wanted to scream. In fact, she did scream, but only after she got back to her room in the dormitory. For the next three days, all she did was daydream about winning.

Having previously told herself she couldn't win, Dorothy was suddenly convinced she couldn't lose. She thought that it would be too cruel of Morgan Chemical to name a girl as a finalist if they did not plan to award her first place. She also found good omens everywhere. She had gotten the telegram from Morgan Chemical on a Tuesday, which was her lucky day, since she had been born on a Tuesday. Also, the time on the telegram was 2:06 p.m., which corresponded to her birthday, February 6.

Dorothy became so sure she would win, she wrote out an acceptance speech and practiced it in front of the mirror in her room whenever her roommate went out. She did not know if the winner would be asked to make a speech, but she wanted to be ready just in case. By the time Thursday afternoon had finally arrived and Dorothy had gone into Manhattan on the train with Miss Parker and Miss Jenkins for the awards ceremony, she could not imagine any result other than her being the Morgan Chemical Talent Search winner for 1963.

The award ceremony was in the Carnation Ballroom at the Roosevelt Hotel on Forty-Fifth Street in Manhattan. A large round table with ten chairs was assigned to each finalist. Dorothy was standing next to her table, waiting for the ceremony to begin. Her nine guests—Miss Parker; Miss Jenkins; her parents; her ten-year-old brother, Jimmy; her aunt and uncle; her cousin Judy; and her science teacher from Kew Gardens Middle School, Mrs. Branson, had all arrived. Dorothy took it as a good sign that the table assigned to her was close to the podium. She assumed Morgan Chemical had put her there so she could quickly go up after they had announced her as the winner.

As Dorothy had expected, the other nine finalists were all boys. Most of them were wearing dark suits that made her feel self-conscious about her choice to wear a bright red dress. She should have known to pick a darker color so she would not stand out so much. She didn't want to look any less serious about chemistry than the boys just because of her clothes.

Dorothy was scanning the faces of her competition when she noticed one boy was alone off to one side of the room. Dorothy recognized him immediately from the fall dance at the New Jersey Military Academy. Although she hadn't talked to him that night, she remembered his face. He was the only Asian student there.

"I know that boy over there. I'm going to go say hi to him," Dorothy said to her mother.

As she walked over to the boy in the military uniform, she imagined all the other finalists must be staring at her. She was sure they were surprised a girl had made the finals. *Soon they will be even more surprised when she wins*, she thought.

"Hi, I'm Dorothy Rodgers. I saw you at the Academy's fall dance," Dorothy said when she reached him.

"Hi, my name's Stanley," Stanley Wong replied. "So that means you go to Parker, right?"

"Yeah," Dorothy said. "I'm the first girl from there to make the Morgan Chemical finals. I guess you're the first also, right?"

"The first what?" Stanley asked.

"Oh . . . I mean, the first student from the Academy," Dorothy said, hoping she had not just insulted Stanley. "You're the first one to make the finals, right?"

"I think so, yeah," Stanley said.

"Actually, I used to go to school in Queens with Donald and Jerry," Dorothy said. "You know them at the Academy, right?"

"Sure, they're good guys," Stanley said.

"Good guys? You really think so? I think maybe we're talking about different people named Donald and Jerry," Dorothy said.

Stanley's eyes lit up, and he laughed a little. Dorothy thought he looked cute laughing. He had looked so serious before.

"Well, okay, maybe they're not exactly great guys," Stanley said with a smile. "But you know, they're my fellow cadets, so I shouldn't say anything bad about them, right?"

"Okay, that's fair," Dorothy said. "Are you here alone?"

"No, my chemistry teacher's here, but he went to the bathroom," Stanley said.

"So, what's your project on?" Dorothy asked.

She did not really want to hear Stanley's answer. She knew learning about other projects could only dent her confidence in the superiority of her own research. But it seemed like the most appropriate question to ask under the circumstances.

"I studied the dispersion rate for aerial delivery of chemical defoliants," Stanley said matter-of-factly.

"What's that?" Dorothy asked, feeling as if she had just heard a string of random words.

"It's a military thing," Stanley said. "Imagine if you're fighting an enemy in the jungle. If you can spray chemicals from planes and helicopters and destroy all the plants and trees around, then it's easier to kill the enemy, right? My research is on what chemicals would be the most effective to spray to do that."

Stanley's project sounded impressive, but Dorothy thought he might have just described a war crime. She had learned in her American Government class that chemical warfare was banned under international law after the First World War.

"Oh. Is that allowed in a war? You can use chemicals to destroy all the trees?" Dorothy asked.

"I think so. Why not?" Stanley asked. "What's your project on?"

"It's on the recycling of plastic," Dorothy said.

"What does that mean?" Stanley asked.

"Well, *recycling* is just another word for *reusing*," Dorothy said. "I researched what's the best kind of plastic to melt down and reuse to make other products."

Stanley looked confused, and Dorothy wondered if she had left something out about her project. Or maybe she had spoken too fast.

"Oh, reusing old plastic. That's really what your project's about?" Stanley asked.

"Yeah. That means less plastic needs to be thrown away, so it should have a lot of benefits," Dorothy said.

"But if old plastic is reused, wouldn't that mean Morgan Chemical would sell less plastic?" Stanley asked.

Stanley's words set Dorothy's pulse racing with anxiety. She felt like she had built a huge dam of confidence to hold back any doubt about whether she would win, and now Stanley had punched a hole in that dam; doubt was spraying everywhere, just like his defoliants. Miss Jenkins had made it sound like recycling would be good for Morgan Chemical, but maybe her project was a threat to the whole business model of the company.

"Well . . . maybe," Dorothy said. "I should go back to my table now. Nice to meet you, Stanley."

"Okay, Nice to meet you," Stanley said.

28

Thursday, October 17, 1963 (7:49 p.m.)

SITTING IN THE CARNATION BALLROOM AT THE Roosevelt Hotel, Stanley Wong was feeling very self-conscious. The tables for the other nine finalists at the Morgan Chemical Talent Search awards ceremony were all full of parents, aunts, uncles, siblings, and teachers. At Stanley's table, it was just him, Major Burnside, and eight empty chairs.

If sitting at a nearly empty table wasn't bad enough, Stanley was wearing his Academy dress uniform. Other than Dorothy Rodgers, the other finalists were all wearing suits and ties.

As a freshman cadet, he had been very proud of his uniform, with its double row of silver buttons on the jacket and thick stripe down the side of the trousers. He imagined he looked like a hero in a war movie. But over time, that excitement wore off, and now he felt slightly ridiculous in it, like he was a little boy playing dress-up as a soldier. He was particularly uncomfortable wearing it at that moment. As if he did not already stand out enough being Chinese, a military uniform made him seem like a different species from the other finalists.

Wendall Klausbach, the winner of the competition in 1951, was finally coming to the end of his long-winded thirty-minute keynote address. Stanley had paid very little attention to the speech, but from the parts he had listened to, he knew Wendall was now a Morgan Chemical research scientist. He had been introduced by Morgan Chemical's assistant vice president for public relations as an excellent role model for the finalists as they considered their future careers in the exciting field of chemistry.

Under different circumstances, Stanley would have been interested in Wendall's description of how his research team had found ways to add additional chlorine atoms to PCB molecules so they would deteriorate at a slower rate. It was very relevant for Stanley's own research. But at that moment, all Stanley wanted to hear was whether he had won the competition.

Getting first place would mean everything to Stanley. He had sensed from his first months at the Academy that he was smarter than most of his classmates. But the grading system at the school made it difficult for him to stand out. A cadet could get an A in many classes just by memorizing a few pages of the textbook. As a result, sometimes even dimwits like Joey Bortz or Lou Douglas would wind up on the honor roll for a semester or two.

The Morgan Chemical Talent Search was a competition for the best students all around the New York area. It was worlds away in terms of difficulty from just getting top grades at the Academy. A competition like this gave Stanley a chance to prove to the school that he was someone special, and that all of his classmates' efforts to diminish him with a silly nickname had just made him work harder.

He knew just being named a finalist, although unprecedented for the Academy, would not be enough to prove that point. The only thing that would get the other cadets' attention would be winning the one-thousand-dollar first prize.

Hearing a light smattering of applause, Stanley realized the keynote address was over. He looked up to see Morgan Chemical's assistant vice president of public relations walking back up to the podium. As the assistant vice president was thanking Wendall Klausbach for his inspiring remarks, the door to the ballroom opened. Stanley looked over to see if waiters were finally bringing in dessert. Instead of waiters with trays, Stanley was shocked to see a man in a black business suit who looked exactly like his father.

Stanley assumed it must just be a look-alike, since his father was supposed to be on the other side of the world. But then the man smiled warmly at Stanley and waved. The intricate tattoo of a dragon's head on the man's wrist left no doubt that it was his father.

Stanley got up from the table and bowed slightly to his father, who responded with the traditional clenched fist greeting of the Ho Fong Triad. Major Burnside stood up as well, looking confused.

"Major Burnside, this is my father, Arthur Wong."

"Nice to meet you, Mr. Wong," Major Burnside said, shaking hands with Arthur. "Fu didn't tell me his father was coming tonight."

"Who?" Arthur asked.

"It's just an Academy nickname," Stanley said before Major Burnside could respond. He didn't want to explain to his father that for the past three years people at his school had been calling him by the name of a fictional Chinese villain.

"Well, Stanley didn't know I was here," Arthur said. "It was a very last-minute decision to come to New York, and I didn't have time to tell anyone before I left."

"How did you know about this ceremony?" Stanley asked.

Before Arthur could answer, an irritated voice uttered the words "excuse me" over the sound system. Stanley looked over at the podium and saw the assistant vice president of public relations staring at them. Most of the people in the audience were also turning in their direction.

"Would the Oriental gentleman who just came into the room please take a seat?" the assistant vice president of public relations said. "We are ready to announce the winner."

Stanley felt embarrassed that his father had been reprimanded. He quickly sat back down. Major Burnside also returned to his seat, and Arthur sat down on the other side of Stanley.

Arthur leaned in close to Stanley and whispered, "I called your school when I got into New York today, and they told me you'd be here. Colonel Overstreet said this is a great honor."

Stanley looked up nervously at the podium, hoping his father wouldn't get in trouble again for speaking during the ceremony. The assistant vice president of public relations was now introducing Morgan Chemical's chairman of the board, Gerald McCormack, to present the award.

Chairman McCormack was a very tall and corpulent man, and he slowly ambled to the podium.

When Chairman McCormack finally reached the podium, he pulled a sheet of paper out of the inside pocket of his suit jacket. Stanley winced when he realized it must be a speech. He just hoped it would be shorter than Wendall Klausbach's keynote.

"Good evening and congratulations to all the finalists, as well as to your families, faculty advisors, and guests," Chairman McCormack began, reading from his speech in a slow and mechanical cadence. "The future of the United States is chemicals. Because of chemicals, crops will grow strong, pests and vermin will die in unprecedented numbers, children will sleep safely in their beds in flame-retardant pajamas, and wars will be won. And you, the future chemists of America, will be leading America's chemical revolution. As chairman of the board of Morgan Chemical, the company that is connecting the world with plastic, I extend to you my personal congratulations on your excellent research projects. You are all winners in our eyes, although, of course, only one of you is actually the winner tonight. So, without any further ado, may I please have the envelope?"

Chairman McCormack looked down quizzically at the sheet of paper in his hand and then turned it over, seeming surprised his speech had finished already. Apparently convinced he had read everything, he then refolded the paper and put it back into his suit pocket. The assistant vice president of public relations carried an envelope up to the podium.

Chairman McCormack took the envelope and started to open it. Did they really need to seal it? Stanley thought, since, befitting a man of his impressive girth, the chairman had huge hands. As he fumbled to get into the envelope, he suddenly pulled a hand back and stuck one of his sausage-like fingers directly into his mouth. Stanley guessed Chairman McCormack had suffered a paper cut.

The assistant vice president of public relations hurried back to the podium and took the envelope with some blood now visible on it. He quickly opened it and handed the card inside to Chairman McCormack.

"As chairman of the board of Morgan Chemical, the company that is connecting the world with plastic, it is my great honor to announce the winner of the Morgan Chemical Talent Search for 1963," Chairman McCormack said in a slightly garbled voice, since he still had the tip of his injured finger in his mouth.

Stanley couldn't wait another second. If anything else happened to Chairman McCormack to delay the announcement, he was planning to run to the stage and get that card.

"And the winner is Brian Richardson of Horace Mann School in Riverdale, New York, for his project on salt water–resistant polymers."

One of the tables off to the side of the room erupted with yelling and applause. Stanley couldn't bear to look at his father or at Major Burnside. He was crushed. He looked over at Dorothy Rodgers, who was sitting close to the podium. Her hands were covering her face, and her mother was gently stroking her back. Stanley guessed she was crying, which was exactly what he felt like doing.

29

Friday, October 18, 1963 (10:10 a.m.)

FOR MOST OF HIS LIFE, RANDOLPH JESSUP JR. HAD LOVED dogs. As a boy he had a bluetick coonhound named Duke he considered his best friend. Leaving Duke at home had been the hardest thing about going away to military school. In fact, one of the few personal possessions he'd brought with him to school was a black-and-white photograph of Duke. He was planning to tape it to the wall of his room, until he found out the Academy did not permit decorations in the barracks. Instead, he slept with that picture under his pillow for months until it was finally confiscated one morning during a surprise barracks inspection.

Randolph Jr. loved that dog so much that during his second year at the Academy, when he learned his father had sent Duke away to live on a farm, he had hidden his head under a blanket and cried for a full thirty minutes. He knew then that his love for that dog was real, since he had not cried at all the year before when he was told his grandfather had passed away.

His fond memories of Duke had led Randolph Jr. to buy his son, Randolph Jessup III, a beagle for Christmas the year before. Randolph III was eight at the time, the same age Randolph Jr. had been when he got Duke. In keeping with his family's naming traditions, Randolph Jr. had named the beagle Duke II.

Despite his name, it turned out Duke II did not share the original Duke's calm demeanor or any of his admirable characteristics of loyalty and kindness. Duke II was a high-strung and thoroughly unlovable beast. The dog took a chunk of flesh out of Randolph III's arm that very first day while he was being posed for a Christmas morning photograph. After that, Randolph III was scared to death of his dog and tried to avoid being in the same room as him. But he screamed and threw a temper tantrum anytime his father suggested they give the dog away.

At roughly the same time Duke II started terrorizing his son, Randolph Jr.'s brief and unsuccessful foray into greyhound racing had collapsed under the weight of nine consecutive months of heavy financial losses. He had intended for the diversification of the family's racetrack empire into greyhounds to be a defining moment in his leadership of the business. Instead, it was a disaster.

While his father had been alive, expanding into greyhound racing was completely out of the question. His father thought that while racehorses were magnificent and regal animals engaged in the "sport of kings," greyhound racing was a ridiculous carnival sideshow. He also thought only the most degenerate gambler would stoop so low as to bet on a dog.

But Randolph Jr. had been confident that greyhounds were the future of racing. Greyhounds were much less expensive to maintain than horses, they did not require jockeys, and they could race much more often. He also thought greyhounds would attract more family business, since he imagined kids would love both the dogs and the mechanical rabbits they chased around the track. The economics of greyhound racing seemed so strong, Randolph Jr. was convinced that adding even one greyhound track to Jessup Enterprises' three horse-racing tracks could double or even triple the size of the family empire. He could not have been more wrong. The move had led to the first money-losing year the company had ever experienced in its thirty-five-year history.

The combined impact of a surly and unmanageable beagle entering his household at the same time that racing grey-hounds were damaging his business had caused a 180-degree change in Randolph Jr.'s attitude about dogs. He now hated them passionately.

A few months after the greyhound racing track closed, Randolph Jr. separated from his wife. She made him take Duke II with him to his new bachelor apartment in Manhattan.

Randolph Jr. was now driving in his Lincoln Continental across the George Washington Bridge to Jessup Enterprises' office in downtown Newark. As always, Duke II was in the back seat, growling occasionally if Randolph Jr. hit a bump or took a turn too suddenly for the dog's liking. Randolph Jr. could not leave Duke II alone all day in his apartment without risking his sofa cushions being ripped apart and his carpet being soiled by the dog's spiteful defecations. So he brought Duke II with him every day to work and let his secretary, Mrs. Phillips, deal with him.

As usual, Randolph Jr. was using his morning commute to mull over new business ideas. Ever since he had gotten his driver's license, he had believed he did his best strategic thinking while he was driving. Even though the plan to diversify into greyhound racing had come to him while he was behind the wheel of his Lincoln, that had not dented his faith in driving as a stimulant for good ideas.

Despite the losses from its greyhound-racing debacle, Jessup Enterprises was in no danger of going under. The horse-racing tracks were still profitable, and the company also made money from the Academy. Although the school was set up as a tax-free, nonprofit institution, it paid Jessup Enterprises a large annual management fee.

Randolph Jr., however, did not just want to be a caretaker of the existing business. His dream was to leave the family empire much larger than when he had inherited it from his father. He wanted to take the Jessup name into new lines of business his father never would have imagined, and the only way that was going to happen was if his thinking time behind the wheel started to bear fruit.

That morning, the thought occupying his mind as he drove was whether to go into the real estate business. Donald's father, Fred, had sat next to him at the Academy's game against Westport and had spent both halves and most of halftime sell- ing Randolph Jr. on investing in his latest project, a two-tower apartment development he was planning to build in Queens overlooking Flushing Cemetery.

Real estate would be an entirely new business line for Jessup Enterprises, because his father had been dead set against investing in it. He thought property was too exposed to the malevolence of the US government, which he believed had been completely infiltrated by Communists and their fellow travelers, like intellectuals and French speakers. He used to say that no matter how attractive a piece of land might look, the government could destroy its value at any time just by put- ting up a public housing project next door. As a result, the

Academy's campus was the only property Jessup Enterprises owned. The company leased its office and the land where it had its racetracks.

Fred, however, had made a very convincing case. When he had explained how his deals were structured, it seemed like making truckloads of money was virtually assured. First, he set up a limited liability partnership for each project into which Fred and his partners would inject as little equity as possible. The partnership would take out construction loans from banks for most of the money needed to build the project, with the banks having no recourse to the individual partners. If the project was a success, the partnership would pay off the construction loans and manage the project debt-free after that.

On the other hand, if the project ran into any trouble, Fred would threaten to walk away and leave the banks to clean up the mess themselves unless they lent him even more money. Since the banks had no appetite for either defaulted loans or operating troubled real estate developments, they would always make enough new loans to fix the problems. As Fred described it, it was basically a foolproof scheme and quite possibly the easiest way to make money short of running a casino.

The only constraint on Fred's business was that he needed a certain amount of equity in his partnerships for them to qualify for construction loans. He explained that, because he had so many projects ongoing at the same time all around New York's outer boroughs, he needed to find investors to help put up some of that equity. The more well established the investor, the larger the construction loans the partnership could take out. That was where Jessup Enterprises' long business history was of great value to Fred. In return, Jessup Enterprises could expect up to a 500 percent return on their money in just a few years.

The proposition was certainly compelling, Randolph Jr. thought. And, based on the size of the donations Fred was making to the Academy, it was clear this was not just all talk, either. In Randolph Jr.'s mind, if people were willing to donate, they must really have a lot of money.

By the time Randolph Jr. had pulled into the Jessup Enterprises parking lot, he had made up his mind. He knew his father never would have approved such a deal, but Randolph Sr. had already been in his grave for close to a decade. For Randolph Jr. to achieve even more success than his father, he knew he had to think in ways his father never could have imagined.

Duke II had fallen asleep in the back seat of the car and was not happy to be suddenly awakened and yanked by his leash into the building. The dog became even more agitated and unhappy after they took the elevator upstairs and he saw Randolph Jr.'s secretary, Mrs. Phillips, coming toward them down the hall. Randolph Jr. found it remarkable that the only human being Duke II seemed to hate more than his son, Randolph III, was Mrs. Phillips, who he had assigned to be his dog's daytime caretaker.

Duke II gave Mrs. Phillips his customary snarling growl. Doing her best not to look afraid, Mrs. Phillips carefully took the leash from Randolph Jr.'s hand.

"A Mr. Arthur Wong has already called for you three times this morning," Mrs. Phillips said.

"Arthur Wong? I don't think I know anyone named Arthur Wong," Randolph Jr. said.

"Well, he seems to know you," Mrs. Phillip said, pulling back her right leg just in time before Duke II could sink his teeth into her calf.

"Really? Maybe it's about some dry cleaning I dropped off the other day?"

"Well, he didn't mention anything about dry cleaning," Mrs. Phillip said. "But he said he needs to speak to you today. He left a number at the Plaza Hotel."

"All right," Randolph Jr. said. "If he's got the money to stay at the Plaza, we'll call this Wong fellow back and see what he wants. But I have another call to make before that."

He first planned to call Fred and ask for a prospectus on the Flushing Cemetery apartments that he could show to the Jessup Enterprises board of directors. He wanted to move quickly. If this deal was as lucrative as it sounded, he did not want to let another investor beat him to the punch.

30

Friday, October 18, 1963 (10:28 a.m.)

AFTER THE NAME OF THE WINNER WAS ANNOUNCED
at the Morgan Chemical Talent Search awards ceremony,
Stanley Wong had stopped listening completely. He had not
paid attention to a single second of the winning student's
short, impromptu speech. He also had not heard the company's assistant vice president of public relations close the
ceremony by saying again that all the finalists were winners.

Stanley knew very well he was no winner. Being a winner
would have meant everyone at the Academy hearing he had
won a thousand-dollar scholarship. It would have meant the
cadets realizing Stanley was in fact smarter and more talented
than all of them. But that was not going to happen now, and
Stanley felt like he had lost more than if he had never participated in the competition at all.

He was supposed to have taken the train back to the
Academy with Major Burnside as soon as the award ceremony
was over. However, seeing as his father had come all the way
from Hong Kong, Major Burnside had decided Stanley could

spend the night in New York and come back to school the next morning.

That night, Stanley and his father did not discuss the science competition at all. Stanley was too disappointed to talk about it, and his father was too busy filling him in on the news from home. Still thinking of his defeat, Stanley only heard fragments of his father's stories. His cousin Edward was getting married. His aunt Agnes had gone to Australia and gotten her picture taken with a kangaroo. Elephant Ears Lee had lost one of his famous appendages in a fight and now might need a new nickname.

Stanley slept on a rollaway cot in his father's room at the Plaza Hotel. In the morning, his triad uncle, Wok Nose Chiu, came to pick him up and drive them to the Academy in an enormous black Oldsmobile sedan. Wok Nose Chiu, who had gotten his nickname from the distinctive shape his nose was left in after his wife had smacked it with the underside of a hot wok, lived in New York and handled the triad's smuggling operations through the ports along the East Coast, from New York to Baltimore.

Stanley's father did not join them on the drive to campus. He needed to stay at the hotel and wait for an important business call. But he promised Stanley he would be at the Academy for the hearing on Monday.

As they got close to campus, Stanley felt the knot that had been in his stomach since that night tightening. He did not want to go back to school. The only thing he had been looking forward to during his fourth year was the Morgan Chemical Talent Search prize. Now there was nothing to be excited about until graduation in May.

On top of that, Stanley was dreading the upcoming hearing. He hadn't seen whether Teddy had fallen or jumped, and he didn't know why Donald was outside Lieutenant Drake's office window. But he knew enough. If Colonel Overstreet realized that Donald was on the window ledge that night, he could find a way to force Donald to admit what had really happened.

Not that Donald appreciated what Stanley was doing for him. Stanley was not sure Donald even had the capacity to be grateful. He just seemed to expect people would do him favors. Even after Stanley wasted two days in the infirmary because of his fake seizure, Donald had not done anything to repay him. In fact, it was just the opposite. Donald had come straight to his room and tried to threaten him.

Stanley was tired of lying, and had started to fantasize about telling the truth at the hearing. He understood the Ho Fong Triad's code of silence was unconditional. His father had repeated that yesterday. Stanley was not to say anything that could get another cadet in trouble. He would need to stay quiet regardless of what lies the other boys might try to spin. But if he followed that order, he wondered if he could go crazy, like a Russian certainly would.

If he ignored the order, surely his father would have to forgive him at some point. Stanley was his only son, and Donald was just some stupid American boy. Maybe his father would not even be angry at all. Perhaps this was just some kind of test, and his father expected him to tell the truth in the end.

Stanley had almost convinced himself to confess, when he realized Wok Nose Chiu was asking him something. He looked out the car window and saw they were already in Newark. He had been lost in his own thoughts since they had left Manhattan.

"What, Uncle?" Stanley asked.

"I said should I turn right here?" Wok Nose Chiu asked him in Cantonese.

"No, just go straight."

Wok Nose Chiu had dropped him off and picked him up at school seven or eight times by now. Even though he had lived in New York for years, he always needed help finding the way. He had also gotten lost in Manhattan. It had taken them more than thirty minutes to find the George Washington Bridge from the Plaza Hotel.

Staring at his lumpy bald head, Stanley wondered about all the information his uncle must be guarding up there. Stanley had heard the story of how Wok Nose Chiu had joined the Ho Fong Triad when he was only thirteen. He was the always hungry eighth child of a very poor family and had tried unsuccessfully to pick Stanley's grandfather's pocket on a Kowloon tram. Impressed by the young boy's moxie, his grandfather had started giving him small jobs to do and soon he was a full-fledged triad soldier. Decades later he moved to America, because the Hong Kong police were looking for him after a jewelry store heist, and the unique shape of his nose made it difficult for him to hide out in the colony. No doubt he was keeping secrets much bigger than what Stanley was being asked to conceal.

"Have you ever seen anyone get killed?" Stanley asked in Cantonese.

"What are you talking about? You think I kill people?"

"No, I didn't mean that," Stanley said. "I just mean, have you seen someone die in front of you?"

"Why would you ask me that?"

"I'm just curious, that's all," Stanley said.

"Well, maybe I'll die in front of you someday if I talk about things like that," Wok Nose Chiu said with a laugh. "I'm sure your father has told you we don't talk about these things."

"Yeah, we keep secrets until the grave, right?"

"Oh, you better keep a secret longer than that! If you start talking in the underworld, who's going to help you there?"

Stanley was not sure if his uncle was joking about the afterlife, but he certainly got the point. There were no exceptions to the Ho Fong Triad's code of silence. He looked out the window and imagined how easy life would be if he had just been born into a regular family.

31

Friday, October 18, 1963 (3:05 p.m.)

GROWING UP, DONALD HAD ASSUMED HE WOULD GO TO the same high school as his brother, Fred Jr., who was eight years older. Fred Jr. had attended the Episcopal Academy, a private coed day school in Long Island. Donald was excited by the prospect of following in his brother's footsteps and going to Episcopal. Based on the dates Fred Jr. had brought home when he'd been there, Donald was sure the school would be full of pretty girls.

The summer after Donald finished middle school, it seemed he was indeed headed for Episcopal. His father had enrolled him there and paid a deposit. But then the plan changed because of his older brother.

Fred Jr. had just graduated from college that summer and had started working in the family real estate business. Since he was fresh out of school, Fred Sr. was not ready to trust him on a big project. So he started him out on a small job in Elmhurst turning a former toy store into a ten-efficiency-unit apartment building.

Although he did not have much faith in his oldest son's business acumen, Fred Sr. thought managing a small-scale efficiency conversion was almost foolproof. He had an experienced construction crew on the job, and they could follow the plans and do the work with very little supervision from management. Even if Fred Jr. did nothing at all at the site, it was likely the project would come in on budget and on time.

But Fred Jr. was eager to show his father he was ready for even greater responsibility in the family company, and he threw himself wholeheartedly into the project. Despite rarely waking up before noon during his previous four years in college, Fred Jr. managed to get to the site every day by 7:30 a.m. He tried his best to add value. Early on, he had painstakingly gone over the plans and had found a way to make each of the units ten percent bigger by trimming unnecessary space from the common areas.

One afternoon, the construction foreman, Ernie Laporte, had shown Fred Jr. some stress cracks his guys had discovered in an upstairs window. Ernie reported they had found similar cracks in most of the windows throughout the building. Having majored in English literature, Fred Jr. was in no way an expert on glass. But he didn't think stress cracks looked like a problem that could be easily remedied. He made the decision on the spot to replace all the windows in the building.

Ernie, who had worked for Fred Sr. for almost twenty years, asked Fred Jr. if he wanted to check first with his father. But Fred Jr. knew how much his father valued employees who took initiative. He thought if he acted decisively to address the cracked window problem, it would prove to his father he could run a building site on his own. Maybe his father would even be able to take a vacation for the first time in his life once he realized his son could handle the business.

On Fred Jr.'s instructions, new windows were ordered, and the cracked windows were torn out of the building and thrown into a dumpster, where they were soon smashed to pieces under a pile of other construction debris. Two weeks later Fred Sr. was sitting in his office on Jamaica Avenue, when a bill from the Jackson Avenue Glass Works arrived. His secretary knew bills with multiple zeroes at the end were to be taken straight to the boss. When Fred Sr. read what he was being billed for, his first reaction was to look around his desk furiously for something to smash. He settled on a glass ashtray that he only had managed to chip by throwing against the wall.

His second reaction was to run down the stairs and take a cab to the construction site. Before the cab had even stopped completely, Fred Sr. threw a few bucks into the front passenger seat and jumped out. He found Ernie Laporte on the first floor and grabbed him by the collar, demanding to know why he had decided to buy new windows instead of just repairing what was there.

Ernie was a very large man who had been a New York State champion wrestler in high school, but he had a calm demeanor and was used to his boss's outbursts. He calmly explained the decision had been made by Fred Jr.

By the time he found Fred Jr. on the second floor, Fred Sr. was apoplectic with rage. He despised cost overruns, and, out of all the reasons costs could escalate on a project, the most unacceptable was making a project better than the tenants required.

A ten-efficiency-unit apartment building in Elmhurst was meant for workers on the Long Island Rail Road. Fred Sr. did not think they needed top-of-the line windows. He was already upset that his son had decided to give each of them ten percent more space, but he had let that decision go as a rookie mistake.

But this kind of irresponsible additional cost was too much for him to excuse.

Ernie had followed Fred Sr. upstairs and held him back from attacking his son with a spackling knife. He screamed at Fred Jr. that he was fired, and that if he ever worked again on one of the family's projects, it would be pushing a wheelbarrow. Fred Jr. threw down his clipboard and stormed out of the building.

Fred Sr. never regretted firing his son because of the window blunder. He did, however, change his mind about sending Donald to the Episcopal Academy, the coddling and undisciplined school that had produced Fred Jr.

For the good of the future of the family business, he decided Donald would attend a military school. He thought a strict military education would whip his second son into shape and prepare him for the kill-or-be-killed world of New York real estate.

Fred Sr. called the Episcopal Academy the next day and told them he was de-enrolling Donald because of the disastrous job they had done educating his older son. After that, all it took was a sternly written letter from his lawyer, Bernie Delk, to get his deposit back. His secretary collected brochures from military schools in the area, and he chose the New Jersey Military Academy, because it would be the easiest one to reach by train from Queens.

His father announced his decision to Donald a few nights later over dinner. Instead of following in his older brother's footsteps, to a day school full of beautiful Long Island girls, in a few weeks he would be leaving home to attend an all-boys military boarding school in New Jersey. Donald was shocked and looked pleadingly over to his mother. But his mother had only just learned of her husband's decision at the same time as Donald.

Donald pictured military school being like the images of army boot camp he had seen in the movies, with sadistic drill sergeants screaming orders. But he knew there was no point in complaining about the change. Once his father announced a decision, it was already final. So just because his older brother thought railroad men deserved nice windows, he had to suffer for the next four years.

As it turned out, he couldn't have been more wrong. Within days of arriving at the Academy, Donald realized the place suited him perfectly. A competitive boy like him could thrive at a military school, because the education was structured around constantly fostering competition among the cadets. Every activity, from shoe-shining to bed-making to fingernail-cleaning, was made into a competition, where the winners got merit citations that could buy rewards, while the losers got demerits that could lead to marching in Jessup Quadrangle. Since the school was constantly sorting the boys into winners and losers, Donald had endless opportunities to indulge in two of his favorite activities: celebrating his victories and mocking the boys he defeated.

In the end, Donald had succeeded at the Academy beyond what he could have imagined the day his parents had first dropped him off. He had risen to cadet captain in the Junior ROTC, had lettered every year in football and baseball, and had achieved a solid B- average in his classes. According to Lieutenant Drake, who doubled as the school's math teacher and college counselor, he had a good shot at getting into Fordham. After all that success, Donald was not going to let Fu Manchu bring him down.

Although Fu Manchu had seen him on the window ledge outside Lieutenant Drake's office, Fu Manchu had no evidence of that. But Donald now had evidence he could use against Fu Manchu. He also was confident that if it came down to blaming one or the other of them, the school would take his side. His father was a big donor and, on top of that, he was not Chinese.

Donald's last class of the day was trigonometry with Lieutenant Drake. Since he was already guaranteed an A, he had a hard time staying awake through the class. The only thing that motivated him to stay upright in his seat was the two demerits he would get if he fell asleep. As soon as class ended, Donald went up to Colonel Overstreet's office on the fifth floor.

Mrs. Kreitzenbach was sitting in the outside office, working on the *New York Times* crossword puzzle. Donald said he had something important to tell the colonel about Teddy Haswell. Mrs. Kreitzenbach slowly got up from her chair, told Donald to wait and not to touch or look at anything on her desk, and went into the colonel's office. Thirty seconds later she came back out and told Donald he could go in.

The colonel was sitting behind his large desk. Donald tried to imagine him killing ten North Korean soldiers all by himself and then ripping a golden Buddha out of their temple. Donald wondered what he looked like back then. Now, with his considerable gut, he certainly did not look anything like the Hollywood version of a war hero.

"I understand there's something you want to get off your chest about Teddy," the colonel said.

"Not really something I want to get off my chest, Colonel," Donald said as he walked up to the colonel's desk. "It's just something I forgot to mention when you called me in before. Maybe it's not even important. I'm not sure."

"All right, what is it?"

Donald started to sit down in one of the guest chairs. Colonel Overstreet raised his hand like a policeman signaling a car to stop, which caused Donald to freeze in place, halfway between standing and sitting.

"Did I tell you to sit down, cadet? You will stand at attention unless I say otherwise."

Donald straightened up quickly and stood at attention, angry at himself. He had come to get the colonel on his side, and now he had already found a way to make him angry.

"Sorry, Colonel," Donald said.

"So, what is it you forgot to mention last time?"

"It's just that Teddy had this problem with Fu Manchu. I mean Stanley. He was fighting with Stanley. It had been going on for a while, sir," Donald said.

"What were they fighting about?" the colonel asked.

"It was about a watch, sir," Donald said.

"A watch?"

"Yeah, Teddy's watch," Donald said. "It was, like, a family heirloom or something and Teddy thought Stanley took it."

"Why would Teddy think Stanley had taken his watch?"

"Because he saw Stanley in our room one time. Stanley said he was just looking for me, but then right after that, Teddy couldn't find his watch. He thought Stanley took it."

"All right, Donald, stand at-ease," the colonel said.

Donald took the at-ease position the cadets had been taught, with his legs apart and his hands linked behind his back, but it made him feel even less relaxed than standing at attention. He had already delivered all the lines he had practiced ahead of time, and now he just wanted to get out of there. As long as he had been standing at attention, it had felt like he was going to be excused soon.

"Do you know why Stanley came to see you?" the colonel asked.

"What, Colonel?"

"You said Stanley was in your room because he had come to see you. I was just curious if you know why Stanley had come to see you," the colonel said.

"Oh, just because we're friends, I guess, sir," Donald said.

"You and Stanley Wong are friends?" the colonel asked, sounding incredulous.

"Yes, sir," Donald said.

"Okay, and you're telling me all this because you think this fight over a watch could have something to do with Teddy's death?" the colonel asked.

"I don't know, sir," Donald said. "It's just that the other day you said we should tell you everything we know that might be important. But I didn't want to say anything then, in front of Stanley."

"Because he's your friend?"

"Yeah, exactly, Colonel," Donald said.

Donald was upset with himself. His father had taught him that while lies might be necessary sometimes in business, telling too many lies at one time was always a mistake. They could become difficult to manage. Donald had been planning to tell just one lie to Colonel Overstreet. Now he had already told two, since Stanley was certainly not his friend.

"Do you know if they ever found this watch when they packed up Teddy's things?" the colonel asked.

"I know they didn't find it yet, Colonel," Donald said. "Teddy's parents asked me about it when they were here. They're really desperate to find it."

"Did Teddy ever tell you he had talked to Stanley about his watch?" the colonel asked.

"Well, he was talking about the watch a lot the day he died," Donald said. "I think maybe Teddy and Stanley met on the roof to hash it out."

"You think it's possible they met on the roof of Jessup Hall? Aren't there more convenient places at this school for two cadets to meet? Why the roof of this building?" the colonel asked.

"I'm not sure, sir," Donald said.

"But Teddy specifically said he would meet Stanley on the roof of Jessup Hall?" the colonel asked.

"Yes, sir," Donald said. "That's definitely a place they could have met."

"Donald, these questions are not that difficult," the colonel said. "Let me ask you very clearly, and please think about my question before you answer. Did or did not Teddy say he was meeting Stanley on the roof of Jessup Hall?"

"The direct answer to your question, Colonel, is that I'm pretty sure he did," Donald said.

"So he did?" the colonel said.

"Yes, maybe he did, sir," Donald said. "Teddy might have done that."

Colonel Overstreet's eyes narrowed into angry slits, and Donald realized he should have prepared a much longer script for this meeting. The colonel's questions were flying at him too fast. And if the colonel kept asking him questions, the lies were bound to pile up.

"But you're absolutely sure Teddy was planning to talk to Stanley somewhere about his missing watch?" the colonel asked.

"Yes, sir," Donald said. "I think he mentioned that to me in the library that night. But I don't remember word for word, exactly what he said, because, you know, I was studying."

"Okay, Donald, I think you need to try to get your memories completely straight before the hearing on Monday," the colonel said. "Take time this weekend and decide exactly what you are one hundred percent sure Teddy told you. Do you understand?"

"Yes, Colonel," Donald said.

"We want you just to tell the truth at the hearing," the colonel said. "If you end up speculating about what could have happened or what Teddy could have said, that won't be helpful. Understand?"

"Yes, Colonel," Donald said.

"You're excused, cadet," the colonel said.

Donald felt a great flush of relief as he turned around and headed for the door. He might not have prepared well enough, and he had told more lies than he had planned to, but overall he was satisfied with his performance. He was sure he had succeeded in planting a seed of doubt about Stanley in the colonel's mind.

32

Friday, October 18, 1963 (5:04 p.m.)

BEFORE ARTHUR WONG LEFT HONG KONG BOUND FOR Newark, he'd called his lieutenant in New York, Wok Nose Chiu, and asked him to find out everything he could about the owner of the New Jersey Military Academy. Wok Nose Chiu turned the matter over to Maxwell Chan, the usual Chinatown private investigator he used. Chan quickly discovered that Jessup Enterprises, the company that managed the Academy, also owned three racetracks in New Jersey.

When Arthur received this information from Wok Nose Chiu on the ride into Manhattan from Idlewild Airport, he was delighted. In fact, he wondered what he had done to deserve such good fortune. After much thinking, he decided it probably was because, eight months before, he had sent money to relatives in China to make a new gravestone for his grandparents. Eight always had been his lucky number.

Arthur immediately devised a plan. He would propose to Jessup Enterprises to partner with him on building a new horse-racing track in Hong Kong. If Jessup Enterprises agreed, they would make the perfect front company for his bid to lease the racetrack land.

He had been looking for a partner to front the bid, because he knew it was going to attract a lot of attention. Whenever the British colonial government leased a prime parcel of Hong Kong real estate close to the central business district, even the Foreign Office in London got involved in scrutinizing the bidders. Arthur realized that the leverage he had over Sir James Hogg-Warren might not be enough for him to get the land. But if he could hide the Ho Fong Triad's interest behind an American horse-racing company, he would have a much higher likelihood of success.

At the same time, if Jessup Enterprises was interested in partnering on the Hong Kong deal, that would give Arthur leverage over the company to make sure Stanley stayed out of trouble at the hearing. It was an opportunity to kill two hawks with one arrow (as his father used to say).

It took several calls to Randolph Jr.'s office to get him to call back. When he did, Arthur introduced himself as the father of a fourth-year cadet at the Academy, and then briefly outlined his business proposition. He was building a horse-racing track in Hong Kong and was looking for experienced partners like Jessup Enterprises. When Randolph Jr. had started to ask questions that showed he was very interested in the idea, Arthur suggested a meeting later that day at the Plaza Hotel. Randolph Jr. had immediately agreed.

Arthur had not been expecting Randolph Jr. to be quite so eager. He assumed he would first ask for documents about the deal or suggest his lawyer take the meeting. He wondered what such eagerness said about the strength of Jessup Enterprises. But it did not matter very much, in any case, since he had no actual intention of cutting Randolph Jr. in on his deal. All he needed was the company's name on his bid for the racetrack land.

If his bid for the land was successful, Arthur would find a way to remove Jessup Enterprises from the deal. He knew his lawyer would be able to create such a complex ownership structure for the racetrack that the colonial government would never be able to untangle what had happened to the American firm they thought was leading the bid. And, by that point, Stanley would have graduated from the Academy.

Randolph Jr. had agreed to come to the Plaza Hotel at 5:00 p.m. To provide the right atmosphere for the meeting, Arthur decided to upgrade from a regular single room to a suite for that one night only. He had been able to secure the hotel's Ambassador Suite, which, from its name and its furnishings, projected exactly the right air of opulence.

The suite had a large living room with two plush satin-covered armchairs and a long sofa in the center, and a well-stocked wet bar on one side. Arthur thought the carpet felt twice as thick as the one in his single room. Anyone setting foot on that carpet would sense immediately that the occupant of the Ambassador Suite was successful.

Arthur also thought it would look more impressive if he appeared to have some executives from his company traveling with him. So he asked Wok Nose Chiu to find two men who could pass as business executives to play the role of his associates. Wok Nose Chiu understood, without Arthur needing to say anything, that his misshapen nose (which made him look more like a retired boxer than an executive) and his poor English made him ineligible to play one of these roles himself.

With fifteen minutes to spare before Randolph Jr. was due to arrive at the Plaza Hotel, the two men Wok Nose Chiu had found for this assignment—his private investigator, Maxwell

Chan, and Maxwell's younger brother, Marvin—showed up at the hotel. As instructed, they were dressed in their best suits and ties. Wok Nose Chiu met them in the lobby and brought them up to Arthur's suite.

Arthur was sitting in one of the armchairs in the suite's living room when Wok Nose Chiu came in and introduced him to the Chan brothers. The brothers had a very simple role to play, Arthur explained in Cantonese. He merely wanted Randolph Jr. to get the impression Arthur had traveled to New York with two of his company's executives. All the Chan brothers were expected to do was to stand up and leave when Randolph Jr. arrived. After that, they would be free to go home. For that very small amount of work, Wok Nose Chiu would give them each ten dollars.

The Chan brothers nodded in agreement with the plan, and Arthur waved for them to come sit on the sofa next to his armchair. As they sat down, Arthur suddenly noticed a strong smell in the air. It was a very familiar aroma, but he could not quite place it.

"What's that smell?" Arthur asked.

The Chan brothers looked confused, seemingly unaware of any unusual odor. Arthur was surprised they would not notice it, because as far as he could tell, the scent was wafting over to him from precisely the area around where the brothers were sitting.

"Come over here and tell me what you smell," Arthur said to Wok Nose Chiu, who was still standing by the door.

Wok Nose Chiu walked over to where Arthur and the Chan brothers were sitting. He dramatically sniffed the air a few times before nodding knowingly.

"Roast duck," Wok Nose Chiu said.

"Exactly!" Arthur exclaimed.

That was why the smell was so familiar, Arthur thought. His uncle Lewis used to conduct his loan-sharking operation out of a roast duck restaurant in the Wan Chai neighborhood of Hong Kong. Arthur had spent many afternoons there after school when he was young, learning how to calculate compound interest and other aspects of the business from his uncle.

"So why does my very expensive hotel suite suddenly smell like roast duck?"

"Oh, that's just Marvin," Wok Nose Chiu said matter-of-factly.

Arthur turned and stared at Marvin on the sofa. Marvin immediately looked away and started to fidget nervously with his watch.

"You didn't notice that Marvin smelled like roast duck when you brought him up in the elevator?" Arthur asked Wok Nose Chiu.

"Of course I did," Wok Nose Chiu said. "Marvin always smells like roast duck. Didn't I tell you he manages the Peking duck restaurant on Canal Street? It's really good. I'll take you there sometime."

"I don't understand," Arthur said. "Why would you bring me someone for this job who smells like duck?"

"What do you mean? Marvin speaks really good English," Wok Nose Chiu protested. "And that's a nice suit."

"I'm sorry, sir," Marvin added haltingly from the sofa. "I only have the one suit I wear to work."

Arthur wondered what it must be like to run an international organization in the legitimate business world. Triad members certainly scored highly in terms of loyalty and dedication, but they were not very attuned to the sensitivities of civilian society. Arthur realized he should not have been surprised Wok Nose Chiu did not understand it would be a mistake to hire someone for this job who reeked like a Chinatown restaurant. Most of the business meetings Wok Nose Chiu attended were in back alleys and behind customs warehouses in the middle of the night. At those meetings, wearing clothes that smelled like food would not pose much of a problem.

As Arthur considered what to do about Marvin and his smelly suit, there was a knock on the door of the suite. Then he heard a loud voice from the hallway that he recognized from the phone call earlier that day as belonging to Randolph Jr.

"Hello? Arthur Wong? Is this Arthur Wong's suite?"

Arthur had assumed the hotel front desk would have called his room first before letting Randolph Jr. up. He told Wok Nose Chiu and Marvin to go into the bedroom of the suite, close the door, and stay in there until the meeting was over. It was better to have only one executive with him than to have a second one who smelled like duck, Arthur decided. Then he instructed Maxwell to go open the door, shake Randolph Jr.'s hand firmly, and introduce himself in good, clear English.

"And don't sit in your roast duck suit anywhere near my bed," Arthur said to Marvin as he started toward the bedroom.

Once Wok Nose Chiu and Marvin were in the bedroom with the door closed, Maxwell walked over and opened the door. Before Randolph Jr. could even get fully through the door frame, Maxwell grabbed his right hand and shook it vigorously up and down several times.

"Nice to meet you, Arthur," Randolph Jr. said as he extracted his hand from Maxwell's tight grip.

"No, I'm not Arthur. My name is Maxwell. I am a business executive in Mr. Wong's company. I have traveled here from Hong Kong with Mr. Wong, who is the gentleman over there," Maxwell said in painstakingly slow and over-enunciated English.

Arthur got up from the armchair and headed quickly toward the door to greet Randolph Jr. He did not want to give Maxwell time to say anything more, since his instruction to use clear English had resulted in Maxwell speaking so mechanically, he'd sounded like a robot in a science-fiction movie.

"I'm Arthur Wong. Thank you for coming on such short notice," Arthur said, extending his hand to Randolph Jr.

As they shook hands, Arthur noticed Randolph Jr.'s dark blue suit was covered in what he assumed was either dog or cat fur. Arthur wondered again about the strength of Jessup Enterprises' finances. In Hong Kong, a successful businessman would never allow himself to show up to a meeting wearing a suit in such a grubby state. Given Randolph Jr.'s appearance, Arthur realized having Marvin there smelling like roast duck might not have been such a problem after all.

"Maxwell, we'll continue our discussion later," Arthur said. "You can go now."

"I should leave now? By myself? Alone?" Maxwell asked, looking toward the closed door of the bedroom.

"Yes," Arthur said firmly.

Maxwell nodded and walked out the door, closing it behind him. Arthur gestured for Randolph Jr. to follow him to the living area.

"Your man there seems a little scared to be alone," Randolph Jr. said.

"Well, it's his first time in New York City," Arthur replied. "But he'll be fine."

Randolph Jr. sat down on the sofa and Arthur went back to the same armchair he had been sitting in before. Arthur remembered he had been planning to order a bottle of scotch for the meeting, but between Marvin Chan smelling like a roast duck and Randolph Jr.'s unannounced arrival, he had not gotten around to calling room service.

"Do you want something to drink? I can call room service. I'm afraid the front desk didn't tell me you were on your way up, so I didn't have time to order anything."

"Yeah, the guy at the desk told me I should just go up, because he wasn't sure the guests in this suite spoke English," Randolph Jr. said. "Anyway, I'm fine. I actually don't have much time, because I had to leave my dog in my car downstairs. If I don't get back soon, it won't be pretty what that dog does to my leather seats."

"You Americans really love your dogs."

"I hate this dog. Got stuck with it in a divorce."

Arthur was always amazed how much personal information Westerners were willing to give away for free in a negotiation. He had met Randolph Jr. a minute ago and already knew he was divorced.

"Before we get down to business, I need to bring up something that involves my son, Stanley," Arthur said. "I'm not sure how much you know about this, but the Academy's investigating the suicide of one of the cadets, and Stanley and some other boys were asked to go to a hearing."

"Let me stop you right there, Arthur. I know all about that situation."

"That's good to know. I wasn't sure," Arthur said.

"The Academy's my school. Nothing happens over there without my say-so."

"So you'll be at the hearing on Monday?"

"Will I be there? I will be chairing that hearing, of course," Randolph Jr. said.

"What a relief to hear that," Arthur said.

This was going to be even easier than he had expected, Arthur thought. If Randolph Jr. was in charge of the hearing, it would be a simple matter for him to make sure Stanley stayed in the clear.

"Naturally, Stanley doesn't know anything about this suicide, but it still makes me very uncomfortable that he has to be involved in such a thing."

"Well, if your boy doesn't know anything, I'm sure there's nothing to worry about."

"Still, as a father, I worry," Arthur said. "That's why it's such a relief to know you will be leading the hearing. In Hong Kong, we say the children of our business partners are like our own children."

"I see," Randolph Jr. said.

"Do you have a son?" Arthur asked.

"I do. He'll be starting at the Academy himself in a few years."

"Well, then you know exactly what I mean. If we move forward with this horse-racing track deal, I'm sure you would expect me to treat your son just like a member of my own family. I hope you'll treat my son the same way."

Arthur knew he was being very heavy-handed, but he wanted to be sure Randolph Jr. understood him clearly. He had instructed Stanley to stay quiet at the hearing so his son could learn a valuable lesson in how a triad member faced an investigation. He wanted Stanley to know exactly what it feels like to hold up to pressure and refuse to squeal.

That was a very important lesson for his son if someday he was to become Dragon Head of the Ho Fong Triad. But Arthur was not willing to risk Stanley getting expelled over this. It was not as if Arthur cared in the slightest about protecting some other boy. His plans for the triad's international expansion hinged on Stanley graduating from a top American university. That was what would give Stanley access to the networks of power he would need in the future. He could not accept any ambiguity about whether Randolph Jr. would be supporting his son at the hearing.

"I hear your message loud and clear, Arthur, and I can assure you, Stanley's not going to have any problems at this hearing. In fact, I understand your boy's a model cadet, so no need to worry. Now, can we get down to racetrack business?"

"Absolutely," Arthur said.

33

Friday, October 18, 1963 (6:31 p.m.)

EVERY YEAR, COACH MULROONEY FACED THE CHALLENGE of scheduling seven games for the New Jersey Military Academy's football team. Only the rivalry game against Westport Country Day had been an annual fixture for decades. The rest of the schedule changed year to year.

Filling out the schedule was difficult, because the Academy had a policy of not playing against public schools. After New Jersey desegregated the state's school system in 1947, the Academy's board of trustees decided games against public schools might attract the wrong sort of crowd to campus. The elite private schools in the area, on the other hand, generally were part of long-standing leagues and were not willing to play a school outside that closed circle. On top of that, the only other military academy in New Jersey, the General Hayes School for Boys, refused to play against the Academy because of the contentious history between the two schools.

With all the limitations to Coach Mulrooney's scheduling, the Academy mainly played against parochial schools. Any given year, at least half of its games were against schools named after Catholic saints or former New Jersey archbishops. These Catholic schools were usually very tough opponents for the Academy. Decades of success enjoyed by Knute Rockne and the University of Notre Dame's football team had inspired many Catholic school administrators to prioritize football. They recruited a lot of hard-nosed boys from tough Irish, Italian, and Polish neighborhoods who liked nothing more than beating up on military school cadets.

Not wishing to put his team up against the pounding of strong Catholic schools week after week, Coach Mulrooney always sought out alternatives. Then, a few years before, a friend who coached football at a different school had let him in on his scheduling secret, which was to find Quaker schools to play. His friend explained that, unlike the Catholics, the Quakers did not prioritize football. In fact, they seemed to be prohibited by their pacifist religion from blocking or tackling too hard.

Coach Mulrooney immediately started building connections with the Quaker school community in the area. Since then, whenever the cadets saw a school with *Friends* in its name on the schedule, they assumed that game would be a walk in the park. Often the Academy would have such a big lead against a Quaker school by halftime that the first-string players would get to take the second half off.

That Friday night, the Academy's opponent was the Middlesex Friends School, a small Quaker school in Edison, New Jersey. When Donald had watched the Middlesex players walk onto Jessup Field, he thought a lot of them looked like little boys dressed up like football players for Halloween. If Teddy had been playing quarterback, Donald was sure the Academy would have won by at least thirty points.

The result was very different, however, with Lou Douglas leading the team. Although the Academy was the stronger team, because of six fumbles by Lou, the score had stayed close all game. With just thirty seconds left in the fourth quarter, the game was tied 20–20, and the Academy had the ball on the Middlesex forty-yard line. There was only enough time left for one more play. Coach Mulrooney, who had called only running plays all day, finally decided to give Lou a chance to pass. Although it was a big risk to let Lou throw the ball, it was the only way the Academy would have any chance to win the game.

Donald was just ready for the game to end. He had lined up all game against a Middlesex defensive lineman who was almost half his size. The guy was so small that the white uniform number 88 that was sewn to his black jersey was too big for his chest. Half of the second 8 stretched around the side of his jersey and ended on his back.

Donald had not been challenged at all by his tiny opponent. Usually he would have thoroughly enjoyed dominating an opposing player like that. However, his mind was spinning with worries about the investigation into Teddy's death. Since he had no family or friends in the crowd to impress, he just wanted the game to end.

"Let's just get this over with," Donald said as the Academy team broke their huddle and got into formation on the line.

Joey Bortz snapped the ball to Lou to start the play, and Lou dropped back to pass. Donald half-heartedly pushed Number 88 a few times until the guy fell backward onto the turf, as had happened thirty times already that day. With his blocking assignment taken care of, Donald stood straight up and looked to see if any of the Academy's receivers had managed to get open. To his great surprise, he saw Lenny Thomas was standing in the middle of the field all alone. It looked like the Middlesex defense was so convinced the Academy would not pass the ball that they had not even bothered to cover Lenny when he ran downfield.

Lou also noticed Lenny was all alone. With Coach Mulroney screaming "Lenny's open!" from the sidelines, Lou decided to take another step back to be sure he would have enough room for his pass to safely clear the defensive line. Unfortunately, that last step resulted in his back foot landing on one side of the small hill that was in the center of Jessup Field. Stepping back onto the hill caused Lou to lose his balance completely as he threw. Instead of the ball flying toward Lenny for an easy touchdown reception, it went straight up in the air.

Donald was so absorbed by the sight of Lou tumbling over the hill that he did not even notice that Number 88 had gotten up off the ground. While Donald stood and watched his quarterback fall, Number 88 ran by him and grabbed Lou's wayward pass just before it hit the ground. He then tucked the ball under his arm and took off running. He did not stop until he crossed the goal line, scoring the winning touchdown for Middlesex as time expired.

Pumping their fists in the air and yelling with joy, excitement, and surprise, the rest of the Middlesex team ran down to the end zone, where Number 88 had assumed a particularly proud victory pose, his legs spread wide apart and the ball, which looked like the size of a large watermelon in his tiny hands, held high above his head. When the rest of the Middlesex team reached him, a few of the bigger players lifted Number 88 off the ground, put him on their shoulders, and carried him to their sideline.

Like most of the Academy team, Donald stood in stunned silence watching the exuberant Middlesex celebration. As much as Donald had wanted the game to end, he had never imagined it could end that way. He assumed the worst would have been a tie. At least, on an individual basis, Donald knew he had won yet again that day. Aside from the unfortunate last play, Donald had dominated Number 88 all game long.

After Middlesex was done celebrating their victory, some of the Academy's players lingered on Jessup Field to talk to their parents or friends who had come to the game. But Donald joined the others who trudged straight to the locker room. He sat down on the wooden bench in front of his locker and quickly pulled off his cleats. He wanted to get into the shower fast, before Coach Mulrooney came in and began his postgame rant. There was no reason he should have to listen to a speech intended for the losers on the team.

As he yanked off his sweat-soaked socks, Donald noticed Lou Douglas, with only a towel wrapped around his waist, heading for the showers. The sight of Lou strolling so casually across the locker room after he'd cost the Academy the game was more than Donald could take. He could feel the rage pumping through his veins. How dare Lou try to take a shower before the winning players like Donald?

"Where do you think you're going, Loser Lou? You're the worst quarterback since . . . ," Donald yelled loudly across the locker room, only stopping his insult partway through because no names of famously bad quarterbacks came to his mind.

The other players in the room stopped what they were doing and looked up at Donald. Lou also stopped and stared at him menacingly.

"Shut up, Donald! You're a loser!" Lou said.

"I'm no loser, you're the loser," Donald said. "You lost us the game tonight, not me!"

"Well, I'll fight you right here and now and show you who the real loser is," Lou said.

Lou took a few steps toward Donald. He looked like he might charge at any second, Donald thought.

Donald suddenly realized he should have thought this situation through a bit more. Lou was small, but he was scrappy. Everybody still talked about Lou's fight two years before with an older cadet on the football team named Larry Orr. Donald had nicknamed Larry "the Stork" because of his long, thin legs.

Larry used to tease Lou all the time about his height until one day when Lou could not take the teasing anymore. He snapped, charging Larry after football practice had ended. True to his nickname, Larry's skinny legs were his undoing. Lou wrapped his arms around those legs until Larry fell to the turf, negating his height advantage and allowing Lou to get in several good hits to his face before some other players pulled them apart.

Donald had no desire to go down with the Stork in Academy lore as cadets beaten up by tiny Lou Douglas. But now he was cornered, and his reputation would also take a hit if he let a nearly naked Lou threaten him in front of the rest of the team. He threw his dirty socks down onto the locker room floor and pointed his right index finger, in as threatening a way as he could, at Lou. Then he stood up to remind Lou how much taller he was.

"If I were the coach, I'd kick you off the team right now," Donald said.

"I'll give you one last chance, Donald. Take that back or I'll make you take it back with my fist!" Lou said.

Donald was impressed Lou had come up with such a cool tough guy line in the heat of the moment. He wanted to come back with something equally intimidating, but he was drawing a blank. Suddenly, he heard the locker room door open. He looked over and saw Joey Bortz walking in with his distinctive waddle, which came from his parents refusing to buy him new cleats after his feet had grown a full size over the summer.

"What's going on?" Joey asked the locker room generally.

"Donald and Lou want to fight," Lenny Thomas said from his seat on the locker room bench.

"Oh, cool. I got a dollar on Lou if that happens," Joey said. "But, Donald, Jerry's out on the field and says he really needs to talk to you."

Donald could not remember ever being so happy to hear Jerry's name before. It gave him the excuse he needed to end the argument with Lou without a fight.

"You're lucky I have to talk to Jerry now," Donald said.

"Oh, we can finish this anytime, anywhere, Donald," Lou said before continuing his stroll toward the showers.

That was another good line from Lou, Donald thought. He realized he needed to spend a lot more time practicing his tough guy insults and threats. For years, his usual threat had been "How'd you like a knuckle sandwich?" But that line was starting to feel dated.

Donald slipped his bare feet into his cleats and clomped out of the locker room and back onto the field. He saw Jerry standing off by himself near one of the goalposts. As he walked over to him, he noticed Jerry's lips were moving slightly, like he was practicing what he was going to say.

"Hey, Jerry. Bortz said you wanted to see me."

"Yeah, thanks for coming out, Donald," Jerry said. "Did you know Fu Manchu's back on campus?"

"What did you think? He was going to stay in New York forever?"

"I don't know. I knew Fu Manchu would come back, but what if he finds the watch in his locker? I mean, I hid it like you said, but he could easily find it, and we could get in big trouble for this."

Jerry was sweating, and he was talking much faster than usual. Donald realized he needed to calm Jerry down fast, before he went off and did something stupid. Jerry had never cracked about the grape juice Donald had spilled on the Stahls' living room carpet in fifth grade, but this was an even bigger secret than that one.

"You hid the watch under Fu Manchu's winter coat like we agreed, right?" Donald asked.

"Yeah."

"Jerry, it's, like, sixty degrees today. You think Fu Manchu's going to need that coat?"

"I guess not," Jerry said.

"Of course not. See? You got yourself all wound up for nothing, right?"

Jerry seemed to relax, and he even smiled a bit. Donald was surprised Jerry did not thank him for coming up with such a smart plan, but he decided to let it pass and not to push for any gratitude.

"Jerry, you just need to calm down. If you keep acting crazy like this, you really could get yourself in big trouble."

"You mean *we* could get into big trouble, right?" Jerry asked.

"Well, you were the one who snuck into Fu Manchu's room. Not me," Donald said.

Jerry suddenly looked terrified. Donald sighed, realizing he would need to calm Jerry down all over again now. As if having to do all the planning of this operation were not enough, he had to manage Jerry's mental state as well. Being a good leader was exhausting, he thought.

"Come on, I'm just joking, pal," Donald said. "You know there's nothing more important to me in the world than loyalty. Believe me, we're in this thing together to the end."

34

Saturday, October 19, 1963 (10:35 a.m.)

SITTING BEHIND HIS DESK ON THE FIFTH FLOOR OF Jessup Hall, Colonel Frank Overstreet held a gold watch in one hand and a handwritten note from Mrs. Kreitzenbach in the other. The note read "1950 Omega Seamaster, gold face and band, long scratch across the dial."

Frank looked back and forth between the watch and the note several times in quick succession. As much as he had hoped to reach a different conclusion, there was no getting around the obvious fact staring him in the face. The note described the watch perfectly.

When Donald had told him about a long-simmering feud between Teddy Haswell and Stanley Wong over a watch, the story had not sounded very believable. Donald never struck Frank as a particularly trustworthy cadet, and it seemed completely out of character for Stanley to steal from a fellow student. In fact, Frank's initial instinct was just to ignore the whole thing.

But Frank decided he owed it to the Haswells to at least check with them if Teddy's watch had gone missing. He had asked Mrs. Kreitzenbach to call them and find out. She had come back into his office twenty minutes later with the news that Teddy's mother had confirmed her son's watch was in fact lost. Mrs. Kreitzenbach had taken a description of the watch. That was the note Frank was holding.

Having corroborated one aspect of Donald's story, Frank felt duty bound to investigate further. He waited until 10:00 a.m. on Saturday, when he knew all of the fourth-year cadets would be out of the barracks for marching practice on Jessup Field, and he sent the Academy's twin custodians to search Stanley Wong's room.

Frank had instructed the Cardozo twins to bring him any gold watch they found in that room. Thirty minutes later, they had come back and placed a watch down on his desk. Tim Cardozo, the more talkative of the two twins, told him they had discovered it tucked under a winter coat in Stanley's storage locker.

Finding Teddy's watch had thrown into doubt all of Frank's theories about what had likely happened that night. He had assumed either the investigators were right, and Teddy really did commit suicide, or that Teddy and some other boys had been fooling around on the roof when a tragic accident had occurred.

This new evidence obviously pointed in a whole different direction. It also raised the disheartening possibility that the Academy's arrogant chairman of the board had been right all along. Maybe the Chinese kid really was the culprit, as Randolph Jr. had immediately surmised that night at Nunzio's.

Frank turned over the watch a few times in his hand and wondered why Stanley would have taken it. If he was keeping it hidden under his winter coat, he clearly realized he couldn't wear it around school.

The watch also looked like it wasn't worth very much. It was old and scratched. Frank remembered seeing soldiers wearing watches like that in Korea, and he guessed it would only fetch twenty dollars at most. He knew Stanley came from a very wealthy family in Hong Kong, so he doubted money was the motivation.

Frank was unsure about his next move. Should he bring in Stanley and ask him to explain why Teddy's watch was hidden in his storage locker? Should he alert Teddy's parents that their missing family heirloom had been found? Or perhaps he was supposed to call the police or the army ROTC?

He usually prided himself on his decisiveness. When he was a young officer in Korea, he had been so quick and resolute in his decision-making that he once shot and killed a Chinese spy based only on a single piece of evidence: the suspicious look on the man's face when he was asked to show his identification papers. The Silver Star he had won for that decision was framed and hanging on his office wall. But, in this instance, Frank could not pull the trigger on what to do next.

If he were still in the military, he could have simply kicked the matter upstairs to his superior officer. But at the Academy, the person above him was Randolph Jr., and Frank was not ready to call him. Randolph Jr. might simply have Stanley arrested. A Chinese cadet being dragged off campus in handcuffs would get the Academy's name splashed all over the papers and set off an avalanche of calls from parents. Most of the parents would not be happy to know there even was a Chinese student at the school, let alone one who was a watch thief and possibly a quarterback murderer.

Frank could not afford to make the wrong decision. Until recently, he had been extremely confident that, with minimal effort, he would be able to keep the Academy headmaster job as long as he wanted it. Compared to leading men in battle, the job was a breeze. But, with each new development in the Teddy Haswell suicide saga, Frank had become less and less confident about his job security.

He would have thought a suicide would be a straightforward problem for a headmaster. Some lonely kid offs himself and so you show a little compassion to his roommate, hold a short memorial service, and then move on as quickly as possible. But by some cruel twist of fate, this suicide had managed to involve boys with some of the richest parents at the school. Not to mention what it had done to the football team. Frank sensed that if he made any serious misstep with this case, he could actually be tossed out by the board.

And this was absolutely not a time he could lose his job. For the last year, he had been expecting his oldest son, Johnny, to get a free college education at the Merchant Marine Academy. But his first ex-wife had just given him the devastating news that Johnny, who was now going by Jonathan, had decided to enroll in art school in Rhode Island instead. Room and board included, Frank was looking at one thousand dollars a year for Jonathan to go paint pictures in New England.

Best not to make any rash decisions here, Frank decided. The hearing into Teddy's death was only two days away. He would bring up the watch during the hearing, and Stanley could explain himself there. There was no reason to assume the worst, since there could well be a perfectly reasonable explanation for why Stanley had the watch. Maybe he bought it, and Teddy just forgot to tell his parents he had sold it.

Frank put the watch and the note under some papers in his top desk drawer, locked the drawer, and then checked his own watch, an army-issued Bulova. He was glad the Cardozo twins had found the evidence so quickly, because he could still make his tee time at the West Orange Country Club.

35

Saturday, October 19, 1963 (3:15 p.m.)

TEDDY HASWELL'S DIARIES FILLED FOUR SPIRAL NOTE-
books. His mother, Marjorie, had read them from beginning
to end many times. Reading each notebook did not take her
very long, because Teddy had not been a prolific writer. Most
pages contained only a paragraph or two and some were filled
with nothing more than stick figure drawings and doodles.

Despite their low word count, Marjorie learned a lot about
her son from reading the diaries. Teddy was always a quiet boy,
and, when he was home from school, he never talked much
about his hopes and dreams. But on the pages of those notebooks he had laid out a whole life plan for himself. He wanted
to play football in college and study business or economics. He
was not sure if he would be able to play as a freshman, but he
expected to be the starting quarterback on his college team by
his junior year at the latest. After college, he planned to join
the army to make use of his military education. At some point,
he would get married and have at least two kids. He might
marry his middle-school girlfriend, Rhonda Macklin, or a new

girl he met in college. After some years in the army, he would retire as at least a captain and then he would go into business. He thought real estate might be the right business for him, from what he had seen of it through knowing Donald. Maybe he would even go into business together with Donald. He also planned on having a beach house someday in Florida just like the one Donald's family had.

Marjorie learned all those things from four notebooks. But one thing she had expected to find in those pages was missing entirely. There was no evidence at all that her son had been depressed. If Teddy had been suicidal, she thought he surely would have written something about that. Based on those notebooks, however, Teddy was exactly who she thought he was, an extremely happy and ambitious young man.

She considered what Donald had said in Colonel Overstreet's office about Teddy being the strong-but-silent type who could not admit to being depressed. But she could not reconcile that theory with what she read. Over four volumes of diaries, there was only one passage where Teddy mentioned feeling sad. It was when his favorite player on his beloved Philadelphia Eagles, Norm Van Brocklin, left the team. If her son's saddest moment at the Academy was Norm Van Brocklin's retirement day, she was sure Teddy really was a very happy boy.

Marjorie was sitting in Teddy's old room on the end of the single bed her son had slept in from the time he was seven years old until he left for the Academy. She remembered buying that bed, along with a Felix the Cat blanket and sheet set, at Gimbels in Newark. Although Teddy got tired of Felix the Cat by middle school, Marjorie knew exactly where that blanket and those sheets were in a cardboard box in the attic.

The notebooks were in a pile next to her and she was flipping through them again, page by page. She stopped on a passage where her son had written that he could do his best thinking at the table in the library that was by a window and had the best view of Jessup Quadrangle. Suddenly, Marjorie felt an overwhelming compulsion to find that library table.

She did not want to analyze this desire too deeply, because it was obvious there was no logic behind it. She knew a seat in the Academy's library could not be expected to provide her magical insight into her son's mind. But Marjorie did not care if she was being irrational. At that moment, she simply felt an urgent need to find the library table with the view of Jessup Quadrangle that Teddy had mentioned in his diary.

As she hurried down the stairs, she called out to her husband, Paul, to tell him she was leaving. It was only when there was no response that she remembered he had left a half hour ago to play golf with some friends. Marjorie was glad Paul was out, because she had no interest in explaining herself to him. Teddy had not even been dead for two weeks, and Paul was already talking about how they needed to move on with their lives. Paul could try to drive and putt away his memories of Teddy on the golf course if he wanted to, but moving on was the last thing on Marjorie's mind. She just wanted to get in her car and drive to the Academy as fast as she could.

Twenty minutes later Marjorie pulled her Ford Falcon into the Academy's parking lot. As she got out of the car, Marjorie was surprised to see a still smoldering butt of a Parliament cigarette in the ashtray. While she drove, she had been completely absorbed by memories of the first time she had brought Teddy to visit the Academy when he was twelve. She did not recall smoking a cigarette. In fact, she had almost no memory of the drive at all. She was not even sure if she had played the radio.

She took a long, deep breath to try to settle her nerves and then made the short walk from the parking lot to Jessup Hall.

She passed a few cadets in their matching white shirts and gray slacks, the same uniform Teddy was wearing when she last saw him alive. She forced herself to keep her eyes down and fixed on the gravel pathway to Jessup Hall, because she knew she would start crying if she looked too long at the vibrant young cadets around her.

Marjorie walked into Jessup Hall and straight to the library, where the librarian was seated behind the front desk. Marjorie remembered hearing once from Donald when he was visiting that he suspected the school's librarian was a Communist agent, because she was always watching the cadets and writing down what they were doing in a notebook. Based on that description, Marjorie had been expecting to see a sullen Ethel Rosenberg look-alike. But she thought the librarian, with her kind face and slim figure wrapped in a fashionable navy-blue coat dress, looked nothing like any Communist she had ever seen on the news.

"Good afternoon. Can I help you?" the librarian asked.

"Hi, sorry to disturb you," Marjorie said. "I imagine parents aren't allowed in here on Sunday, but I'm Teddy Haswell's mother."

Marjorie wondered when she would be able to say her son's name without choking up. As usual, she could feel her eyes welling up with tears.

"Oh, Mrs. Haswell, I'm so sorry about your son," the librarian said. "He was a wonderful boy."

"Thank you. That's nice to hear."

Marjorie wiped her eyes and focused on keeping her composure. She was tired of crying in front of people.

"I'm Rosemary Duncannon, by the way. Is there something I can do for you?" Rosemary asked.

"This is probably going to sound crazy, but Teddy mentioned in his diary that he used to like to sit at a certain table in the library," Marjorie said. "He said it was where he could do his best thinking. I just wanted to see if I could find that spot. I'm not really even sure why, but it just suddenly felt important to me."

"It doesn't sound crazy at all, Mrs. Haswell. What did Teddy say exactly about it?"

"He wrote in his diary it was by the window with a good view of Jessup Quadrangle."

"Well, then I know the table," Rosemary said. "And come to think of it, I do remember finding Teddy studying there a lot."

Rosemary stood up and came around the front desk. When she reached Marjorie, she put her hand on Marjorie's shoulder.

"Thank you for being so understanding," Marjorie said. "I know I probably should have called first and not just shown up here like this."

Marjorie followed behind Rosemary to the center of the library, where there were three long tables. Rosemary stopped and pointed at the empty one by the window.

"This must be the one," Rosemary said.

Marjorie went over and looked out the window. She could see a few cadets marching with their rifles on their shoulders in Jessup Quadrangle. She knew from Teddy's stories that they were being punished for amassing too many demerits. She then sat down and slowly ran her hands along the table's smooth wood surface, trying to imagine her son studying at the same spot. As she daydreamed about Teddy reading a book at that very spot, her fingers ran across a rough and uneven area on the side of the table. She looked down and saw the initials *D. T.* had been carved into the wood.

"I guess Donald used to come here also," Marjorie said, pointing out the small carving to Rosemary.

"I think you're right," Rosemary said with a deep sigh.

"I hope I didn't just get Donald into any trouble?"

"Oh, believe me, there's no need to worry about Donald," Rosemary said. "I know him well enough to know he'd never admit to doing this. He'd just deny and deny and deny some more."

Marjorie could hear the sharp edge in Rosemary's voice. Clearly, her displeasure with Donald went beyond just this one carving. Marjorie was surprised, because she had assumed from Teddy's stories that Donald was the star cadet on campus. She thought the faculty must all love him.

"Were you here the night Teddy died?" Marjorie asked.

"Yes, I was. What a horrible night!"

"Then can I ask you something? In Teddy's diary, he mentioned he was going to pull some kind of prank in Jessup Hall that night with Donald," Marjorie said. "Teddy was worried the boys were going to get into trouble. You didn't notice them doing anything strange that night in the library, did you?"

"Did he write anything about them going to the roof?" Rosemary asked.

"No, it just said Jessup Hall," Marjorie said. "I asked Donald about it, and he made it sound like nothing. That they didn't really have an idea anyway, and they just decided to study instead. Maybe I'm crazy to be so fixated on it, but it's just, if the boys were pulling a prank . . . Well, you know, that could have been the reason."

"That doesn't sound crazy at all," Rosemary said. "And Donald didn't say anything about them sneaking off somewhere?"

"No, he said they were just studying all night until . . . you know," Marjorie said.

"Well, I suppose we'll all find out more on Monday, won't we?"

"What could we find out on Monday?" Marjorie asked, confused why Rosemary would expect new information to come to light over the next two days.

"Oh, I just mean since the hearing's on Monday, we should know more after that," Rosemary said. "If Donald or any of the other cadets know something, I'm sure Colonel Overstreet will be able to get the truth out of them."

Marjorie could feel her temper rising. Colonel Overstreet had promised her and Paul that the Academy would launch an investigation, but they had not heard anything more after that. The thought crossed her mind that Paul knew about the hearing but was keeping it from her. It would be very much like Paul to try to decide what was best for the both of them without consulting her. After all, he had gotten a vasectomy fifteen years ago and only told her about it the day after the operation. A man who could do something like that to his wife could certainly decide not to inform her about a hearing.

"I had no idea there was going to be a hearing. What time will it be?"

"Oh, well, okay, I'm so sorry," Rosemary stammered. "I just thought . . . Well, I assumed . . . Perhaps I should just check with Colonel Overstreet first."

"Please," Marjorie said, staring straight into Rosemary's eyes.

"Ten," Rosemary said.

36

Saturday, October 19, 1963 (7:05 p.m.)

DONALD'S FATHER, FRED, WENT OUT OF HIS WAY TO AVOID being associated with any political party. Since he understood the country was divided roughly fifty-fifty between Democrats and Republicans, he couldn't see any benefit to offending roughly half of his potential tenants and business partners by choosing sides. Also, by having no known political affiliation, he could simply agree with the views of whoever he was speaking with, ensuring all his business contacts believed he was on their side, politically speaking.

Given his fundamentally apolitical approach to life and business, it was very unusual for Fred to attend a political party fundraiser. However, that night he was making an exception. He had agreed to buy a seat at a fifty-dollar-a-plate dinner to raise money for the New York Republican Party. Richard Nixon was speaking on the topic of "Integrity in Politics."

Randolph Jessup Jr. had invited Fred to the event earlier in the day when they had spoken on the phone about the Flushing Towers project. Ordinarily, Fred would have quickly come up with an excuse not to go (especially after he had heard the fifty-dollar price tag), but he could not pass up the chance to spend an evening with Randolph Jr. The only way for Fred to appease Queens Savings Bank and get them to give him some breathing space on his past-due loans was to sign on a new partner for the Flushing project as soon as possible.

Randolph Jr. had asked for a prospectus on the project over the phone, which in Fred's experience meant he was seriously interested. If someone was just wasting Fred's time and pretending to have money to invest, they usually would not ask for documents. Now Fred just needed to close the deal.

The fundraiser was in the Carnation Ballroom at the Roosevelt Hotel. Fred had stopped at the registration desk on his way in, where an eager young Republican Party operative had informed him of his table assignment in exchange for his fifty-dollar check. He was at Table 17 with Randolph Jessup Jr. and eight people he did not know.

Although Fred had arrived at the hotel a few minutes early, the ballroom was already quite full and buzzing with hundreds of different simultaneous conversations. Fred scanned the room and saw that Table 17 was among the outer ring of tables farthest from the speaker's dais.

He walked over to his table, but he did not see Randolph Jr. About half the seats at the table were already taken, but Fred did not want to commit yet to a chair, since his plan was to position himself directly next to Randolph Jr. He picked out a man who was also standing alone near the table and went over to talk to him. Fred introduced himself, mentioning, as he always did, that he was one of the biggest property developers in Queens.

"Nice to meet you, Fred. My name's Tom Stephens. I'm in the import-export business out in New Jersey."

Fred was surprised by Tom's very English-sounding name, because he spoke in a heavy Spanish accent. He was also fascinated by a long, thick scar on Tom's face that ran from his forehead, down along the right side of his nose, and then took a sharp turn from near his nostril straight across his cheek to his right ear.

"You were also invited by Randolph?" Fred asked, trying not to stare too directly at the scar.

"Yes, I've known Randolph and his family for years," Tom said. "Randolph and I basically grew up together."

"Where are you from?" Fred asked.

"Summit, New Jersey. Same as Randolph."

"I mean where are you from originally?" Fred asked, thinking it was obvious Tom could not have picked up his accent in New Jersey.

"What do you mean?" Tom asked. "You don't know where Summit is?"

"Sure, I know Summit, but I mean what country are you from?"

Tom suddenly looked angry. As a salesman, Fred prided himself on his ability to read people, but he had no idea what had upset Tom.

"Sorry, I need to talk to someone over there," Tom said, walking away.

Confused, Fred was watching Tom walk off when he felt a hand on his shoulder. He turned around and saw it belonged to Randolph Jr.

"What did you do to make Tom so angry?" Randolph Jr. asked.

"I have no idea," Fred said.

"You didn't ask him about his scar, did you? Did you mention the Bay of Pigs? Oh no, I really hope you didn't say anything about the Bay of Pigs!"

"The Bay of Pigs? Why would I mention that?" Fred asked.

"You're sure? Tom looked really angry, and the Bay of Pigs is the only thing I can think of that would set him off like that."

"You mean he got that scar at the Bay of Pigs?"

Randolph Jr. looked around suspiciously, as if he were concerned someone might be listening in on their conversation. Then he leaned in close to Fred.

"It's better not to ask questions like that," Randolph Jr. whispered. "I know him from some racetrack business we tried to do in Havana before the whole Castro disaster happened. His life's pretty top secret, if you know what I mean. Anyway, have a seat. Dick Nixon should start talking any minute now."

Randolph Jr. pulled out the chair closest to where they were standing. There was one empty seat next to his, but Randolph Jr.'s body was between Fred and that chair, blocking him from getting there.

He suddenly noticed a man coming fast from the other side of the table who seemed to be headed straight for his desired seat. Fred was determined not to lose out on a chance to spend two hours sitting next to Randolph Jr. pitching him on Flushing Towers, especially since he had paid fifty dollars for that privilege. He quickly reached around Randolph Jr. and managed to get his fingertips on the back of the chair, to claim it, just half a second before the other man could get there. The man glared at Fred, but when he realized Fred had no intention of moving his fingers off that chair, he gave up and retreated.

Once Randolph Jr. sat down, Fred was able to get around him, pull out the chair he had claimed, and take a seat. He could see a number of dignitaries were starting to gather around Richard Nixon on the dais. Since Fred was not sure how much pitching he would be able to do once the speeches started, he decided there was no time to waste. Fred leaned over to Randolph Jr. and put his hand on top of his forearm.

"So, I spoke to my lawyers at Delk, Delk and Associates and they're almost finished with the prospectus on Flushing Towers," Fred said. "They'll send it to your office in the next few days."

Fred really just had one lawyer, Bernie Delk. Bernie's firm consisted solely of Bernie; his alcoholic son, Gordon, who never came to the office; and a retired postal worker (their "associate") who Bernie hired to make court filings. But Fred liked to use the firm's name to give the impression he had a full team of lawyers behind him.

"That's great, Fred. But actually, there's something else I need to speak to you about."

"You're interested in a different development?"

"No, it has to do with the Academy," Randolph Jr. said. "I guess you've heard about the hearing we're going to have on our quarterback's death. I believe your son, Donald, is involved."

"Yeah, I got a call from Frank Overstreet about that," Fred said.

Fred had understood that Donald would testify at the hearing because he had been Teddy's roommate. That had sounded reasonable to Fred. Who would know better about what was bothering Teddy than his roommate? Fred thought. So he had not given it a second thought after he'd finished the call with Colonel Overstreet.

"It seems we have a Chinese cadet at the Academy, did you know that?"

"I had no idea," Fred said. "Donald never mentioned that. Do you mean a Chinese from China?"

"Well, what other kind of Chinese is there? Anyway, from what I'm hearing, this Chinese boy might have been on the roof of Jessup Hall at the same time Teddy was up there thinking about ending himself."

"Seriously? What was he doing up there?"

"Not a clue," Randolph Jr. said.

"But you think this Chinese kid could have done something to Teddy?" Fred asked.

"Frankly, I have no idea. I didn't even know there was a Chinese boy at my school until a week ago, so it's not like I know everything that's going on over there," Randolph Jr. said. "But it turns out this isn't just any Chinese boy. His father came to visit me today and made me a very interesting business proposition."

"What kind of business?"

Fred was having a hard time following Randolph Jr. He thought the Chinese were all Communists, which meant they shouldn't make business propositions.

"My kind of business, of course," Randolph Jr. said. "Because of this business proposition, it's essential that this Chinese boy not get into any kind of trouble that will make his father upset with my school."

"I see," Fred said.

A Republican Party official was now at the microphone and telling the audience to settle down and take their seats. Fred was not sure how much more time he would have to close Randolph Jr. on the Flushing Towers deal. He wished Randolph Jr. would quickly finish his story about the Chinese boy.

"So, what I'm saying, Fred, is I would appreciate it if Donald didn't say anything at this hearing that could get this Chinese kid in any kind of trouble."

"I completely understand, Randolph. I'll speak to Donald and make sure he protects this Chinese boy."

The official at the podium was now going over the highlights of Richard Nixon's résumé. Soon he and Randolph Jr. would need to be quiet or risk being shushed by the others at their table.

"So, in terms of the timing of your investment in Flushing Towers . . . ," Fred said, letting his sentence trail off so the fact that he was asking a question would be implicit.

"We need to listen to the speeches now, Fred. But I really do appreciate your help with this Chinese kid," Randolph Jr. said. "I'm sure you understand this is one of those if-you-scratch-my-back situations."

Fred waited to see if Randolph Jr. would complete his sentence with "I'll scratch yours," but Randolph Jr. apparently was done speaking. He was now fully focused on the dais. Did Randolph Jr. really mean only his back was going to be scratched?

37

Sunday, October 20, 1963 (6:51 a.m.)

DONALD'S MENTAL IMAGE OF HIS GRANDFATHER Friedrich was based on a single photograph he had seen in his Great-Uncle Johan's apartment. He saw it the year before Johan died and around the time Johan decided to stop taking the subway or the bus. *Full of Catholics!* he would say. Since Johan would not travel anymore, Donald had gone with his father to visit him for his seventy-fifth birthday. Donald remembered his father telling him it wasn't really Johan's birthday, but it was "close enough." Donald was thirteen.

Johan was a widower by then and was living in a very small efficiency apartment on Broadway and Seventeenth Street in Manhattan. Donald remembered his father had offered many times to lease Johan a bigger apartment in one of his buildings in Queens at discounted rent, but Johan refused to leave Manhattan. He would say he hadn't come all the way from Bavaria just to live in Elmhurst or Astoria. He only wanted to live in the "real" New York.

Since they had forgotten to bring a birthday gift, Donald's father had left him alone with Johan for a few minutes to go buy a bottle of scotch at a liquor store nearby. As Johan struggled to put on a necktie to look presentable for his rare visitors, Donald poked around the tiny apartment and noticed a faded black-and-white photograph in a gold frame on top of a tall stack of yellowing copies of the *New York Times*.

The photograph showed two men sitting on a sofa surrounded by fifteen young women (Donald had counted). Donald recognized one of the men as a young Johan and guessed the other was his late grandfather Friedrich. But what had really caught Donald's attention were the women. Most were in sexy dresses, sleeveless and short, and two of them were not wearing dresses at all, just some kind of lacy lingerie.

With his teenage hormones racing, Donald asked his great-uncle about the photograph, and specifically about all the women. That was when Johan told him the story of his grandfather Friedrich and the Impressionable Dwarf.

Donald learned that Friedrich and Johan had spent their childhood in the small Bavarian town of Unterkleinstadt, dreaming of New York City. A distant cousin had gone there in the 1880s, made a fortune investing in property, and returned to live as the richest man in town. The two brothers were determined to follow in their now wealthy cousin's footsteps. Their plan seemed simple. They would go to the new world, get rich, buy property, and get even richer.

Friedrich had gone to America first at the age of sixteen. He left at that young age because a rumor was going around that all Protestant boys his age were being rounded up to join the Bavarian army. Friedrich needed to leave town fast to avoid the Catholic conscription officers. Friedrich agreed that he would invite Johan to join him once he had uncovered the best way for them to strike it rich. After several missteps on his way to wealth, Friedrich finally struck gold when he turned a dilapidated pub he had purchased for one hundred dollars, the Impressionable Dwarf, into a German restaurant and bar that also offered certain other services involving the young ladies in the photograph. In case the photograph was not enough, Johan's smug wink made the nature of those services very clear to Donald.

The business was soon literally making bag loads of money every night, and Friedrich sent word to Unterkleinstadt that the time had come for Johan to make the journey over to America. Within a year, the two brothers were working together at the restaurant; a few years after that, they imagined they might already be even wealthier than their rich cousin who had gone back to Bavaria.

The brothers decided the time had come to use the nightly success of the Impressionable Dwarf to pursue their ultimate dream of becoming New York City property barons. All they had to do was invest wisely and within a few years they would be hobnobbing with the Astors and the Vanderbilts at high-society parties in the lavish mansions they saw along Fifth Avenue. They would create a property empire, putting up beautiful buildings of brick and stone throughout the city, buildings like the ones they remembered from visiting Munich in their youth, and make princely sums in the process.

But it was not to be. Before they could even buy their first piece of land, Friedrich got married to a fellow immigrant from Unterkleinstadt, a stern and religious woman named Anna. She set as a firm and nonnegotiable condition to the marriage that Friedrich sell his interest in the disreputable restaurant and move with her out of Manhattan to a quieter and more God-fearing part of New York. Anna also dictated that

Friedrich could never go into business with his brother so long as Johan was still running the Impressionable Dwarf. Friedrich reluctantly accepted her conditions, sold his share of the business to Johan, and moved with Anna to the most God-fearing town in Queens: Flushing.

With that move, the brothers' dream of a property empire was finished. It turned out Johan lacked the business savvy of his brother and was never able to save enough money to buy any land on his own. Friedrich did manage to buy several tracks of vacant land, but, under Anna's always watchful eye, only in the most respectable and quiet parts of Queens. His life cut short by the Spanish Flu, Friedrich was never able to build anything on that land. A few years after his brother died, Johan had to sign over the deed to the Impressionable Dwarf to settle a gambling debt. After that, he worked at various low-wage jobs, usually given to him as favors by former satisfied customers of the restaurant.

His Great-Uncle Johan's story that day had been a revelation to Donald. Before then, his grandfather had been barely a stick figure in his imagination. Just a collection of generic details. He came from Bavaria. He married his grandmother. He bought some land. He died of the flu. That was all he knew.

The photograph had transformed Friedrich into a fully formed, flesh-and-blood character to Donald, and a cool one at that. Whenever he thought of his grandfather after that day, it was the dapper-looking bachelor Friedrich, surrounded by beautiful young ladies, pondering his future real estate empire in Manhattan.

That morning, in his room in the Academy barracks, Donald had woken up just as dawn was breaking over Newark. His skin was clammy, his Academy pajamas felt damp, and his eyes were stinging like he had barely slept all night. Suddenly, he felt nauseated and he quickly sat up in bed to avoid vomiting. As he propped himself up against the wall behind his bed, Donald remembered something that made his pulse race. At some point, in the middle of the night, his grandfather Friedrich had been in his room.

Donald had no idea if he was remembering a dream or if he had been visited by a ghost, but his grandfather had been sitting at the foot of Teddy's bed, talking to him. He was sure it was him.

He looked exactly like he did in the photograph Donald had seen in Johan's apartment, but in color and in different clothes, and without the fifteen nearly naked women around him. He was wearing a navy-blue suit and a red silk necktie. Not a suit from back in his day, like he wore in the photograph, but a fashionably modern suit, an expensive-looking one as if he might have bought it at Bloomingdale's on his way to the Academy. His hair was also done in a modern style, like Cary Grant in *North by Northwest*. If his grandfather went for a stroll down Fifth Avenue, no one would realize he had just arrived from 1913.

Donald remembered trying to get up from his bed, but he couldn't move at all. Just to be sure his muscles were working again now, Donald waved his hands in the air and wiggled his toes under the sheets. He was no longer paralyzed.

He was not sure how long his grandfather had been in his room. Donald had asked him why he had come, and his grandfather said it had been a difficult journey, but he needed to tell him something very important. He wanted Donald to know he was the key to fulfilling Friedrich's dream. Only Donald could carve out a place for their family among the great business families of Manhattan. Spanish flu had taken him before his time, and his son, Fred, had squandered his opportunity already. Fred Jr. was like his own brother, Johan, kindhearted, but he lacked vision. He could only depend on Donald.

Donald struggled to fight back and defend his father. He wanted to say his father was a great businessman and had done his best with what he had been given. But suddenly he could not speak. The paralysis had spread to his mouth as well.

His grandfather said Fred had wasted his inheritance on cheap apartment buildings on the most remote edges of the great city of New York. The family empire must be rooted in beautiful, impressive structures built in Manhattan. And he said Fred had disgraced the family by obscuring their Bavarian roots. A true son of Bavaria would rather die than pretend to be Swedish, Friedrich had said.

Then his grandfather was gone. Donald could not remember if he had just disappeared or if he had gotten up from Teddy's bed and walked out the door. After that, Donald, trapped in his bed and unable to move or speak, must have fallen back to sleep somehow. He was not sure how long it had been since his grandfather's visit.

Donald got out of bed and walked gingerly to the window. After last night's paralysis, he did not trust his legs completely yet. His bare feet were sweating and they felt sticky against the linoleum floor. Donald was scared. What if his father somehow found out about his conversation with Friedrich? His father was a genius of real estate, and he had given Donald everything: a nice home, an education, even a bright future. Despite all that, Donald had not been able to defend him against his grandfather's horrible accusations. He had wanted to, but he couldn't get any words out, so maybe his father wouldn't believe he had even tried?

He opened the room's one small window and felt the cool air flow in and start to dry his clammy forehead. He breathed in the fresh air deeply and felt his fears shift from his father back to the hearing. If his grandfather was right, and he was the family's only hope, he had to be doubly sure nothing went wrong on Monday.

38

Sunday, October 20, 1963 (11:18 a.m.)

ALL MORNING, DONALD HAD A SENSE THAT FRIEDRICH might still be nearby. Other than that, it was just a typical Sunday morning. He ate two bowls of Cream of Wheat in Jessup Cafeteria, made fun of Lou Douglas for thinking the ranch in *Bonanza* was called the "pond of roses," and ignored Chaplain Roberts's sermon during mandatory church services. But that whole time, Donald kept looking around, thinking he might see his grandfather again. Since Friedrich was dressed like a modern businessman, no one would realize he was a ghost. He could have just gone into downtown Newark for breakfast, and he was planning to come back to campus later.

After church services, it was time to call his father. He did that every Sunday morning, and it would seem suspicious if he chose that day not to call. But he was starting to sweat with anxiety because speaking to his father was the last thing he wanted to do. What if his grandfather had decided to visit his family's house in Kew Gardens after he had left Donald's room? Maybe Friedrich had ratted him out to his father, telling him all the awful things he'd said and how Donald had not defended his father at all.

Donald was in the Jessup Hall stairwell heading down to the basement, where there were three pay phones the cadets could use to make collect calls home on Sunday mornings. Joey Bortz was going downstairs with him.

As Donald went around the bend in the stairwell, a freshman cadet with bright red hair and a face full of freckles, who was going up, almost ran directly into Donald. Although the freshman managed to swerve at the last second to avoid a head-on collision, his foot grazed the tip of Donald's right shoe, smudging his perfect shine.

"I'm so sorry, sir!" the freshman said, looking and sounding terrified.

"Jeez, be more careful before you kill somebody," Donald said.

The freshman looked at Donald, then at Joey, and then back at Donald. After a few seconds, it slowly seemed to dawn on him that by some miracle he was escaping punishment. He hurriedly saluted them both and ran away as fast as he could up the stairs.

Donald decided he should clean off his shoe then and there, since some of the faculty were obsessed with shoe-shine quality. He pulled a handkerchief out of the pocket of his slacks and started trying to smooth out the smudge.

"Wait a second. What in the world's going on around here?" Joey said.

"What do you mean?" Donald asked.

"You're Donald, right? You live to peer-discipline stupid kids like that," Joey said. "And you saw his hair, right? And all those freckles?"

Peer-discipline was the Academy's word for hazing younger students. It was strongly encouraged by the school's faculty as an important part of building character and leadership skills among the student body, and Donald was known as the most enthusiastic peer disciplinarian at the school.

Donald realized Joey was right. It was not like him to let a freshman get away with something so egregious. Particularly not one who was clearly asking for trouble by walking around with such bright red hair. But between his grandfather's surprise visit and the stress of the hearing, he really was not his usual self that morning.

"Oh, I guess I'm just distracted these days," Donald said, still wiping his shoe. "But don't worry. I know what the kid looks like. I'll get him later."

Joey edged past Donald and continued down to the basement. Donald quickly folded his handkerchief, put it back in his pocket, and followed Joey to the pay phones. When he saw only one of the phones was free, Donald sped up and beat Joey to it.

"Let me use the phone first. My dad's going out soon," Donald lied. He wanted to get this call over with fast.

Without waiting for Joey to agree, Donald picked up the available phone, the middle one in the row of three. He dialed 0 and then told the operator that he wanted to make a collect call to his father's number. His father had had a separate line installed in his home office, and that was the number Donald always called on Sunday afternoons.

He knew it would be pointless in any case to ask to be connected to the main home number. His father did not authorize his mother or any of his siblings to accept collect calls. After a few seconds, he heard his father come on the line.

"Hi, Dad. How's everything?" Donald said, trying to sound as casual as possible.

"It's great, as always," his father said. "I think we'll be breaking ground on Flushing Towers in just a few months. That project's going to be a new landmark for Flushing, that's for sure."

So far, so good, Donald thought. Surely if Friedrich's ghost had visited Kew Gardens, his father would not have led with Flushing Towers. But another thought also flashed through Donald's mind. None of his father's buildings, and certainly not one stuffed full of compact rental units in Flushing, would ever deserve the title "landmark."

"I'm glad you called, Donald," his father went on. "I need to talk to you about this hearing tomorrow."

"You know the hearing's about Teddy's suicide, right? It's not really a big deal," Donald said.

"Yeah, I know all about it, Donald. Your headmaster filled me in."

Colonel Overstreet had mentioned he would tell their parents about the hearing, but Donald hadn't expected his father to take any interest in it. He was sure his father would be too busy with work.

"I'm not even sure why they want me at the hearing, Dad. I was just Teddy's roommate."

"Well, it's good you're going to be there, Donald, because I need you to do something that's very important for the future of the company."

"What do you mean?" Donald asked.

As his grandfather had said, what was most important for the future of the company was keeping Donald safe and sound. And he had already taken care of that himself.

"You know this Chinese boy in your class, right?" his father asked.

"Yeah, we call him Fu Manchu," Donald said. "But there's no need to worry about him, Dad. I already took care of everything."

He wanted to tell his father about his brilliant plan, and its flawless execution, but it was too risky. Joey was behind him, and there were cadets on either side using the other phones. They all would be able to hear every word out of his mouth.

"I don't know what you mean by 'taking care of everything,' but I need you to listen to me very carefully, Donald," his father said. "This Chinese boy cannot get in any trouble tomorrow. It's very important you make sure of that."

"I don't understand, Dad. You want Fu Manchu *not* to get into trouble? Why?"

"There's a new investor ready to come in on the Flushing Towers project, and it's important to him that this Chinese boy not have any trouble tomorrow. I don't know why exactly, and I don't care. But if it's important to one of my investors, then it's important to me. And if it's important to me, then it's important to you. You got that?"

Donald could feel trickles of sweat running down his temples. If he had to protect Fu Manchu, who would protect him?

"Dad, Fu Manchu was on the roof that night also. Maybe he knows something about why Teddy fell? How can I protect him when I wasn't even there?"

"I don't care about any of that, Donald. Whatever happened, happened. You just do whatever it takes to make sure this Chinese boy stays out of trouble."

"But what if Fu Manchu tries to get me in trouble?" Donald asked his father.

"How could he do that? You just said it yourself that you weren't even there. Don't be paranoid, Donald."

"But, Dad," Donald pleaded.

"Just do what I say, Donald," his father said. "This family is not a democracy!"

Donald knew that "this family is not a democracy" meant a conversation with his father was over. For someone who often said the American political system was the greatest one on Earth, his father didn't seem to have a lot of faith in democracy.

"I've got to go, Donald. I'll be at the hearing tomorrow to make sure everything goes well."

"Okay, Dad," Donald said weakly.

His father seemed more concerned with Flushing Towers than with Donald's safety. But Flushing Towers was just another low-rent building in Queens, barely one step above public housing. Donald, on the other hand, was the future of the family business. If Donald was expelled from school and his future was ruined, who did his father expect to carry on the family legacy?

Donald wished he could say all those questions to his father, but he knew he wouldn't be allowed to get out more than six or seven words before his father cut him off. It was not a democracy.

Donald hung up the phone and stood motionless, his hand still on the handset. The thought of disappointing his father terrified him. He needed to find a way to reverse whatever trouble for Stanley he already had set in motion and protect himself at the same time. And he only had twenty-four hours to do it.

39

Sunday, October 20, 1963 (4:38 p.m.)

THE NEW JERSEY MILITARY ACADEMY HAD BEEN selected for the first time ever to march in the Macy's Thanksgiving Day Parade. Macy's always invited one local military school, and for the past ten years in a row that honor had gone to the General Hayes School for Boys in Morristown.

The previous year, however, some cadets from the General Hayes School were accused of loosening the moorings of the giant Dumbo helium balloon that opened the parade. Halfway along the route, Dumbo got loose from his handlers and briefly flew free over Sixth Avenue before being impaled by the giant flagpole protruding from the tenth floor of the Time & Life Building. The sight of a rapidly deflating Dumbo with a pole through his chest traumatized hundreds of children who were watching, and a photo of the incident made the front page of the next day's *New York Daily Mirror* with the headline "Macy's Kills Dumbo."

Macy's took that kind of publicity poorly and launched an investigation that reported directly to the company's president. Its investigators eventually turned up photographs taken during the pre-parade preparations that showed General Hayes School cadets touching Dumbo's moorings. That evidence was enough for Macy's to impose a five-year parade ban on the General Hayes School.

The New Jersey Military Academy had been more than happy to step in and replace its rival. To make Macy's invitation even sweeter, this year President Kennedy and the First Lady were expected to be in the parade (just in front of the balloon turkey).

To ensure the cadets represented the school well, Colonel Overstreet ordered them to practice on Jessup Field every Saturday morning and Sunday afternoon until Thanksgiving. Coach Mulrooney usually drilled the cadets on parade formations, but for this event, Colonel Overstreet put the Academy's chemistry teacher, Major Burnside, in charge. He had marched with his battalion in President Eisenhower's inaugural parade in 1953.

When parade practice ended, Stanley Wong looked around for Donald because he wanted to talk to him about the hearing. Although he couldn't find Donald, he spotted three of Donald's friends from the football team—Lenny Thomas, Lou Douglas, and Joey Bortz—leaving the field together.

Stanley ran over and asked them if they knew where Donald was. None of them had seen him. Lenny guessed he might have used his regular excuse for getting out of weekend activities during football season, which was a perpetually sprained ankle. Lou thought Donald might have claimed he was having appendicitis, which he had done six or seven times since he'd gotten to the Academy. Joey speculated he may have faked a dead relative.

Stanley had to stop himself from laughing. It was clear Donald's own best friends considered him to be a habitual liar. If Colonel Overstreet wanted to know if Donald could be trusted, all he needed to do was ask any one of Donald's friends.

Stanley walked back to the barracks alone. When he reached his room, he saw that Dicky had beaten him back from parade practice. Dicky was already in his usual spot under his desk, reading a book. Stanley went into the room, closing the door behind him, and sat on top of his perfectly made bed.

Stanley knew he should study for his chemistry exam on Monday, but he was not in the mood. After the disappointment of the Morgan Chemical Talent Search, he didn't want to think about chemistry ever again. He decided he would just sit on his bed and stare out the window for a while.

"Hey, Stanley, is anything missing from your locker?" Dicky asked from under his desk.

As usual, on the rare occasions when Dicky spoke, the sound of his voice took Stanley by surprise. Stanley had become accustomed to having a roommate who could go days at a time without saying anything at all.

"What do you mean?" Stanley asked.

"I forgot to mention it before, but I saw Jerry Stahl in our room the other day," Dicky said. "I think he was looking around in our lockers."

"What did he want?"

"I'm not sure. He didn't see me, so I didn't talk to him," Dicky said. "It was the day you were in New York."

"But you saw him going through our lockers?" Stanley asked.

"No, I just heard him," Dicky said.

Stanley understood why Jerry had not seen Dicky. But he was surprised Dicky would not have said anything if he knew Jerry was going through their stuff.

"You didn't try to stop him?" Stanley asked.

"No, but he was only in the room for, like, a minute. I didn't really have time to do anything," Dicky said.

Stanley got off the bed and went over to his locker. He did not keep anything of real value in there, and since he had never inventoried his belongings, he was not sure how to check whether something was missing. Should he count his underwear and socks?

"Did Jerry take anything from you?" Stanley asked.

"I don't think so," Dicky said.

Stanley looked at each shelf in his locker, and everything seemed to be there. He decided not to worry about it. Dicky's information was too sketchy in any case for him to make an accusation against Jerry.

"I don't think he took anything from me, either," Stanley said.

"Okay," Dicky said. "That's good."

Stanley decided to go and look for Donald in the barracks. He went to the door and opened it and then immediately jumped back with shock. Donald was standing right on the other side of the door in the corridor.

"Hey, Fu Manchu, I was just coming to see you," Donald said. "Is Shower Shorts in there?"

Stanley took a deep breath to try to steady his pulse. Not only had he almost run straight into Donald, but in Hong Kong, it was a bad omen to think of someone and then immediately see that person.

"Dicky? Yeah, he's studying," Stanley said.

Donald walked by Stanley and into his room. He nudged Stanley slightly as he passed him, which Stanley could tell was intentional. As usual, Donald was trying to intimidate him.

"Scram, Shower Shorts!" Donald yelled in the direction of Dicky's desk.

As Dicky crawled out from under his desk, Stanley sat on the edge of his bed. He took another long, deep breath to prepare himself for what was to come. Conversations with Donald were never pleasant, but Stanley needed to speak to him about the hearing. Stanley did not want any surprises.

40

Monday, October 21, 1963 (9:30 a.m.)

FRANK OVERSTREET KNEW JESSUP AUDITORIUM WAS A much bigger venue than was needed for the hearing into Teddy's death. However, his options had been limited. He wanted to hold the hearing during regular class hours so the faculty who were involved could not ask for overtime pay. So all the school's classrooms were unavailable.

He had then gone down the list of other places on campus that were big enough to hold around twenty people. He did not want to use Jessup Cafeteria, since there might not be enough time between the cleanup from one meal and the preparation for the next to hold a full hearing.

Besides, he was reluctant to bring it up with Mrs. Jorgenson, the Academy's cook, who ruled over Jessup Cafeteria with an iron fist. For a seventy-year-old woman who was not even five feet tall, Mrs. Jorgenson was very intimidating. Frank had once seen her make the school's English teacher, Major Clark, apologize in front of the whole kitchen staff for wastefully eating only half of his serving of beef Stroganoff at lunch (*"while there are children starving in China!"*). After that incident, he noticed Major Clark started bringing his lunch to school in a brown paper bag. Frank did not want to join Major Clark on Mrs. Jorgenson's bad side.

Finally, Frank had considered Jessup Chapel, but had decided that since the Academy was affiliated with the army, that might violate the principle of the separation of church and state. Through a process of elimination, he was left with Jessup Auditorium.

First thing in the morning, he had sent the Cardozo twins to set up the auditorium. Their instructions were to put five chairs behind a long table for the panel, three chairs along one side for the cadet witnesses, and then a row of chairs in front of the panel for the parents of the witnesses. Since he had never presided over a hearing like this, the seating formation was based on what Frank remembered from a court martial he had attended in Korea.

Frank had sent Mrs. Kreitzenbach out that morning with five dollars from his petty cash envelope to pick up doughnuts. When she came back with twelve glazed doughnuts in a box from Joe's Bakery, he had her type out a sign that read *For Parents Only* and take the doughnuts and the sign to Jessup Auditorium.

He had considered offering the parents coffee as well, but the Academy's coffeepots and mugs were under the control of Mrs. Jorgenson, and he knew how much she disliked special requests. Parents would just have to use the drinking fountain if the doughnuts made them thirsty.

Thirty minutes before the hearing was due to begin, Frank took Teddy's watch out of his desk drawer and put it in his pocket. Then he left his office and went down to Jessup Auditorium to check on the preparations. As he walked through the auditorium's main door, he was very surprised to see Teddy's parents standing in the middle of the room.

Frank had intentionally not invited the Haswells to the hearing. According to the army-issued field manual to military justice that he had carried back from Korea, friends and relatives of the victim should not be allowed to participate in hearings, as their emotions could prejudice the outcome. Although Teddy was not a "victim" per se, Frank presumed the same principle applied to suicides.

Frank noticed Mrs. Kreitzenbach coming in from the back door that led to the auditorium's storage room. She was followed by the Cardozo twins, who were carrying a long table. They were walking directly toward him.

"We need a table for the doughnuts," Mrs. Kreitzenbach said when she got within earshot of Frank. "This one's too big, but it's the only size they have in the back room. Do you want me to send the twins to get a smaller one from the library instead?"

"I don't care about the table, Mrs. Kreitzenbach," Frank said. "Look who's here."

As instructed, Mrs. Kreitzenbach quickly scanned the auditorium. Then she turned back to Frank with a quizzical look.

"I only see Teddy Haswell's parents," Mrs. Kreitzenbach said.

"Exactly," Frank said. "Why are they here?"

"Is that a trick question, Colonel? Aren't they here for the hearing?" Mrs. Kreitzenbach asked.

"I mean, who invited them?" Frank asked her. "I told you very clearly that I would handle the invitations for the parents."

Frank knew Mrs. Kreitzenbach was very capable of disregarding his instructions. She had been at the Academy for thirty years, serving as secretary to six different headmasters over that time, and she made it very clear to Frank, in a multiplicity of ways, that she considered him to be no more than a temporary holder of the position. As such, she viewed his orders as something between requests and suggestions.

In fact, Frank got a daily reminder of Mrs. Kreitzenbach's independent streak every morning with the delivery of his coffee. Although he always asked for two sugars, each day of the week it came with a slightly different level of sweetness, one sugar one day, no sugar the next, and three sugars the day after that. Frustrated after six months at the Academy, Frank had looked into firing her, but he had been told by the brigadier general on the Academy's board that Mrs. Kreitzenbach was untouchable. She had a kind of gold-plated status with the army because she had been Douglas MacArthur's secretary and lover sometime back in the 1920s, when he ran West Point. Since the rumor was that she still had MacArthur's deep affection and home number, firing Mrs. Kreitzenbach was out of the question.

So Frank was left with no choice but to accept that his orders would not always be faithfully executed by his secretary. This time, he suspected Mrs. Kreitzenbach might have overruled him about the parental invitation list to the hearing.

"Well, I certainly didn't invite them," Mrs. Kreitzenbach said with a look that managed to express both confusion and anger at the same time.

"Excuse me, sir, but can we put the table down now?" Tim Cardozo asked in a strained voice.

"Sorry, Tim, of course," Frank said. "Mrs. Kreitzenbach, show the twins where to put that table and then set the doughnuts out please."

As Mrs. Kreitzenbach led the twins away, Frank heard a loud and familiar voice coming from behind him. He turned around to see Randolph Jr. entering the main door of the auditorium with Donald's father, Fred, and a man who he presumed was Stanley's father. Frank was surprised to see those three walking in together.

As headmaster, Frank knew he should greet all the guests. He considered whether to start with Randolph Jr. and the other men with him or with Teddy's parents. Neither prospect was appealing. Either talk to the Academy's insufferable chairman or the bereaved parents of a dead cadet. He chose the men.

Randolph Jr., Fred, and Stanley's father were standing close together talking when Frank walked over to them. None of them turned around to look at Frank even though he was sure they must have noticed him.

"Thank you for coming today, gentlemen," Frank said after announcing his presence by clearing his throat.

"Frank, we'll be with you in a few minutes. We're discussing some important business now," Randolph Jr. said, only briefly glancing at Frank before returning to his conversation.

It took Frank a second or two to process how rudely he had just been dismissed. This from a man who had gotten out of serving his country because his ankles were not thick enough. Frank took a deep breath and tried to focus his mind on the alimony and child support checks he would need to send out next week. As much as he wanted to grab the nearest folding chair and break Randolph Jr.'s thin ankles, he could not lose this job right now.

Frank turned around and headed straight over to Teddy's parents. Talking to them could not be any worse than what he had just endured.

Teddy's father, Paul, greeted Frank with a handshake. His mother, Marjorie, on the other hand, noticeably hung back with an angry expression on her face.

"You must be surprised to see us here, Colonel," Marjorie said in a clearly challenging tone.

"Actually, we can leave now if it's a problem," Paul said. "When my wife heard there was a hearing today, she really wanted to come. But I understand if we're not allowed to be here."

"What are you talking about, Paul? You can leave if you want to, but I'm not going anywhere!" Marjorie said.

"I just want to make sure, Marjorie," Paul said before turning back to Frank. "The librarian told my wife about it. I hope you don't mind?"

"Oh please, Paul, why would you even ask that?" Marjorie said. "Why should he mind?"

"Well . . . ," Frank began. "You said the librarian invited you? Mrs. Duncannon?"

"Yes, I guess she's one of the few people at this school who understands who really needs to be at a hearing like this," Marjorie said.

Frank clenched his fists so tightly, he could feel his fingernails digging into his palms. *This school is out of control,* he thought. Cadets were dying and lying to him and stealing things from each other. A pompous civilian was acting like he ran the place all by himself. A secretary he was not allowed to fire decided which of his orders she would follow and which she would ignore. And now the school's librarian was making executive decisions about who should attend an official Academy event.

The man he had been in Korea, who had won a Purple Heart and a Silver Star, would never have put up with this nonsense. Frank just hoped his desire to roughly frog-march both of Teddy's parents out of Jessup Auditorium was not too visible on his face. Now that they were here, he had to try to be cordial. He knew if the Haswells got too upset, they might go to the Newark police and ask them to reopen their investigation, which could lead to the Academy's board losing confidence in him. Although he had in fact lost control of the school, he did not need the board to know that.

"So, it's all right then?" Paul asked.

"Well, what I was going to say was, under military procedures, in this type of case, family members aren't usually invited," Frank said, struggling to maintain a civil tone. "But since you're here already, you're welcome to stay."

"Thank you, Colonel," Paul said. "That's nice of you."

"Of course we're welcome to stay, Paul," Marjorie said. "This hearing's about our son. What did you think he was going to say?"

"Well, I'm sorry, Marjorie, if it bothers you so much that I'm polite, and I understand how things are handled in the real world," Paul snapped back at his wife. "Maybe if you needed to be out in the real world, you would understand better."

"My son died. That is the real world," Marjorie said.

"That's not fair, Marjorie. You know what I mean," Paul said.

Frank was getting flashbacks to the final days of his own last marriage. He was thinking how best to extract himself politely from the middle of this marital dispute, when he saw Lieutenant Drake, the Academy's math teacher, come rushing into the auditorium.

"Is Colonel Overstreet here? Has anyone seen the colonel?" Lieutenant Drake yelled, sounding extremely upset and almost out of breath.

"My God, what is it?" Frank said, hurrying over to Lieutenant Drake.

When he got closer, Frank saw that one leg of the lieutenant's trousers was ripped toward the bottom. There was a bloody wound visible on his partly exposed calf.

"What in the world happened to you, Lieutenant?" Frank asked.

"There's a vicious dog going crazy out there, Colonel," Lieutenant Drake said. "I tried to catch it, but it attacked me! Phil got his shovel, but he wants your permission before he kills it."

Frank was not sure what to say. Even in Korea, nobody had ever asked for his permission to kill an animal before.

"Forget it!" Randolph Jr. said, running by Frank and Lieutenant Drake on his way to the door. "Nobody's killing my dog!"

Frank hurried after Randolph Jr., with Fred, Stanley's father, and Lieutenant Drake following behind him. Stepping through the door onto Jessup Quadrangle, he could hear the steady barking of a dog. Fifty feet away stood Phil Owens, the Academy's hulking groundskeeper, brandishing a shovel at a small barking dog cornered against Jessup Hall. Randolph Jr. shrieked, "Drop that shovel, you idiot!"

Frank could not believe what he was witnessing. This day was turning into a disaster, and the hearing hadn't even started yet.

41

Monday, October 21, 1963 (10:25 a.m.)

RANDOLPH JR. MANAGED TO SAVE HIS VICIOUS BEAGLE, Duke II, from the Academy groundskeeper's shovel. Once all the canine commotion had died down, Colonel Overstreet sent Lieutenant Drake to the infirmary to have his bite wound examined, and he asked everyone else to go back inside Jessup Auditorium. Randolph Jr. first made a detour to lock Duke II in his Lincoln in the parking lot.

Rosemary Duncannon had arrived at Jessup Auditorium after the dog incident was over. The people in the auditorium had broken up into several different conversation circles. Rosemary considered going over to greet Teddy's mother, but she was engaged in a loud, and not very pleasant-sounding, conversation with a man she assumed was Teddy's father. Rather than join a circle, Rosemary stood off to the side and observed, waiting for the hearing to begin.

A few minutes later the three cadets came in, escorted by Mrs. Kreitzenbach. Although Rosemary had not met their parents before, she had already guessed which adult in the room was related to which cadet. The entrance of the boys caused the conversation circles to break down into smaller groups, as each boy went off to talk to his own parent.

Several minutes passed until the Academy's chairman of the board, Randolph Jessup Jr., joined Donald and his father at the back of the auditorium. Soon she could tell they were having a very animated conversation. She was too far to over-hear, but Donald was facing her and seemed to be doing much of the talking.

Finally, Lieutenant Drake came into the auditorium, limp-ing slightly with one pant leg rolled up almost to the knee and a bulky white bandage wrapped around his calf. She wondered what possibly could have happened to him. Colonel Overstreet circulated among the conversation groups to announce the hearing was ready to begin.

Rosemary took the seat next to Colonel Overstreet, behind the investigative panel's table. As she sat down, the colonel leaned over to her and whispered that she should not have invited the Haswells. He then immediately leaned away, clearly not open to any conversation on the topic.

Rosemary lowered her head and crossed her arms tightly across her chest, as she always did when she felt under attack. She had realized years ago in school, when they studied the fight-or-flight response to danger, that she completely lacked that instinct. Her response was more like a possum's. She would curl in on herself and just hope the danger would pass.

She knew she had made a mistake by mentioning the hear-ing to Teddy's mother, but it was not completely her fault. She had been very clear with Colonel Overstreet that she was not the right choice to serve on this panel. He had ordered her to be on it anyway.

Colonel Overstreet banged his fist against the table, softly at first and then harder until he had the attention of the whole auditorium. The last people still standing and talking—Donald, his father, and Randolph Jr. in the back—went to take their seats.

"Sorry for the delay, but we're ready to get started," Colonel Overstreet said.

The rest of the panel—Randolph Jr., Lieutenant Drake, and Major Burnside—joined Rosemary and Colonel Overstreet behind the long table. The three cadet witnesses sat in chairs on the side, and the parents sat in a long, single row directly in front of the panel table.

"Thank you for coming this morning," Colonel Overstreet continued after everyone was seated. "First of all, let me just say—"

"Hold on there, Frank," Randolph Jr. interrupted. "If you don't mind, I'll chair this hearing. I am chairman of the board of this school, after all."

"Of course," Colonel Overstreet said.

Rosemary tried to keep her eyes fixed forward, but she could not stop herself from quickly glancing at the colonel. She had never seen his face so red. He was clearly seething inside at the slight to his authority.

"If you know me at all, you know I don't like to waste time," Randolph Jr. continued. "So I promise you, this hearing's not going to take very long. I decided we should have it because this is the first time since my father founded this school that a cadet has committed suicide. Well, just for accuracy's sake, I should mention there was a boy named Edward or Edmund something or other who may have killed himself about ten years back, but even if he did, that was during summer break, so it was a very different situation. This is the first time a cadet has killed himself right here on the Academy's campus. On our sacred ground, so to speak."

Marjorie raised her hand in the air and waved it back and forth to be sure to get Randolph Jr.'s attention. Rosemary could see the pain and the tears in her eyes.

"Yes, Mrs. Haswell, is there some kind of problem already?" Randolph Jr. asked, not bothering to hide his irritation.

"Well, it's just that I wish you wouldn't keep saying my son killed himself. It very well could have been an accident. Isn't that what this hearing's about?"

"Thank you for that comment, Mrs. Haswell, which also reminds me that I forgot to mention the ground rules for this morning. I'd like to ask parents to hold any questions or comments until the end," Randolph Jr. said. "But since you've already raised this, let's agree going forward just to refer to Teddy's death as . . . Well, how about . . . 'the Incident'? Whenever we're talking about it, we'll just say 'the Incident.' Would that be all right with you, Mrs. Haswell?"

Marjorie silently nodded. Rosemary realized Colonel Overstreet may have been right not to invite Teddy's parents. This might not be easy for them to watch.

"So we will move on now," Randolph Jr. said. "I had been planning to ask each boy a few basic questions about that night, just to start us off, but then some rather alarming information came to light this morning. It seems that one of these boys had a very serious beef with Teddy. We need to address that issue right away or we'll just be wasting our time here."

Colonel Overstreet leaned over and put his hand on Randolph Jr.'s arm to get his attention. Rosemary also leaned in that direction so she could overhear what Frank was going to say.

"Randolph, I think we need to be very careful before we start making any accusations," Frank whispered. "As I told you before, Stanley Wong's one of the top cadets at the Academy."

"I'm not talking about Stanley Wong, Frank," Randolph Jr. whispered back.

"Apologies for that interruption," Randolph Jr. said, turning toward the three cadets. "Donald, please stand up and tell everyone here what you were telling me just now in the back of the room."

Donald stood up and put his hands in his trouser pockets. He had his usual overconfident smirk on his face, and Rosemary felt a sense of loathing welling up from someplace deep and primal inside her. Whether it was Donald, or Roger Turnbull back at Millburn Elementary School, smirking bullies made her skin crawl. She knew she needed to put those feelings aside. She was on an investigative panel and wanted to be as objective as possible. But Rosemary sensed that might be impossible. Looking at him standing there ready to testify, her feelings were extremely clear. She detested Donald.

"Cadets, if you're asked to stand, you'll stand at attention," Colonel Overstreet said.

"Yes, sir," Donald said, straightening up with his arms at his sides.

"Go on now, Donald," Randolph Jr. said.

"Okay, sure. But about what exactly, sir?" Donald asked.

"About what we were just talking about a minute ago," Randolph Jr. said.

"Oh yeah," Donald said. "Well, the thing is, Jerry and I are from the same hometown, and we used to be friends when we were little kids. And, well, to tell you the truth, ever since we got to the Academy, Jerry's always wanted to be my roommate. He used to ask me about it all the time. It's like Jerry just couldn't accept that I would rather live with Teddy than him. He would say things like 'Why do you like Teddy more than me?' even though, if you think about it, that's pretty obvious, right?"

"That's not true!" Jerry yelled. "Donald asked me to be his roommate. I never asked him!"

"Were you given permission to speak, cadet?" Randolph Jr. said.

"Oh, do you mean I should stand up if I want to say something?" Jerry said, starting to get up from his chair.

"No! Sit down!" Randolph Jr. said. "That was obviously a rhetorical question. I didn't give you permission to speak."

Jerry meekly sat back down. Rosemary could see he looked terrified.

"Go on, Donald," Randolph Jr. said.

"I think Jerry was just really jealous of Teddy. You know, since Teddy was my roommate since freshman year and all. So then I find out Jerry had filed a room-transfer application just a few days after Teddy killed . . . I mean . . . after 'the Incident.' People always say I'm very perceptive, and that seemed really suspicious to me."

"Donald told me to do that!" Jerry yelled. "He told me to file that application."

"Cadet!" Randolph Jr. said, staring at Jerry. "If I have to tell you again to stay quiet, that will be . . . Actually, I don't know what the demerit system is like these days, but it will be a lot of demerits, I promise you that. Do you understand, cadet?"

"Yes, sir," Jerry said, sounding thoroughly defeated.

Rosemary could see tears in Jerry's eyes, and she wished his mother, who had come alone to the hearing, would go over and comfort him. She knew everyone at a military academy was supposed to act strong and stoic, like it was really the army, but these were just boys, after all. If his mother went to him, nobody would stop her, Rosemary thought. But looking at his mother, Rosemary did not expect that to happen. She appeared to be too shocked to move much at all.

"So," Randolph Jr. said, turning back to Donald. "What did you mean when you said it seemed suspicious that Jerry had filed a room-transfer application?"

"Well, it's suspicious that he was ready to transfer into my room so soon after Teddy died, right? But actually a lot of things seemed suspicious to me. Like I said before, people say I'm very perceptive," Donald said.

"For example?" Randolph Jr. asked.

"Well, I thought it was strange from the beginning that Jerry found Teddy's body. I mean, it was around eight o'clock, right? We're all supposed to be in the barracks or in the library at that time. So, what was Jerry doing in the quad? It's suspicious, right? It never made much sense to me, and believe me, I thought about it a lot. And then Jerry kept saying all this weird stuff about Stanley, like how he saw Stanley on the roof at the same time as Teddy. It just seemed like Jerry was trying really hard to make it look like Stanley was to blame for . . . you know, the Incident."

Rosemary thought back to when Jerry told her about seeing Stanley on the roof that night. She wondered if he had used her to spread false information. Maybe Jerry knew she would go tell the colonel about that.

She looked closely at Jerry, who was now quietly sobbing in his seat. It took two seconds of watching Jerry for Rosemary to decide he had not tricked her. Jerry could not possibly have come up with such an evil and devious plan. He may have wanted to be Donald's friend, but the story Donald was spinning did not make any sense to her. The idea that he could have killed Teddy and then set up Stanley to take the blame, all that just so he could move into Donald's room, seemed absurd.

"Wait a second, Donald," Colonel Overstreet said. "You told me Teddy thought Stanley took his watch. So, it seems to me you were also very eager to cast suspicion on Stanley."

"I only said that because that's what Jerry told me," Donald said. "Teddy never actually told me that himself."

"So everything you told me in my office was a lie?" Colonel Overstreet asked.

"No, sir, it wasn't a lie then, because I thought it was true," Donald said. "It only became a lie later when I found out it wasn't true."

"I'm confused, Donald," Colonel Overstreet said.

He reached into his pocket, pulled out a gold watch, and put it down on the table in front of him. Rosemary suddenly felt like she was in an episode of *Perry Mason*. She never would have guessed Colonel Overstreet had such a flair for the dramatic.

"How do you explain why I found Teddy's watch in Stanley's locker?" Colonel Overstreet asked.

"Because Jerry put it there. And Dicky Daniels saw him do it," Donald said. "If you call Dicky in here, I know he'll tell you that himself."

Jerry's crying suddenly became so loud, everyone in the room looked over in his direction. Rosemary worried he might be having a hard time breathing. She saw Jerry's mother finally get up and start to walk over to her son.

"We need to take a break now," Jerry's mother said. "And I need to call my husband."

42

Monday, October 21, 1963 (11:05 a.m.)

RANDOLPH JESSUP JR. ANNOUNCED THE HEARING WAS
going into recess. Then, together with Colonel Overstreet,
he escorted Jerry and his mother out of Jessup Auditorium.
Donald didn't want to look at Jerry, so he kept his eyes fixed
straight down on his well-shined shoes. But he had no choice
but to hear him, since his former best friend had been wail-
ing like a wounded animal.

After they left, everyone else sat silently in their seats for a
while. As it dawned on them that the recess might last for some
time, they stood up and soon the old conversation circles were
re-forming. Donald walked with his father to the back of the
auditorium.

"Jerry Stahl. I still can't believe it. I didn't think that kid
had it in him to do something like that," his father said.

"Yeah, I guess you never really know a guy," Donald said.

"I wonder if we're going to need to find a new dentist now,"
his father said.

Donald didn't care that Jerry's father was the family dentist. He was thinking about how well his testimony had gone, even better than he had expected.

He had agreed on the plan the day before with Stanley. As long as Stanley didn't say anything about seeing him on the ledge, Donald would make sure the suspicion fell on Jerry. Personally, Donald still preferred his previous plan, where Stanley would take the fall. But since his father had made him take that option off the table, sacrificing Jerry was the only way to go.

Jerry had been a good friend to him back in Kew Gardens, and Donald didn't like hearing him cry. But he was sure Jerry would be fine eventually, since there couldn't be any actual evidence he had done anything to Teddy. All he needed was someone other than him and Stanley to be the focus of the hearing. Jerry had served that purpose perfectly.

"Well, the main thing is, Flushing Towers should be able to go forward," his father said. "That's what's important for the family."

No, Dad, I'm what's important for the family! Donald wanted to scream. He couldn't believe his father, as great a businessman as he was, still could not see the big picture. Getting through this hearing was about protecting Donald, the hope of the family, not about protecting some second-rate Queens apartment building. Donald's grandfather understood that, and he had been dead for almost fifty years.

Staring at his father's face, he realized his father simply wasn't capable of dreaming big like Donald and his grandfather. His father was perfectly satisfied being an outer-borough developer of Swedish heritage, living in the biggest house on the nicest block in Kew Gardens. Donald would never be satisfied with a life like that. Once he ran the business, it was going to be so much more. He would run a company that would make people walking on Manhattan sidewalks look straight up at glistening towers of glass. And he would do it all from a penthouse apartment or a huge mansion on the water in East Egg, not a two-story Tudor-style house in Kew Gardens.

Suddenly, the image came into his mind of the painting of George Washington crossing the Delaware that he had seen in his history textbook. He pictured himself like that, leading the family company across the East River to conquer Manhattan. He imagined Janet Riverstone in the boat next to him. A girl like that could never be kept in Queens. She needed to be in Manhattan, to be seen and appreciated by the city's elite. His grandfather Friedrich and his Great-Uncle Johan were in the boat too, with the fifteen beautiful young ladies from the Impressionable Dwarf. They were smiling with pride that their family was finally assuming its rightful place in the world. And Donald's brothers were there also, but in the back of the boat. His grandfather had already selected Donald to lead the family.

Donald could see it all so clearly. But he knew better than to say anything to his father. His father would never understand. But his grandfather would.

43

Monday, October 21, 1963 (6:20 p.m.)

SITTING AT HER FORMICA KITCHEN TABLE, ROSEMARY Duncannon could not get the image of a crying Jerry Stahl out of her mind. His look of shock and anguish had made Rosemary want to cry herself.

The hearing that morning had stopped so that Jerry's mother could call her husband from Colonel Overstreet's office. After that, it never resumed. Rosemary spent the rest of the day at her desk in the library, too distraught over what had transpired to stick to her usual schedule. She even skipped her 4:15 reshelving, despite staring all afternoon at an overflowing book trolley.

About an hour after the hearing was over, Rosemary saw two men, one in a white lab coat and another in a business suit, rush into Jessup Hall and go straight to the elevator. Thirty minutes or so later, those two men reappeared, coming out of the elevator with Jerry and his mother trailing behind them. They all quickly left the building, and Rosemary heard one of them slam the large steel-and-glass doors to Jessup Hall on the way out.

Mrs. Kreitzenbach came down later to the library and told Rosemary what had happened upstairs. Those two men were Jerry's father and the family lawyer. After getting the call from his wife, Jerry's father had left a patient in his dental chair and driven straight from Queens to the Academy, stopping only to pick up his lawyer along the way. They had agreed with Colonel Overstreet and Randolph Jessup Jr. that the investigation would be handed back to the Newark police and that, pending the outcome, his parents would take Jerry home.

Rosemary could not picture Jerry as the prime suspect in a murder investigation. It was obvious to her that Jerry was not a killer, much less one who could push another cadet off a roof and then cover his tracks by pretending to discover the body.

She was so upset, she had closed the library early at five. As much as Rosemary hated committing such a dereliction of her librarian duties, she didn't think the cadets would mind. She was sure they all would be too preoccupied trading gossip about Jerry and the hearing to want to study that evening. Rosemary got to the admissions office on the third floor of Jessup Hall just as Natalie was locking up, and they had gone home together for the first time ever.

Since getting home, Rosemary had been sitting in her kitchen. Natalie had kept her company for a while, but Rosemary was not in the mood yet to talk. After a mostly silent thirty minutes together, Natalie had left to get a pizza from Uncle Sal's down the street.

Rosemary's bag was on the kitchen table and for the third time that evening she opened it, took out a scrap of newspaper, and read it slowly. When she had seen the item in the *Newark Star-Ledger* that afternoon, she had surprised herself by ripping it out. It was completely unlike her to damage library property. But something about having this scrap of paper in her bag gave her a sense of hope.

That scrap of paper was still on the table when Natalie came into the kitchen carrying an Uncle Sal's pizza box.

"What are you reading, Rose?" Natalie asked as she put the pizza box down on the table.

"Oh, it's just an article from today's paper. I shouldn't have torn it out," Rosemary said.

"Yeah, I can see it's from the paper, Rose. I mean, what's it about? I saw you looking at it before," Natalie said.

"Well, actually, it's a job advertisement," Rosemary said. "Seton Hall is looking for a librarian."

"You know someone who is looking for a job?" Natalie asked, leaning over to try to read the paper herself.

"I think I might be," Rosemary said.

It scared her to say those words, since she was not sure how she would feel if she discovered Natalie was looking at job announcements. Maybe even just tearing out a job advertisement before saying anything at all to her girlfriend about changing jobs was a betrayal of her trust.

"Seriously? You'd be able to leave Jessup Library to somebody else?" Natalie asked.

"I just feel like maybe a military academy isn't where I truly belong anymore," Rosemary said. "These boys don't need me. In fact, most of them spend their four years trying to read as few books as possible. To them, I'm just the cranky lady who tells them to be quiet."

"That's not true, Rose," Natalie said. "What about Stanley Wong? You've made a real difference for him."

"But you know he's an exception. And besides, for every Stanley, there's a Donald. Can you believe I found his copy of *Crime and Punishment* in the library weeks ago and he still hasn't come looking for it? I'm not sure he even knows it's missing."

"And if any boy could really use a dose of Dostoevsky, it's Donald," Natalie said, laughing. "But maybe he's just not a reader. That's not your fault, Rose."

Rosemary smiled, but she knew her desire to leave the Academy ran much deeper than just the cadets' disinterest in books. A vibrant young man full of promise had died in the Academy's care. His family deserved to have the Academy do everything in its power to determine what had really happened that night to their son.

Rosemary had tried to put her faith in the Academy to do that. She thought that if any institution could be trusted to uncover the truth, it should be the Academy, with its honor code and strict rules and a faculty full of decorated army officers. But Rosemary realized at the hearing that the Academy did not deserve her faith. No serious investigation could conclude that poor, bumbling Jerry Stahl might have pushed Teddy off a roof over some sort of disagreement about a watch and a room assignment. If the Academy could accept such an obviously absurd explanation as the most likely reason for the tragic death of one of its own, it was not the honorable institution it proclaimed itself to be.

And then there was Donald. Rosemary was still as convinced as ever that Donald knew what had occurred that night on the Jessup Hall roof. Other boys may have been involved as well, but Donald was Teddy's best friend and roommate. They had left the library at around the same time. They were together that night in Jessup Hall, she was sure of that. That fact should have been as clear to Colonel Overstreet and Randolph Jessup Jr. as it was to Rosemary, but neither had hesitated to let

Donald point the finger of blame at Jerry. Not only were they unable to get the truth out of Donald, they did not even seem to try.

Rosemary worried that if she explained all that to Natalie, her partner would try to convince her she was overreacting. She would tell Rosemary to trust the Academy to do the right thing, just like she had done before. But Rosemary knew she could not trust the Academy anymore. So she decided that, for now anyway, she would give Natalie a slightly different explanation for wanting a new job.

"Are you angry that I'm considering leaving the school? Of course, if you want me to stay at the Academy, I will," Rosemary said.

"Are you kidding?" Natalie asked. "If a job at Seton Hall gives us a reason to move out of this tiny dollhouse, I'm all for it!"

44

Monday, October 21, 1963 (6:20 p.m.)

ARTHUR WONG WAS SAYING GOODBYE TO STANLEY IN the Academy barracks. He had found a flight leaving that evening from Newark Airport to Chicago that would be the first leg in his long journey back to Hong Kong.

After the Academy's hearing had ended that morning, Arthur returned to Manhattan for a business meeting with a bond certificate–counterfeiting ring that operated out of the back of a dim sum restaurant on Mott Street. Since the meeting was at one o'clock, the counterfeiters politely offered to arrange for a working dim sum lunch, but Wok Nose Chiu had turned that offer down. He insisted that for Arthur's last meal in New York, he had to try the Peking duck restaurant on Canal Street that Marvin Chan managed.

They reached the restaurant around two thirty, and Marvin served them lunch in the same smelly suit he had worn to the Plaza Hotel. It was clear that Marvin was much more skilled at slicing a duck than pretending to be an international businessman. They took ninety minutes to finish off a full banquet course for two.

Arthur and his lieutenant then picked up his bags at the hotel and drove back to New Jersey. Arthur had expected to have at least an hour with his son before his flight, but Wok Nose Chiu got badly lost on his way to the George Washington Bridge, so Arthur's final visit was reduced to just a few minutes.

Since he did not know parents were prohibited on campus without the headmaster's permission, Arthur just walked straight to the barracks from the parking lot and knocked on doors until another cadet guided him to Stanley's room. Stanley had not been expecting to see his father again. He considered telling him that his being there was against school rules, but he realized that would be pointless, and possibly dangerous for him as well.

"Who's that?" Arthur said, pointing to a pair of legs poking out from under one of the gray metal desks.

"That's my roommate, Dicky," Stanley said. "Dicky, my father's here."

"Nice to meet you, Mr. Wong," Dicky said without getting up from under the desk.

"Is he okay?" Arthur asked his son, switching to Cantonese.

"Yeah, he just likes it under there," Stanley said in Cantonese as well.

"Stanley, I wanted you to know you made the triad proud today with your silence," Arthur said.

Praise from his father was a rare and precious commodity, and Stanley could not help but smile. But he did not feel like he had done the right thing. Certainly not after he had heard Jerry was going to be investigated by the police.

"But you know that boy today, the one who was crying, I think he could go to prison," Stanley said. "And I know he had nothing to do with any of it."

"Stanley, that's not our problem. His family should have protected him. Send just the mother to a hearing like that? That was a very bad mistake," Arthur said. "But it wasn't our mistake and it's not our problem to solve."

Stanley was not surprised by his father's reaction. He seemed to have no capacity to feel guilt at all. It was as if his father were the exact opposite of the characters in all the Russian novels Stanley had read that semester.

"Do you understand me, Stanley?" Arthur asked.

"I guess so," Stanley said, not sure what his father thought was hard for him to understand.

"Stanley, Uncle Wok Nose told me he thought you were struggling to understand the Ho Fong Triad's code," Arthur said. "I hope after today you understand more about why we have that code."

"What do you mean?" Stanley asked.

"Our code comes from the simple fact that the people in power in this world cannot be trusted to treat you fairly," Arthur said. "That includes the people who run this school. I raised you to respect your teachers, but you are old enough now to hear the truth. You saw the ridiculous hearing your school held today. Blaming a helpless boy who could not hurt a fly. That was their idea of justice? Well, as you get older, you will learn it's the same in adult society as well. All these proud institutions holding on to power and pretending they know what's best, but most of them operate with no principles at all. For the Ho Fong Triad to survive in such a world, should we rely on these institutions to treat us fairly? Do you think they would be fair to us, Stanley?"

"I guess not," Stanley said.

"Of course not! We would be fools if we trusted them. That's why we protect our own. We handle justice ourselves. We don't cooperate with the authorities, because we don't trust them. Do you understand, Stanley? There's a reason why you are safely in your room tonight and will be going to MIT next year and that other boy's in trouble."

Stanley stood still, silently processing everything his father had just said. It was true that the school's investigation was a farce. Nobody could seriously believe Jerry was responsible for Teddy's death. He felt a shiver down his spine thinking about what could have happened to him if his father had not come from Hong Kong. He did not know exactly what his father had done, but he was sure no one else would have protected him. In fact, he imagined everyone at the school would have been very happy to see Fu Manchu take the fall for Teddy's death.

Stanley suddenly felt ashamed to have ever wished he could just be a normal boy and not the son of a triad Dragon Head. The Ho Fong Triad was his family and it was the reason he still had a promising future.

"Thank you, Father," was all Stanley could think to say.

"I should go now, Stanley," Arthur said. "My plane doesn't leave for a few hours, but you know how Uncle Wok Nose drives. I will probably see all of New Jersey before I reach the airport!"

Stanley felt stupid that just a few minutes before he had wanted to scold his father for coming to the barracks without proper permission. Of course his father would not follow the Academy's stupid rules. He was the Dragon Head of a major Hong Kong triad, after all. Stanley wished he could hug his father, but in his family, hugging was reserved only for his mother. Instead, they exchanged Ho Fong Triad clenched fist salutes.

"Father, do you think I will make a good Dragon Head someday?" Stanley asked.

"I know you will, Stanley," Arthur said.

Stanley hoped he was not smiling too much, since he wanted to look strong in front of his father, not like a grinning fool. But he could not stop smiling nonetheless. Since the day he had learned the truth about his family, Stanley had feared taking on the position of Dragon Head. Breaking rules without remorse was not his strong suit, and he wished he could be a scientist, a doctor, or a lawyer. Anything other than a triad leader. But now it seemed like the most important job there could be.

"Now that I've seen how this school is run, I'll tell Uncle Wok Nose to check on you more often," Arthur said as he turned toward the door.

"But, Father, you should know I may not get into MIT," Stanley said.

"Oh, you will, Stanley. Didn't I just tell you we take care of our own?" Arthur said, smiling back at his son. "And please say goodbye to the boy under the desk for me."

45

Saturday, May 16, 1964 (7:05 p.m.)

IT HAD BEEN A VERY HARD FALL AND WINTER FOR
Dorothy Rodgers. First, she had lost the Morgan Chemical
Talent Search. She had convinced herself she was destined to
be the first girl winner, but instead they gave the prize to just
another boy. Since Dorothy didn't plan on studying science
in college, that contest had been her one chance to stamp
brilliant at science on her permanent life record.

A few weeks later her political hero, John Kennedy, was
killed in Dallas. Dorothy had been obsessed with politics for as
long as she could remember, and she had gone through many
political crushes. Her first crush was on the Democrat candidate for the Kew Gardens seat on the New York City Council
when she was ten. The night her candidate lost, Dorothy had
cried herself to sleep. After that, she fell hard for Mayor Robert
Wagner. Twelve-year-old Dorothy had spent hours passing
out Wagner leaflets on Jamaica Avenue. But looking back,
she realized her feelings about those candidates had just been

mild infatuations compared to how she felt about President Kennedy.

Kennedy made her feel hopeful and excited about the future in a way no politician ever had before. When he ran against Nixon in 1960, Dorothy had been in her first year at Parker. She had asked her parents if she could take an extended leave of absence from ninth grade to go campaign for Kennedy in Alabama and Mississippi. Her parents had refused to even consider the idea, and she had still not completely forgiven her father for calling her "crazy as a loon" for suggesting it.

The day Kennedy was shot, Miss Parker had gathered all the girls together in the school's auditorium to give them the horrible news. Many of the girls started to cry, but only Dorothy had wept so hard that she had to be taken to the school infirmary and kept overnight for observation. Dorothy was so devastated, she was excused from classes for a week and went home to Queens to mourn.

When she came back to school, Dorothy had lost all interest in the place. She resigned from all her club positions, which resulted in several of them, including the current events club, shutting down completely. She had decided it would be best to spend the final semester of her high school career quietly in mourning.

Her dark mood only started to lift last month when she had received a letter from Stanley Wong asking her to be his date for the Academy's commencement ball. They had been exchanging letters since they had met that night at the awards ceremony, but Stanley had never let on before that he thought of Dorothy as anything more than a friend.

She was so flattered by his invitation, she caught herself smiling the rest of the day. She immediately wrote back and accepted his invitation. She knew MIT, where Stanley was going next year, was very close to where she would be at Wellesley. Although Dorothy realized it was far too early to think of such things, that certainly would make it convenient if a romance developed between them. After such a long mourning period, it felt good to be excited about something again.

Dorothy's reaction to Stanley's letter surprised her. Before then, she had always said formal dances were a silly custom. Girls would spend all day getting dressed up and doing their hair and makeup just so some boy could brag about having the prettiest date. It struck her as being a male chauvinist tradition that should have died around the time women got the vote. But with a date as smart as Stanley, going to a dance did not seem so silly after all.

Standing next to Stanley now in Jessup Auditorium, Dorothy felt truly happy. She thought her long pink taffeta dress looked even better than she remembered from when she had tried it on at Gimbels. Stanley looked very sharp in his uniform, and he was even funnier and nicer in person than in his letters. As if that were not enough, she was having one of her best hair days in weeks, with the front curls of her bob hanging perfectly across her forehead.

Even Jessup Auditorium looked better than it had when she had come last October for the Academy's fall dance. The only decorations that time had been sad-looking paper palm trees taped to the walls. For the commencement ball, the Academy had gone to much more effort and strung multiple strands of white lights across the ceiling. There were also lights on the small stage where the Fort Dix army orchestra was playing.

Stanley had just suggested they go to the snack table to get something to drink when Dorothy noticed a familiar face. She was sure the blond girl crossing the room was Janet Riverstone from Kew Gardens Middle School. She stood out from the crowd in a tight sleeveless black dress that was far sexier than anything a Parker girl would ever wear.

"Janet!" Dorothy yelled.

Janet stopped walking and stared at Dorothy. Dorothy could tell it took Janet a second or two to recognize who she was. Once she did, she smiled and came straight over.

"Dorothy Rodgers! Oh my God, I haven't seen you in ages. What are you doing here?" Janet said.

"I'm here with Stanley," Dorothy said, gesturing to him.

"Oh," Janet said, slowly looking Stanley up and down as if she were carrying out an inspection. "Isn't that interesting? Does Stanley work here?"

"I'm a fourth-year cadet at the Academy," Stanley said.

"Yeah, maybe you can tell that by his Academy uniform," Dorothy said.

Stanley chuckled and Janet looked uncomfortable. Dorothy knew exactly why Janet did not realize Stanley was a cadet.

"I'll go get some punch," Stanley said.

"Sorry, I didn't know they had Orientals at the Academy," Janet said, once Stanley was out of earshot. "But he's cute in his own way. How did you meet him?"

"We were both finalists in a big science competition," Dorothy said.

"A science competition? That's such a Dorothy Rodgers way to meet a boy! I see you're still as brainy as always," Janet said.

"Who are you with?" Dorothy asked.

"Donald, of course! We're kind of dating now," Janet said. "Did you know his family owns apartment buildings all over the city?"

"But I heard a rumor last summer you were with Ricky Dunstan," Dorothy said.

"Well, Ricky's parents kicked him out of the house because he was stealing from them or something. Can you believe that? He had to move upstate to work on his uncle's farm. So he's not exactly dating material anymore, if you know what I mean?"

Dorothy noticed Donald walking across the dance floor. He was weaving his way around dancing couples.

"I see Donald over there," Dorothy said, nodding toward him.

Janet turned in that direction and yelled "Donald!" so loud that many of the couples on the dance floor stopped and looked over at her. Janet waved both of her hands in the air until Donald realized the source of the high-pitched scream. He walked over to them, looking irritated.

"I was looking for you for a long time, Janet," Donald said.

"So sorry, honey. But look who I ran into on my way back from the bathroom," Janet said. "Can you believe it? Three old Kew Gardens Rams back together again."

"Oh, hi, Dorothy," Donald said, not looking happy to see her.

"Hi, Donald," Dorothy said. "I didn't know you and Janet were together."

"Yeah, and nobody else knows Janet here, so you don't have to say anything about how you know her, okay?"

Dorothy had no idea what Donald was worried she might say, but she just ignored it. She was fascinated watching Janet position herself so close to Donald that he had no choice but to put his arm around her shoulders. She wondered if she would ever feel comfortable enough to try a move like that with Stanley.

"I thought Cindy Grubb would be here, but I haven't seen her," Donald said.

"Oh, Cindy didn't come back to Parker after winter break. She's back home taking night classes now," Dorothy said.

Cindy had written to her after winter break, confirming what Dorothy had already suspected. She had gotten pregnant over the previous summer during a fling with a Teaneck Country Club lifeguard. By Christmas she was showing, so her parents had pulled her out of school. Instead of going to Montclair State next year as she had planned, Cindy would be taking care of a baby.

"Who's Cindy Grubb?" Janet asked.

"Nobody you know," Donald said.

"And speaking of Kew Gardens Rams, where's Jerry? I haven't seen him yet," Dorothy said.

"Oh, you didn't hear? Jerry's not at the Academy anymore," Donald said.

"Really? Why?" Dorothy asked.

"Well, he got in really big trouble and ended up getting himself kicked out," Donald said.

"No, I can't believe that," Dorothy said.

She was shocked she had not heard that news from her mother. Jerry's father was her family's dentist, and his office receptionist was one of the biggest gossips in Kew Gardens. Since her little brother, Jimmy, was getting cavities all the time from eating too much candy, Dorothy thought her mother should have heard about Jerry on one of her trips to the dentist.

"That doesn't sound like Jerry," Dorothy said. "What did he do?"

"Well, officially he got expelled just for theft," Donald said.

"Just for theft? He did more than that?" Dorothy asked.

"Well, it also kind of seemed like he might have killed another cadet," Donald said.

"Oh my God!" Dorothy said, shocked Donald could seem so calm delivering news like that. "Jerry might have killed somebody? Seriously? That can't be true."

Stanley walked up to them carrying two Dixie cups. He handed one cup to Dorothy and the other to Janet. Dorothy couldn't believe they had exchanged letters all semester, and Stanley had never mentioned once that Jerry Stahl might be a murderer.

"Stanley! How could you not tell me about Jerry? You know I grew up with him," Dorothy said.

"Oh, you guys are talking about that?" Stanley said.

"Well, in the end there wasn't any proof about the murder stuff. He probably didn't do it, but who knows? Someone can seem like a great guy, but you never really know what's going on inside their head, right? Maybe Jerry had a whole different side to him that we never saw," Donald said.

"You know, I always thought there was something off about that guy, and my mother says I'm a really good judge of character. I'm not surprised at all," Janet said.

"So, what happened to him? Can Jerry even go to college now?" Dorothy asked.

"I don't know if he could get into college, but I guess it doesn't matter anyway because his dad made him join the army," Donald said.

Dorothy looked at Stanley, thinking he might have something to say that would make this shocking news about Jerry make more sense. But Stanley was just staring down at the floor.

"Jerry Stahl in the army. Seriously? I can't really imagine that," Dorothy said.

"Well, have you heard about what's going on in Vietnam?" Donald asked.

It was just like Donald to think he had some special information about Vietnam. Dorothy had been following the situation in Vietnam closely since the French had pulled out in 1954.

"Of course. I read the *New York Times* every day," Dorothy said.

"Well, I hear Jerry's over there now. I'm kind of jealous of him. If I didn't have to go to college, I'd love to be over there myself. I could win some medals and it would be good for my career if I ever went into politics," Donald said.

Six months ago Dorothy would have been sure Donald was joking. Back then Kennedy was in office, the March on Washington had just happened, and it seemed as if only the brightest people would be going into government. She felt confident all the world's problems would be solved during her lifetime. But now Kennedy was dead, Barry Goldwater was running for president, and her certainty about the future was gone.

46

Saturday, May 16, 1964
(7:19 a.m./6:19 p.m. Saigon time)

EVER SINCE JERRY STAHL WAS EXPELLED FROM THE NEW Jersey Military Academy, his mother had advised him not to dwell on the past. His school days may have come to a sad and unfortunate end, she would say, but he could still have a bright future. He just needed to keep his eyes focused straight ahead and not look back.

Although Jerry was not convinced his mother was right about the brightness of his future prospects, he tried to follow her advice about the past. He did his best not to think about what had happened at the Academy, but he was not always successful. Sometimes, if he let his guard down, memories would find a way to slip into his mind. Mostly they were of Donald lying at Teddy's hearing. Those thoughts would make him feel like he was suffocating under a heavy wool blanket, so he fought against them as best as he could. He found it helped to imagine himself digging a deep hole in the backyard of his family's house in Queens, shoveling those memories into the hole, and then covering that hole with a thick layer of cement. It also helped that in recent months he had not had much time for thinking.

When he had first left the Academy, he had lived at home with nothing to do. That time in his life had felt like torture. During the day, television was not enough to distract him from his alternating feelings of self-pity and rage. And every night, when his father came home from his dental office, Jerry had to feel the sting of his father's bitter disappointment in him.

Ever since Jerry was a young boy, his father's dream had been that someday his only son would get a dental degree and join his practice. In his father's mind, Jerry's expulsion from the Academy had crushed that dream forever. Jerry's mother tried to convince her husband that their son could still get a high school degree and go to college and then study dentistry. She even filled out the papers to enroll him at Kew Gardens High School and left them on her husband's dresser for his signature.

But Jerry's father had decided it was pointless for Jerry to continue his education, because dental licenses were reserved only for people of the highest integrity. He was sure the New York State Board of Dentistry would never give a license to a watch thief.

His father had decided that the only hope for his son was to enlist him in the army. If military school had failed to make a man of strong character out of Jerry, then only the real military could do the trick. Even if his son might never become an actual dentist, he could still learn to live up to the high moral standards demanded of the dental profession by serving his country.

His father discovered, however, that it was not a simple matter to get Jerry into the army, since his expulsion from the Academy also meant that he had been expelled from the Junior

ROTC. Ordinarily, ROTC rejects were not permitted to join any branch of the military, since they had already proven that they were unfit for service.

But Jerry's father had found a way to circumvent that problem. His patient list included the sweet-toothed, and therefore cavity-prone, congressman who represented New York's Sixth Congressional District. The congressman came in for a filling about a month after Jerry's expulsion. Just before starting the procedure, Jerry's father held his stainless-steel dental drill a few inches from the congressman's face and asked for his help getting Jerry a waiver from the enlistment ban on ROTC rejects. The congressman immediately agreed to look into it.

When he got back to Washington, the congressman learned from a friend on the House Armed Services Committee that the military was about to do away with the enlistment ban in any case. As the country was getting more deeply involved in the conflict in Vietnam, the country's military leadership had changed its mind and decided that most ROTC rejects would probably still make perfectly fine soldiers. So the congressman called Jerry's father and gave him the good news that, because of the escalating hostilities in Vietnam, his son would be allowed to join the army after all.

Jerry had not taken that news well. He had hoped that since the Newark police had already cleared him of murder and dropped the theft charges, his father would eventually forgive him and relent on subjecting him to any more time in a military environment. But by that point, his father was determined that Jerry needed to go to war in order to come back a better man.

On January 6, 1964, the day that Jerry should have been starting his last semester at the New Jersey Military Academy, he instead arrived for boot camp at Fort Dix in Trenton, New

Jersey. Since he had gone to a military school, Jerry thought he knew what to expect at boot camp. It turned out the drills the cadets had been put through at the Academy were like country club calisthenics classes compared to boot camp.

To make things worse, Jerry was assigned to a company under the command of Drill Sergeant Ed "the Brow" McCloskey. The Brow was famous at Fort Dix for two reasons: he was considered the most sadistic drill sergeant on the base, and he had only one eyebrow, an extremely unkempt and bushy one that started very close to the top of his left eye and extended well up onto his forehead. He had lost the other eyebrow when his first wife threw a whole frying pan's worth of bacon grease on his face during a fight about his drinking.

The two different reasons for the Brow's fame became interlinked for recruits because they found it almost impossible to stop themselves from staring either at the Brow's one extraordinary eyebrow or at the lack of an eyebrow on the other side of his face. Any recruit caught staring would then be subjected to an extra dose of his sadistic instruction.

From five o'clock to ten o'clock, seven days a week, the Brow put Jerry and the rest of his company through endless marching, exercises, combat training, and riflery practice. As he led the recruits through the drills, the Brow would pound into their heads that, even though they had come to boot camp as worthless and weak little boys, they were all that was standing between the good South Vietnamese and the rabid dogs of the Viet Cong. Only by wiping out the Viet Cong could they become men of character worthy of wearing the uniform of the US Army. Those words were repeated over and over again with impressive consistency. Jerry had even watched the Brow deliver that speech while pressing a recruit's face down into a mud puddle with his boot.

Jerry couldn't believe he used to find Colonel Overstreet intimidating. Compared to the Brow, he was a pussycat. He wished his former classmates could witness the Brow in action even just for an hour so they would realize the Academy was just a make-believe army. Each night, as Jerry lay in his bottom bunk, for his few waking seconds before he passed out, he would fantasize that Donald was there at boot camp with him and had developed an affliction where he simply could never look away from the Brow's eyebrow.

When boot camp was finally over, the army deemed that a bruised, exhausted, and eight-pound-lighter Jerry was now in fighting shape and ready to be deployed to Vietnam. He flew there in three different US Air Force transport planes, traveling from Fort Dix to Tacoma to Japan to Saigon. Before that, the farthest Jerry had been from Queens was Philadelphia.

Jerry had been assigned to the Army Chemical Corps, specifically to serve on a four-person defoliant-spraying helicopter team. When he'd first heard his assignment, Jerry had been excited, because the Academy's chemistry teacher, Major Burnside, used to tell his classes gripping stories about his exploits in the Chemical Corps during the Korean War. Major Burnside had made it sound like the Chemical Corps were basically a bunch of secret agents who used their expert knowledge of science to confuse and repel the enemy with chemical agents and gases.

After a few weeks in Vietnam, Jerry decided the Chemical Corps must have changed a great deal since Major Burnside's time. His helicopter team consisted of a pilot and a copilot, who were both officers; a sergeant who manned the machine gun; and Jerry, a lowly private, second class, who was the valve man. Their helicopter had been fitted with a two-hundred-gallon tank connected to a long spray boom, and the valve man's job was to fill the tank with defoliant chemicals, open and close the valve to release the chemicals on the pilot's orders, and occasionally clean the tank and the boom. So far, the job had not required him to use any of the science he had studied at the Academy.

Their helicopter was now flying a few hundred feet over rice paddies and small villages just north of Saigon. Dusk came early in May near Saigon, and the rice paddies were bathed in a soft orange light coming from where the sun had just set.

The team had already sprayed their entire load of defoliants over an area of suspected Viet Cong activity, and they were headed back to base. Jerry had brought a few extra ten-gallon canisters of defoliant on board in case he needed to reload the main tank. He was now using one of those metal canisters as a makeshift chair. Looking down between his legs, he could read the words *Morgan Chemical* emblazoned across the top of the canister.

It was another stiflingly hot and muggy day, so Jerry had positioned his canister seat to take maximum advantage of the breeze. As always, both doors of the helicopter were wide open—on Jerry's side so that the nine-foot spray boom could extend out from the tank, and on the other side so that Sergeant Nate Thomas could keep watch on the landscape below with his machine gun. Jerry sat himself inches from the open door on his side so that he could feel the wind in his hair, which had finally grown back after boot camp.

Since arriving in Vietnam, Jerry had done a good job keeping his bad memories of the Academy sealed in the imaginary cement-covered hole. Although the specific duties of a valve man were not very exciting, they kept him busy all day and, between that work and his constant fear of being shot or blown up, his mind was usually fully occupied.

But that day was different. Sitting on the Morgan Chemical canister and listening to the whirring of the rotator blades, Jerry could not stop thinking about how he had ended up on that helicopter.

He knew exactly why the memories had been able to escape their hole on that particular day. Although he did not usually pay much attention to the date, that morning he noticed the calendar in the mess hall showed it was May 16. As a former member of the Academy's spirit club, he knew that back in Newark, the Academy would be holding its commencement ball.

At one time, he believed he would be going to the ball that night with the beautiful Cindy Grubb. What an idiot he was, Jerry thought. She was never going to go with a guy like him. That was just another lie that Donald had gotten him to believe.

Of course, compared to everything else Donald had done to him, tantalizing him with the false hope of a date with a beautiful girl was a relatively small offense. And Jerry did not care anymore about the commencement ball. The thought of his classmates playing soldier, proudly adorned in their dress uniforms, seemed ridiculous to him now.

What gnawed at him was not that Donald had lied to him. Donald was a liar, so that was to be expected. It was the fact that the lies were unnecessary. Jerry had been such a fool, he would have helped Donald anyway, without all the manipulation. It had been that way since the first grade. Jerry had always gone along with whatever Donald wanted, because that was the only way to be his friend.

Jerry realized now that the many hours he had spent obsessing over the past had just been a huge waste of time. It was not a collection of his mistakes and other people's lies that had ruined his life. It was just one big decision. He had decided he wanted to be Donald's friend.

Because of that one decision, he was stuck in this hellhole of a country. His father was convinced that only the military could mold him into a man of honor and principle, worthy even of the noble profession of dentistry. If his father was right, then being accepted into the army had given him a second chance at integrity.

But Jerry had begun to suspect the military might not be such a good character builder after all. The Academy told everybody it produced cadets with the highest integrity, with steel rods in their loins, and yet a liar like Donald was still there. The Brow claimed the army could do the exact same thing.

But something felt wrong to Jerry about what his team was doing. He heard some guys at the base saying the coordinates they got could be six months old before they went on a mission. Sometimes the coordinates were not even complete, so in the end, the pilot just had to guess where they should release their load. When Jerry opened that valve, he had a feeling nobody really knew whose fields they were destroying below their helicopter. It could be a Viet Cong camp or it could be a village full of innocent people, for all they knew.

Jerry did not want to disappoint his father any more than he had already. But if the military was building the kind of character needed to be a dentist, maybe Jerry just was not cut out to be a dentist after all.

The sudden sound of machine gun fire jerked Jerry back to his present reality. The pilot veered the helicopter violently to the left, causing Jerry to lose his balance and almost tumble out of the open door. He had to grab on to the spray boom to keep from falling out of the helicopter. He looked down into the rice paddies. The light was almost gone now, but he could just make out ten or fifteen men running on the narrow mud paths between the paddies, and he saw flashes of light that he guessed were machine gun fire.

"Shit! There's a whole pack of VC down there!" Sergeant Thomas yelled as he continued to fire his machine gun nonstop.

Jerry suddenly felt like his right foot was on fire. The pain was excruciating and he had to bite down hard on his lip to keep from screaming. He looked down and saw that small holes were being blown through the helicopter's aluminum floor all around him. He knew he had taken a bullet in his foot. Guys at the base had told him that Viet Cong machine guns could pierce a helicopter's hull, but it was the first time he was experiencing it.

"I've been hit!" Jerry yelled as he sat back down on the Morgan Chemical canister.

Bullets blew holes into the side of the empty chemical tank inches from where Jerry was sitting. He bent over and covered his face with his hands to evade shrapnel. Jerry wished he knew a prayer, but he had never paid any attention at the Academy's mandatory Sunday church services. He heard Sergeant Thomas scream out in pain. Jerry peeked through his fingers to see the sergeant falling facedown onto the helicopter floor.

"Hold on!" the pilot yelled. "I think we're going down."

GRAND PATRONS

Anita Jahan Bose

Ann Louise Elliott

Asif Sherani

Ben Lamberg

Dale and Julie Bennett

Heung Sik Choo

Hidaya Tazi

Jhinuk Hasan Fulton

Jigme Shingsar

Joanna Syroka

John D. Bennett

John Seo

Jukka Pihlman

Kenneth G. Lay

Matthew Ruddick

Nona Pucciariello

Noorjahan Bose

Pamela K. Sutherland

Silvia Melendez Briskie

Stuart Kinnersley

Supriyo Malaker

Thomas Jeffrey Karr

Tom Wright

William McNulty

Xueman Wang

INKSHARES

INKSHARES is a reader-driven publisher and producer based in Oakland, California. Our books are selected not by a group of editors, but by readers worldwide.

While we've published books by established writers like *Big Fish* author Daniel Wallace and *Star Wars: Rogue One* scribe Gary Whitta, our aim remains surfacing and developing the new author voices of tomorrow.

Previously unknown Inkshares authors have received starred reviews and been featured in the *New York Times*. Their books are on the front tables of Barnes & Noble and hundreds of independents nationwide, and many have been licensed by publishers in other major markets. They are also being adapted by Oscar-winning screenwriters at the biggest studios and networks.

Interested in making your own story a reality? Visit Inkshares.com to start your own project or find other great books.